Joan Bakewell is a journalist and broadcaster. She lives in London and has two children and six grandchildren.

All the Nice Girls

JOAN BAKEWELL

virago

VIRAGO

First published in Great Britain in 2009 by Virago Press
This paperback edition published in 2010 by Virago Press

Copyright © Joan Bakewell 2009

The moral right of the author has been asserted.

*All characters and events in this publication, other than those
clearly in the public domain, are fictitious and any resemblance
to real persons, living or dead, is purely coincidental.*

Grateful acknowledgement is made for permission to reprint from
the following material: 'Cargoes' by John Masefield, used by permission of The
Society of Authors as the Literary Representative of the Estate of John Masefield;
'I'll See You Again' by Noel Coward, used by permission of Methuen Drama, an
imprint of A& C Black Publishers Ltd, and of NC Aventales AG, successor in the
title to the Estate of Noel Coward; 'Sally' by Will E. Haines, Leo Towers and
Harry Leon, used by permission of the International Music Network, Ltd.

A CIP catalogue record for this book
is available from the British Library.

ISBN 978-1-84408-531-6

Typeset in Palatino by M Rules
Printed and bound in Great Britain by
Clays Ltd, St Ives plc

Papers used by Virago are natural, renewable and
recyclable products sourced from well-managed forests and certified
in accordance with the rules of the Forest Stewardship Council.

Mixed Sources
Product group from well-managed
forests and other controlled sources
www.fsc.org   Cert no. SGS-COC-004081
© 1996 Forest Stewardship Council
FSC

Virago Press
An imprint of
Little, Brown Book Group
100 Victoria Embankment
London EC4Y 0DY

An Hachette UK Company
www.hachette.co.uk

www.virago.co.uk

For Thomas, Katie, Louis, Charlie, Max and Maisie

Author's Note

This is a novel grounded in fact. In the 1940s I was a schoolgirl at Stockport High School for Girls when it joined the Ship Adoption Scheme and adopted a merchant ship. Its captain and his wife became great benefactors of the school during the war and beyond. I have drawn on my memories of those years to construct a fiction: there is no connection whatever between the lives I have given the characters in my book and the headmistress and staff of my school, either in the 1940s or its successor school thereafter. Nor is there any connection with the master and crew of the ships we adopted. Staveley is the fictional name I have given to an imaginary town between Manchester and Liverpool.

The School

1942

The shuffling of shoes, identical pairs of shiny black shoes. The murmur of young voices, words inaudible, the scraping of rush-seated upright chairs on the polished parquet floor. The pupils of Ashworth Grammar School for Girls were arriving in the echoing hall for their daily nine o'clock assembly. Unlike the girls, the teachers were not in uniform, but there was a sameness to the sensible shapeless skirts, hand-knit jumpers and peach-coloured lisle stockings. Each group was ushered in by its form mistress, who had already marked the register that recorded their attendance. That morning one of the girls in the lower sixth was not yet present: her brother had been reported missing in action. She would be in later, when her aunt had arrived to comfort her mother. So, all was normal.

Miss Maitland, the tall, straightbacked headmistress, mounted the rostrum, announced the opening hymn. She surveyed her school with quiet satisfaction, knowing each girl by name and watchful for any fidgeting. Despite wartime shortages of cloth and clothing, she was almost elegant, arriving at school each morning in a pert little hat, with matching bag and gloves, leather when everyone else had knitted theirs. She had harvested her clothing coupons and managed with some deft home dress-making to set her own style of fashion and appearance. Her taste ran to Gor-Ray suits, whose box pleats she ironed each morning with a damp cloth.

She lived with her widowed mother but wouldn't acknowledge how sad this was – after all, there were plenty like her. Rather, she had an aura of purposeful achievement. In later decades she might be described as having a career, but no one spoke like that in 1942. It was enough to have a life.

The removal of the pert little hat had left the fine golden hair flat on top of her head, but it curled towards her collar in a hint of Veronica Lake. Like the rest of the school, she went regularly to the cinema and was not immune to its glamour. Her porcelain skin she treated each night with Pond's Cold Cream, and by day with a dusting of Bourjois face powder.

That early-March morning she looked at her girls with particular pleasure. Her pale blue eyes were set wide above high cheekbones, a neat straight nose and wide but thin lips. She might once have been marked out as a beauty, but her concern was with her school, and beyond it, of course, with the country and the war. This, though, was her domain. She sang the hymn in a warm contralto, while the girls, absolved from the rules of silence applying in classrooms and corridors, threw themselves vigorously into the familiar phrases. The major chords and their own voices gave several a private rush of pleasure. And today Miss Maitland had another delight in store for them. She had an announcement to make.

From her position on the platform she surveyed the assembled ranks: navy gymslips, white blouses, prefects distinguished by badges of office, sporting heroines in their yellow plaited girdles. At the back of her mind she was aware that the sixth-formers were restless. They were starting to look like young women. They wore skirts and shirts and the school tie, a status symbol that confirmed their authority when they disciplined the younger girls. More importantly, it made them the equivalent of the grammar-school boys they eyed furtively on street corners when school had finished for the day.

Ashworth Grammar School for Girls in Staveley, one of the thriving industrial towns that circle Manchester, ran smoothly on strictly conventional lines. Girls had circumscribed contact with the opposite sex because boys were a different breed, destined for a different way of life. Nice girls must be kept apart and safe. But Miss Maitland knew that social controls were breaking down. The bolder girls shared the back-row seats at the cinema with schoolboys of their own age and indulged in exploratory fumbling, which, given the limited space and their heavy clothes, never found much flesh. Nonetheless she was reassured that within the school childish innocence persisted. The girls would grow slowly into their adult selves.

'The school is going to adopt a ship.'

There was an immediate tremor of excitement. Then as the significance of what she had said sank in, there were

3

shrill cries of surprise and girls whispered behind their hands. Now they had the prospect of one-to-one contact with boys older than themselves, who were serving in the war, 'the hand of friendship' meant contact with serving sailors in uniform, officers with gold braid on cuffs and shoulders, men who'd seen the enemy, even been in battle. Letters. Meetings. No wonder the hall was swept with whispers.

Even the teachers, sitting neatly, hands clasping hymn books, leaned forward to catch each other's eye and raise enquiring eyebrows. Their minds were spinning, too, trying to work out what might be involved.

Miss Maitland brandished a letter. An outbreak of hushing restored the now electric silence.

'I have this morning received a communication from her master, Captain Josh Percival. Because of wartime regulations, I can't tell you her name: for the time being we are asked to refer to her only as "our ship". And the scheme is already afloat.' The nautical reference added a flash of jaunty gaiety, quite unlike her usual tone. She allowed herself to smile, and her girls listened.

'This is another of our contributions to the war. I'm already proud of the trouble each class is taking with its collections of used wool and aluminium pans – and paper seems to be piling up everywhere! But, as you know, I can put up with a little untidiness in the interest of victory.'

The other teachers seized the chance for a covert smile of their own: Miss Maitland was always scathing about the mess in the staffroom.

'But this new effort involves the entire school coming together to forge personal links with one of our valiant merchant ships. I shall ask form mistresses to arrange letter-writing to different members of the crew. We shall make comforts for them, too, and despatch parcels to cheer them up. The collectors among you can look forward to stamps from exotic places. Most of all, we shall be welcoming them here whenever they're docked in Liverpool. Later, when it's considered safe enough, there may be visits to the ship.' By now Miss Maitland was almost laughing, enjoying the girls' hum of interest.

The previous week, concerned by the bad news from the front, she had written to the British Ship Adoption Society in London and asked for the school to be involved. She assumed the project was seen as a way of boosting morale on board the merchant fleet, which was battling to get food supplies through the German blockade. It would boost patriotism at home, too, and, perhaps, Miss Maitland thought, a taste for geography, among the girls. A telegram had arrived the day before, informing her that a formal bond had been registered by the authorities.

More than whispers had broken out at the back during assembly: a bout of serious giggling among the lower sixth. The rustle of interest that Miss Maitland could tolerate was being overwhelmed by snorts of laughter she could not. Echoes of her younger self stirred. But she knew the rules. She disciplined herself and would not allow standards to slacken among the girls.

Hastening to quell the outbreak she announced the next music: 'Jesu Joy of Man's Desiring'. It set off more squeals. The senior girls were now engulfed in a wave of hysteria, cotton hankies stuffed into mouths, hands held over eyes. The delicious pleasures of transgression were beyond control. Knowing there would be a price to pay, the two who had started it coughed and struggled to straighten their faces. Slowly the surge of spontaneity subsided.

Back in their form room it wasn't long before Polly and Jen were summoned. Grace Bunting, the secretary, conducted the administration of the school's affairs from a neat little sentry-box of a room adjoining Miss Maitland's study. This was her first job since secretarial college and she had a girlish adoration of her superior. She was readily at her command and, when not actually needed, fussed around in her room, freshening the flowers, setting out the *Manchester Guardian*, filling the cigarette box, little tasks she took pleasure in fulfilling. She knew when to take a wet umbrella and set it to dry alongside Miss Maitland's galoshes. She was watchful for books out of place, even enjoyed the intimacy of mentioning, were it to happen, that the headmistress's petticoat hem was showing. Miss Maitland indulged her, even leaving an odd glove or an opened book to be retrieved, her thanks making Grace glow with pride.

Grace identified with the girls. Some were not much younger than her but she was already earning money. A favoured few had been shown the sapphire and diamond ring that went with the recent newspaper announcement of her engagement – little flicks of her left hand had become an instinctive mannerism. She waved it at Polly and Jen now, and made a *moue* of disapproval as she fetched the naughty girls.

6

'Margaret and Jennifer are here, Miss Maitland.' And to them a conspiratorial 'She's in one of her moods, so don't provoke her.' As if they would.

The girls edged into the inner sanctum, and drank in its splendour. The richness of polished wood glowed from panelled walls and floor, while the bookcases held impressive volumes with tooled leather bindings. Bright splashes of colour – an Indian rug, a run of silk cushions on a small sofa – gave the room, with its tall windows, a faint hint of the exotic.

So far the war had made one conspicuous difference to the school building. To guard against the effect of bombing, its corridors and stairwells had been strength-ened by sturdy wooden scaffolding. Chunky timbers lined corridors and stairs, cloakrooms and gymnasium. When the younger girls swung on them, hooting like monkeys, they got splinters in their hands. 'Serves them right,' said the staff, who grudgingly administered first aid.

None of this disfigured the headmistress's enclave. She had preserved its pre-war state to remind them all of the school's Edwardian elegance. The main business of the room was in the centre: the desk, of solid bur-nished oak, its roll top displaying a nest of shelves and, below, a neat settlement of documents, a glass paper-weight, a bottle of Quink and a small lacquer tray that held Miss Maitland's three fountain pens. A silver photo-graph frame held a picture of a young man. The girls knew not to look at it and they never saw Miss Maitland do so either. So much not-looking made it the most power-ful object in the room.

'Margaret and Jennifer, there's no excuse for your behaviour, but I'm prepared to hear what you have to say.' Miss Maitland stared at them hard. Using their Christian names in full carried authority and disapproval. Polly, a tall willowy blonde, slouched on one leg. Jen, with red cheeks and bright black eyes, stood four-square, compact but intense. Miss Maitland tried to recall whether she herself had been like this when she was young: bold and awkward, bright but chastened. She rather feared she had been lanky and dull. Neither girl looked at her, suddenly taken with the state of their shoes.

'Well?'

'We're sorry, Miss Maitland.'

This was Polly, who hated to be in the wrong. Miss Maitland, knowing as much, kept her thoughts to herself and acted out her disapproval. 'What caused such hilarity? Tell me.'

Clearly, Polly felt the weariness of guilt. She gave a wretched, helpless shrug.

'Don't shrug your shoulders, Margaret, and stand up straight. Jennifer, what have you to say?' For a moment she delighted in her power.

'Nothing, Miss Maitland. We were just laughing at . . . you know . . . the news of the ship, sailors . . . er . . .' She glanced helplessly at the panelling, the leather books, the distant unused sofa.

Miss Maitland held all the cards. She could afford to mellow, and she did. She crossed her legs in their fine silk stockings.

'Now, you are usually intelligent, polite girls. I have

8

high hopes of your doing well, and I look to you to be an example to the school.'

Polly let out a long sigh.

'And I don't want any insolence.' Suddenly she sat up and gave way to a passion that came from somewhere she hardly knew. 'I spoke to you of how we can support the brave men of our services, some of them still boys, who face danger and death every day. They are out there enduring brutal conditions, confronting the enemy, surrounded by the turmoil and fear of war. Do you know what that means? Can you begin to *imagine* what that means? For them, for their families, and . . .' she paused '. . . for those they love, those they leave behind. Many heroes will make the final sacrifice so that our lives might be safe. They lay down their young and beautiful lives – but all you can do is disrupt and sneer. You're despicable with your cheap behaviour.'

This was now well beyond any routine telling-off. Polly and Jen were transfixed.

Miss Maitland was silent, breathless, seeking to calm herself. She stood up and turned away from them, brushing non-existent fluff from a pleat of her skirt.

Now she turned back. 'I look to senior girls like you to set an example, to show patriotism and pride in our country and its serving men. Now, leave this room and never let me hear that you have been disrespectful or dismissive of this enterprise again. Is that understood?'

Polly and Jen were shocked. There was an intimacy about their headmistress's manner that discomfited them. They saw her as vulnerable and didn't want her to be.

'Yes, Miss Maitland.' Jen nodded vigorously. 'Understood.'

And Polly, tugging at the tail of her sixth-form tie, added, 'Sorry, Miss Maitland,' and meant it.

As they filed out through the heavy oak door, they didn't look towards the sepia photograph on the desk. It showed a young man in First World War uniform smiling breezily at the camera, and, scrawled along the bottom, 'To Cynthia'.

On the way back to the classroom, Polly broke away and ran off. Jen returned to the lesson, sidling into her desk and refusing to meet the others' questioning eyes, or answer the hissed enquiry, 'Where's Polly?'

Miss Jessop was analysing Lamartine's 'Le Lac', and Jen gave herself up to the intensity of the poem.

Aimons donc, aimons donc! de l'heure fugitive,
Hâtons nous, jouissons!
L'homme n'a point de port, le temps n'a point de rive;
Il coule, et nous passons.

Yes. 'Let us love, let us love . . . let us be happy, time is fleeting': wasn't that exactly right? That was what they all wanted to do, to love and live to the very limit before this terrible war took away every chance of happiness. That was what the poem was telling them, and what the teacher was urging them to do. How odd that a long-dead French poet should know exactly how they felt right now.

*

Polly had fled to the cloakrooms, where Jen found her at break, hunched over, her shoulders bent almost to her knees, surrounded by the smells of shoes and coats, the stuffiness of young bodies that, in line with some government ruling, had just one bath each week. Polly hugged her knees, finding comfort in her body's heat. Jen's arrival brought on the tears again and she reached into her pocket for her handkerchief, already damp, and screwed it into a ball. She rocked to and fro.

'She wants us to be happy about the ship – she does, Polly. It's because she cares that she gets so upset. Please . . .' Jen took Polly's hand and squeezed it.

The roar of girls released from classrooms swept round them. Glass bottles of milk rattled in the crates as girls snatched them and grabbed at the rows of currant buns. Polly stood up and allowed her friend to lead her outdoors to join the others. Quiet, subdued, she resumed her place at the centre of their little group as they hung around, gossiping.

Jen quietly explained Polly's tears. 'Her brother Gerald's with the Atlantic convoys.'

Every Friday Jen went to the cinema with her mother, Ruby. It was part of the routine. Two years ago, in 1940, when she'd sat round the wireless with the rest of the family and heard Mr Churchill declare he had 'nothing to offer but blood, toil, tears and sweat' it had sounded as though, with one big combined effort, a colossal tug-of-war, they'd have the Germans beaten and return to the lives they knew. But it hadn't been like that. Six months later they had stood in the back garden and watched in

11

the distance the great orange glow that didn't flicker or change, just held fast throughout the night. Miles away Manchester was burning, like a huge sun in the sky. Jen's parents had worried silently about what had happened to aunts and uncles in places like Stretford and Gorton. They had no telephone so they'd only find out if someone in uniform appeared the next day. They had come up from the Anderson shelter in the garden, among the spiders and damp soil, and were grateful to feel safe. Liverpool was further away but they knew it was hit all the time because of the docks.

The war had been going on for two and a half years and it felt now as though they were losing. Some of the soldiers who had survived Dunkirk had come back silent and staring. Jen remembered a stranger taken in by her aunt sitting in a deck-chair in the garden. She was hoping for stories of derring-do and heroics but her aunt had shooed her away. 'Take him a syrup sandwich, if you must,' she'd said and Jen had carried the plate to the cramped little square of grass that hadn't yet been dug for vegetables.

Since then things had got even worse. Jen looked at her parents, whose grim, expressionless faces showed no hope, little good humour. Her dad, usually her ally, had become moody and sullen. Her mother was withered and worn-out, her hands lined and dry from cleaning other people's homes. Out of doors, she wore the same shapeless black felt hat pulled over hair held perpetually in place by a net, and a pair of brightly striped knitted gloves, a present from Auntie Vera last Christmas and so much worn that the tips of the fingers had had to be darned. The wool didn't match, and the patches resembled an animal's paws. Ruby clung to her daughter for comfort and reassurance.

It was amazing how quickly Jen's routine had been set with those early raids: German bombs by night; everyone into the shelters; clear up in the early hours; have a cup of tea and go to school. There were modest pleasures in the evening once homework was done – *ITMA* on the wireless, choir practice, Guides – but she was in bed by ten to get some sleep before the sirens sounded. Once the Blitz was over, the routine cinema trip was back.

A fine rain blew into their faces as they hurried to the bus stop. Mr Leather, the newsagent, was among those waiting with his son. They must have been there for some time because the rain had soaked darkly into the shoulders of his gabardine.

'Let's hope the queue's not too long.'

'No, not in this weather. I've lost my brolly.' He gave a snuffle of pleasure as the dimmed lights of the bus loomed out of the dark, and they embarked. This week there was special excitement; everyone had known what was coming from the trailers. And there was indeed a queue outside the Essoldo: the whole neighbourhood was turning out. Tickets were first come first served – you could only book seats on Saturday night – it was as well they were early. Jen saw Miss Fletcher, form mistress of Three B, right at the front, holding a man's arm. That would be worth reporting back. They must have come out straight after their tea. The queue moved slowly towards the darkened door, the rain seeping into their shabby clothes.

Inside there was a comforting fug. Cinemas had rare permission to light their foyers and were the most glamorous places Jen knew. The style and the sudden brightness after the dark and rain made her gasp. The walls bore reliefs of swooping couples dancing, a little like Fred Astaire and Ginger Rogers. The damp steamed off everyone's clothes and some people even took off their macs to stand around the ticket booth in their cardigans. They looked almost naked, unseemly somehow. Jen and her mother took their tickets from the girl in the booth – Peggy, Mrs Johnson's daughter, from along their street. She'd left school only the previous year and already had this responsible job. She had painted nails too. Ruby frowned at that.

They got to their seats while the organ was playing. It was floodlit and set on a platform that rose and fell in the pit before the screen where a dot bounced along the top of the words so the audience could join in the songs. Mr Leather and his son, Miss Fletcher and her man – everyone was swaying and singing, all made one by the good humour. Jen and her mother's voices, sweet and piping, swelled with the rest. The final song in the medley changed the mood from cheery to something more thoughtful: 'We'll meet again' they sang, knowing that some of them might not meet again the husbands and boyfriends fighting in North Africa or Singapore. They sang as though it was a hymn.

Then they were agog for the newsreel: Gaumont British. A week ago the news that Singapore had fallen to the Japanese had stunned them into horrified silence. Now the news told how some hundred thousand

14

Japanese Americans were being rounded up and sent to a special area. That seemed fair enough and there were murmurs of approval. Jen thought she heard, 'Quite right too,' from her mother. Then, thankfully, the commentator's voice switched from solemn to bright: the Board of Trade had said skirts must be shorter, women's shoes must have lower heels and men would not be allowed double-breasted suits or turn-ups on their trousers. They showed the new dresses, skirts reaching only to the knee. Jen's mother was a bit tight-lipped. But if the government had decreed it, it would be so. Finally sixteen-year-old Princess Elizabeth was seen registering for war service, smiling and confident. It was a tonic for them all.

Then, at last, what they'd all been waiting for: the big picture. There was a buzz of pleasure as the smoke from a multitude of cigarettes curled into the light from the projector and people settled down for *In Which We Serve*. They watched in tense silence. The film told of a ship serving in the war, its captain and crew, how the ship sank and some of the sailors survived in an open boat. The one played by Bernard Miles died, but Richard Attenborough's character, who'd been a coward at first, was brave by the end and died a hero's death. It was so sad and heroic. They were spellbound by how real it was, how like the life they were living. And Noël Coward, who played the captain, and Celia Johnson, as his lovely wife, well, they were just like the posh people whose homes Jen's mother cleaned. And Celia Johnson wore such lovely clothes. Jen wasn't the only girl in the audience to be envious.

At the end, when a voice paid tribute to the sailors of the Royal Navy, 'above all victories, beyond all loss . . . they give us, their countrymen, eternal and indomitable pride', everyone stood and cheered, and remained standing, in silence, while the organ boomed the national anthem.

As they trooped out it was clear that lots of people had been crying. One woman was still sobbing uncontrollably. The murmur went round that her son had been drowned in an Atlantic convoy last autumn, but no one liked to intrude. It didn't seem polite. Her friend handed her a hanky and steered her to the door. 'She needs to pull herself together,' Jen's mum whispered. She'd be better once she got home. You had to keep going. They all knew that.

But Jen was thinking about the ship and the sailors, not the ones in the film but the ones they would get to know at school. The ship they were adopting. She would be in touch with the war she'd seen on the screen; she would meet heroes. She would be like their girlfriends and families in the story – she could even pretend her teachers were like Celia Johnson. It was all going to be so exciting.

The Decision

2003

It looks as though there's going to be a war, far away in a place no one knows with people getting killed and blood and guts all over the television screen. Millie sighs in despair.

She folds the *Guardian* and sets it among the art books on her table. She doesn't want to have to get concerned all over again: she did it long ago when she was part of a group that helped American draft dodgers: Vietnam was a conscripts war. This won't be, though. Professional soldiers out there risking their lives. What makes young people join the services: why would they? She can't imagine. Do today's young men want to be warriors, proving their courage in the face of the enemy? How sad an outlook for young boys perhaps with nothing better to do with their lives. Their frail lives. Life is frail, Millie knows that.

She sighs and sits back into the deep comfort of her leather chair, fingering the stray strands of hair that have escaped from the clip at the nape of her neck. She is neat in body and in mind but right now she has things to think through. Pale curtains keep the dark from tall windows: she loves this moment, this empty time in the late afternoon, when the night closes in on winter evenings, when she can sit and let her thoughts wander. But not today. Millie has afternoon care of her two-year-old granddaughter, Freya, whenever Kate, her daughter, is having her dialysis. The rumour of war has drifted into her mind, prompted by a disputatious item she had heard earlier on Radio 4.

Perhaps even now Tony Blair is thinking through whether to send young men to die. She feels as though she and the country are sleep-walking into some vague and shifting future. She's glad it isn't her decision, that nothing is being asked of her. She has a far more immediate decision of her own to make.

She has been to see a specialist, one of the team dealing with Kate's illness.

As Millie entered the inner sanctum – broad spaces of hushed carpets – she had been gripped by a sense of panic. Her daughter has a failing kidney, and she knows that Kate's best chance of a reasonable life is a kidney transplant from a live donor.

But everyone was behaving as though she had already offered her body up for surgery, and was quite sanguine about it. It seems a foregone conclusion, but it isn't at all. She has swiftly agreed to take the tests. She doesn't like to be taken for granted and a part of her feels rebellious, the difficult daughter living on in the ageing woman. All in good time, she says to herself as she waits to meet the consultant.

18

There is a shadow haunting this decision. Two years earlier her husband Dominic, whom she had loved for so long, died in hospital. His illness was short and unexpected. Being a scholar, she did what scholars do, researching all the information she could in libraries and on the internet. Nothing she found could save him. Nor could the hospital. He was a mere sixty-two and had slipped away unobtrusively, without saying goodbye, without her there to hold him. Plans for their retirement together – travelling the world, seeing all the great art they loved – were suddenly snatched away and a chasm of loneliness opened up before her. It makes her quick to blame; it makes her suspicious of hospitals. It makes her fearful.

The consultant, Mr Charles, had a shock of grey hair crinkled like a pan-scourer, neat hands and fingernails, precise movements, an odd yellow tie with birds on it. Was he an ornithologist in his spare time, she wondered, this man who expected so much of her? What nonsense. There'll be no risk. She's not even ill. It's Kate who's ill. Millie's here to talk and to listen. And to take the tests.

'Well, Mrs Carson,' he embarked on the formal delivery of medical information, 'I know you've been unable to establish whether in the past anyone in your family suffered from polycystic kidney disease. I'm delighted you've agreed to take the appropriate tests.'

Millie bowed her head in a sort of aquiescence, and picked up a stray paperclip from his desk.

'Of course, once we've done the tests, if we find your kidney does match, you'll have a very delicate decision to make. I want you to take your time. Discuss it with the family.'

She interrupted his words suddenly, startling him, and even herself. 'No, I have no one to talk to. No one.' She paused. He was waiting for her to continue but it wasn't easy. Something seized hold of her. She tried to think of Kate and how she could save her but the thought vanished into the panic. Her throat tightened. She swallowed hard before she could speak. 'You see, my husband, Dominic, the only person I could have shared this with, died two years ago. I want to talk to him now – I need to. He was the only one who would have understood. But he's not here.' Millie held Mr Charles's gaze. Her loss was none of his business. He is a renal expert, waiting to conduct the tests to which she has agreed. She fought to stop the tears brimming in her eyes. She rallied and smiled wanly. 'I'm sorry – I've wrecked your paperclip,' and she laid the coil of wire on his desk.

Freya is scrambling towards the tempting fringe of a pale silk cushion when the doorbell rings. 'Come on, Freya, let's see who it is.' Millie already knows. The nursing home has phoned ahead to warn her. It is moving out of its current building, and in clearing the cellar has found a box that once belonged to her mother. It's a laundry basket, leather straps frayed and pliant with age.

Millie signs the smudgy papers offered by the delivery man and drags the box into the middle of the room, where the child is bearing down on a coffee table on which stands a large and perfect glass bowl. The home of an art historian is no place for sticky fingers and Millie rushes to distract her.

'No, Freya, not there! Let's explore inside this box.' She

shakes open the wicker lid, dust powdering into the air, curious despite herself.

Inside there is yellowing tissue paper – things have been wrapped and stacked. A neat pile of old school magazines from the 1940s. She skims through them: Gothic headings, dim photographs of plain women in shapeless clothes, a framed watercolour – rather good – accounts of visits to coal mines, silk mills, a gasworks. Was this what passed for entertainment in those days?

'Oh, Freya, look at these!' Six turtle shells, small ones, terrapins, perhaps, each painted a bright colour. She holds one out to the child. A zoologist had passed this way then, someone bringing back specimens and bequeathing them to . . . who knows? She looks for labels or descriptions. There are none. Freya casually bangs the yellow shell against the curved leg of a Victorian chair.

A black photograph album with a silk tassel. Groups of girls massed round a surprisingly stylish woman. A clutch of papers, some old greetings cards, bits and pieces jumbled together. A map. Why had her mother not explained what all this was about when she was still alive? Or thrown it all away? But Millie's mother never talked about her life.

'Oh, just look. You'll like this.' She doesn't know what children like any more. She's out of touch, but this is a two-foot model of some sort of Arab dhow. The child reaches out for it. 'Gently now.' As she hands it over, Millie notices someone has written across the base 'From MS 898/S34'.

She hears a key turn in the lock. That'll be Kate. Time to investigate all this later. Millie hustles everything back into the basket. 'C'mon, Freya, Mummy's here.'

The Ship

1942

Josh Percival sat back in his cabin, poured himself a whisky and swirled it slowly, the drops clinging to the sides of the glass. It was early morning, still dark, and raining. He looked down into the depths of the drink, abstracted, his mind's eye blank. 'Good God!' He stretched and threw back his head. He was a tall man and the confines of the ship had given him a premature stoop. He was always more comfortable on deck. He gulped the lowland single malt – Bladnoch. He cherished such private luxuries: he had tasted this whisky first on that weekend in the hills of Dumfries where he'd met Jessica so long ago. He had another swig. So long ago.

Only in port and in moments such as this did he have any sense of the burden of effort and resolution heaped on the people of Liverpool. He knew he would be among them soon, see their tired eyes and sagging shoulders, the weariness of surviving, the remorseless pressing forward with each successive task. The rain was pounding down outside, but what else could you expect? This was good

22

old Lancashire. And wet, dark, misty, wonderful Liverpool, almost as proud as his own Glasgow. He couldn't see much of it from the porthole now, and had seen even less as they had come into dock late last night. It had been tricky to navigate, so many ships coming and going, lights at a minimum, passing and setting out, all part of the same enormous enterprise. The city itself was shrouded in darkness, canopied in rain, but he had sensed it there, its strong, throbbing heart, the black trappings of its industries, the stubborn humour of its people, all there behind the rain, not noticing its persistence, and the all-embracing damp. A great welcome, he thought, after what he'd been through.

He was thankful they'd got back at all. They'd been attacked only two days out of Halifax, carrying a cargo of steel and timber. The sea was running a good swell and there was a full moon, no clouds: he knew that meant danger. Even as he had nudged the SS *Treverran* into the wide waterways of the harbour he had known that the German U-boats would be waiting. Canadian air cover could reach only so far out of Halifax and the RAF only so far from Britain. It left a gaping opportunity. Their convoy had taken a week to assemble, with escort ships of the Canadian and Royal Navy on either flank protecting a dozen merchantmen like his own. What had seemed such a mighty flotilla as it moved out of home waters was soon little more than flotsam on the mighty ocean.

The hit had caught the ship next to the *Treverran* full on, an almighty boom, then a blaze of sparks and fuel. It lurched and, within minutes, had begun to go down.

Each of the *Treverran*'s crew looked up grimly, took in the horror with sudden violent prayers. They might be next. 'They've bought it, poor buggers, not a bloody chance.' Some saw a single lifeboat lowered, but the *Treverran* steamed on. It wasn't their job to rescue: that was for the escorts. They saw figures clustered on the tilting deck, jumping into the sea . . . and still the *Treverran* steamed on. Soon the spreading fire lit up the night sky, signalling their presence for miles. They continued to slide stealthily forward. The cargo must get through. The survivors would be picked up – if they were lucky. That was the theory. Everyone watching knew it might not work out like that. 'God damn it . . . poor sods.' And they kept their course.

Now Josh shot the last of the whisky neatly to the back of his throat. It helped burn away dark thoughts. Soon the crew would be signing off and going their different ways. Only Tim Beesley and Robert Warburton – first and second mates – with the company apprentice, Charlie Rawlings, would return to the *Treverran*. They were very different from each other, but he'd come to trust them. The older two were almost like sons to him now – like his own lad, Peter. They rubbed along well together – even if Tim was a bit touchy about life back home. 'Whole country's buggered by class,' he'd rage, when he'd been drinking.

Josh had cut him short, 'No politics on board,' though he'd known well enough that Tim was right.

'Yoo-hoo!' Jessica leaned out of the window and waved at a distant figure walking towards them along the pavement below. Her white shirt sleeves ballooned over the sill. Against all rules, she had taken off her uniform jacket, which hung now on the back of her chair. 'Yoo-*hoo!*'

'Hold on a mo, Jess! How can you be sure it's him?' This was Babs, her secretary, with whom she shared an untidy flat. 'You'll look such a clot if it's someone else.'

'Worth the risk. If it's him, good – if not, whoever it is will just think I'm cracked!' She would have leaned out further, but her sturdy build and the stiffness of the old sash window prevented it. 'Yoo-hoo! It's me! Is that you?'

Jessica was too old to behave like this – she was a grown woman with a husband at sea and a son serving in the Royal Navy – but the skittishness of girlhood persisted, a boisterous good humour learned in the Guides, at the tennis club and from the Youth Hostel Association.

'Oh, heck, it's not him. Damn!' Her well-corseted bulk collapsed into the green leather chair she had infiltrated into the spartan décor of the Wrens' office. It had come from the nursery at home and had been with her all her thirty-eight years.

'Now some bod out there thinks you tried to pick him up.' Babs spoke above the sniggering of the other girls.

'Perhaps I should go out and make sure he's not disappointed, eh? Is he handsome?' asked a languid blonde, battling with a typewriter at a corner desk. It was the cue for them all. Up from their places they sashayed across the room, making for the two windows Jessica had thrown open to the late winter chill.

Molly, devoted follower of Ginger and Fred, had chosen to tap-dance her way through life. Now she swung herself, toes and heels clicking, across the dark green lino. Mavis, with a passion for the sultry Rita Hayworth, tossed her shoulder-length hair, lit a cigarette, drew in the smoke with high drama and glided after her. 'Is this the one for me, d'you think, girls?'

By now the stranger was at the doorway below and, looking up, saw the bright, eager faces of wholesome young women, not of the sort they talked about at sea but lovely as could be. He waved and went on his way, smiling. Shore leave. Wonderful.

The little cyclone of gaiety was passing. 'That's enough, people. Joke's over. Now, for God's sake, let's do some work, or we'll get it in the neck!' Jessica was torn between excitement and formality. War work had that effect on her. She had volunteered right at the start and her fluent French had ensured that within weeks she had been commissioned as an officer in the Wrens. Josh had been impressed and a little afraid for her. How would she, with her volatile temperament, respond to the discipline? Now she was at Derby House in Liverpool, strategic headquarters for the battle of the Atlantic, working every day in the vast meandering bunker tucked away behind the Pierhead, the powerhouse of naval planning where shipping movements were plotted day and night by relays of uniformed Wrens and WAAFs. It was the inner sanctum. The Commander-in-Chief, Western Approaches, had his office there.

Both Josh and Jessica deplored the war, of course, but Jessica also relished the changes it brought to her. She had never thought she would have a paid job. Women of her class, privately educated, no intellectual pretensions, stayed at home and ran the household. But now everything had changed. Domestic staff were harder and harder to find. Village girls were drawn to clerical or shop work in the local towns – they wore smart black shoes with Cuban heels, frilly blouses, and became quite chatty, even familiar, with the customers. Something was infecting them, something challenging and risky, bold and courageous, and it was infecting Jessica too. The war was terrible, but her place in it was good. All this she knew but did not speak of it to Josh.

Her staff thought they made an odd couple: Josh with his rolling Scottish ways, the master of a merchant ship, she from the comfortable south. They didn't know that, as a young man, Josh had had a taste for monied folk, with big houses, who drank coffee and martini. Nor how, when he, tiring of local girls haunted by the shadow of John Knox, had been smitten by Jessica's easy abandon, how she had made love with as much gusto as she brought to hockey and lacrosse. To start with their marriage arrangements had been unconventional but suitable: he away at sea, but with a sure anchor in the Surrey hills where they'd made their home, while she, in solid domestic comfort, stirred to excitement whenever he came on leave. But now Jessica was in the war, too.

Today, making proper allowance for his having to deal with all the administration that went with discharging the cargo and handing over to the shore staff, she calculated he could be with her by the end of the day. But her spirits began to rise much earlier, and with them the mood of her office.

Josh rang from the dock office on the quay. It was seven o'clock and Jessica was in her draughty flat tucked away behind the Pierhead. The only telephone was downstairs in the hall where it was answered by Mrs Scragg, who kept a spider's watch on her tenants. She shouted up the echoing stairwell and Jessica came clumping down, eager but apprehensive, and took the receiver.

'You've docked, then.'

'Yes, I'm here right enough.'

'That's good 'cos guess what . . . I'm free – I'm due a weekend off! Isn't that wonderful?'

'It is. Just what I was hoping.'

'Where shall we meet?'

Mrs Scragg was wary of men visiting the flats she let to women, even the married ones. Besides, Jessica's was tiny, with stockings and knickers drying over the bath . . . and Babs.

'What do you say we meet in the Grapes, eh, on the corner of Argyll Street?'

'It's a bit grim – noisy and smoky. I'd like not to have to shout above the rabble.' Jessica had genteel reservations.

'Well, we're all rabble, these days.'

'You know what I mean.'

He did. Jessica hadn't abandoned the snobbery of her upbringing. But Josh wanted to meet her where there would be plenty of noise and all sorts of other people meeting as their ships docked. Twenty had arrived today and sailors had been coming ashore in large numbers, heads down against the slanting drizzle, making for pubs and welfare hostels, even, the lucky ones, for home. Josh felt their surging energy, wanted to be part of it.

In the end he indulged her. It would be something for

her to tell the girls. They met in the bar of Liverpool's finest hotel where his pay packet would run to a round of pink gins. Wren officers liked putting on the style and didn't often have the chance. In peacetime the Adelphi's plush and gilt greeted trainloads of punters arriving at Lime Street for the Grand National, but the race meeting had been cancelled for the duration.

The lights in the bar were subdued and the drift of meeting couples spread a murmur across the dusty shadows of the interior. Josh and Jessica met briskly, exchanged an awkward, perfunctory kiss.

'Heard from Peter?' It was his first question as they settled into ageing armchairs.

'Nothing, but he only sailed a couple of weeks ago.' They looked around the neglected bar rather than at each other.

'How was it?' she asked.

'Terrible.' He laughed harshly. He was holding her hand tightly and now gave it a soothing stroke, which told her not to ask for more. Not just yet. 'It seems to be getting worse. Bloody terrible.'

She didn't need to ask what that meant. Her job at Derby House made her privy to the mounting Atlantic losses. Some forty ships had been sunk in the previous month alone. 'But you're here, and I've a couple of days off. That's some kind of miracle.'

'Aye, well, we need as many of those as we can get.'

'Yes.'

In the silence they began to feel that quiet knowledge of each other which had sustained their many years together. It was as if blood was returning to a numb limb.

Within the familiarity of their marriage they could stay with their own thoughts.

'Bumped into my old mucker Bertie Conrad at the dock office. He suggested we take his old banger and his golf clubs and go to Hoylake for the day. Can you come? Would that be good?'

'Let's do it tomorrow.'

Two gins later, Jessica phoned Babs and told her she wouldn't be back. Josh booked a room in a cheaper, shabbier hotel behind the station and together they made a clumsy and affectionate attempt at pretending the war was making no difference at all.

Waking to a morning of thick drizzle, they turned on rumpled sheets and lay together, half entwined, as they had over the years. He stirred against her, his gaunt frame finding comfort in her ample curves, and she yielded to him, still half asleep.

Later, he lay thinking of how they'd met, years ago, at that bizarre house-party on the shores of the Solway Firth – he'd been dragged there by a jovial friend he'd fallen in with at a seedy Glasgow party – and Jessica, then a boisterous girl, had caught his eye. When he manoeuvred his way to her side, she had gauchely teased him about his beard and pipe. Eventually he had prised her away from the braying voices of her companions and enticed her to the wide beaches of Carrick Bay. As the slow tide lapped their toes he had told her how, long ago, further down the coast two women had been tied to posts and drowned by the incoming tide for failing to acknowledge King Charles II. She had been moved by the tale – 'Imagine! To drown slowly like that ... How dreadful.' Her eyes had bulged with the horror of it. He remembered it now – a fear he had come to know all too well.

Later they picked up Bertie Conrad's car – a Ford 7, black, as all cars were – and Josh hoisted his clubs into the back. The gentle lovemaking of the morning had made them kindly towards each other. The world had slowed, giving them space. It made them smile. They drove to the Royal Liverpool, the famous course lying on the coastline of sandy scrub and dunes. It offered naval officers courtesy entrance for the duration of the war but, fearful that the privilege might not extend to the merchant fleet, Josh made a point of being engagingly pleasant to the girl at the desk.

This was what they always enjoyed – being in the open together, playing some sport or other, and now Jessica strode out in her tweed split-skirt and fringe-tongued brogues, her hair looped into a crocheted snood like factory girls wore. Josh's shabby corduroys and polo-necked sweater were universal off-duty rig. His long body shaped well over the tee and he made his drive with an easy style. He took pleasure in doing things well. Only a few couples were on the course, pausing always at a certain point out towards the coast. Josh and Jessica did the same, on the eleventh and twelfth holes, watching in the distance a shadowy line of ships – cargo ships, converted liners, corvettes, even a battleship – moving across the waters of Liverpool Bay, a measured, almost elegant progress. Then they turned back to their game.

It was only on the drive back that they flared into unexpected confrontation.

'Why didn't you tell me? Why on *earth* didn't you tell me?' Jessica was sitting upright in the passenger seat, and looking accusingly at Josh.

'I *am* telling you . . . I'm telling you now.'

'I suppose I'm not invited, am I?' She knew the answer but wanted to make him feel guilty.

'Use your loaf, Jess. It's an entirely new venture and I don't know yet how it works.'

Jessica's crabbiness transferred to the road. 'Mind out! That lorry's not going to give way . . .' The choking traffic intensified as they neared the docks; few private cars but everything else on wheels that could carry freight to and from the quays – machinery, pit props and steel had to be loaded into holds that had recently discharged frozen meat, bauxite and fuel oil.

'I read about it in a paper I picked up at the dock offices before we sailed last time and it sounded like a good idea, a way of keeping in touch with the Home Front.'

'I thought I was your Home Front?' A flinty smile broke the tension. He gave her gloved hand a squeeze and swerved to avoid an army transport vehicle coming out of a side-street with little warning.

'Damn!' He moderated his tone: 'Look, the Ship Adoption Society puts us in touch with schools and we exchange letters or visits. It's meant to boost morale and teach the children geography. I wrote to the secretary and when we docked there was a letter from the headmistress of the Ashworth Grammar School for Girls.'

'What? Girls? Don't be daft.'

'It wasn't up to me. I know it seems a bit rum, but the lads'll like it.'

32

'It sounds a bit posh for your lot. Young ladies!'

'You were a young lady yourself once.'

'And look what I got up to!'

Josh gave her a long, hard stare, neither hostile nor intimate. They'd had to marry: there was simply no other way once Jessica had realised she was pregnant.

She laughed uneasily. 'Make sure they stay like that, then. Where is the school?'

'Over Manchester way, an hour on the train. I thought I'd take along my first and second mates, Robert and Tim. Possibly the young apprentice, Charlie Rawlings, too. They could do with an eyeful of feminine charm.'

'And what about you?'

'Oh, I'm just meeting the headmistress to make the arrangements. Some whiskery old trout, no doubt. I'll go across first thing tomorrow.'

'What about the ship? Are you telling me that a bunch of giggling schoolgirls are to be told all about your cargo, the convoys, where you're heading? I can't imagine what Derby House will make of that.'

'Not at all. They'll write to the ship using a code – we're MS 898/S34. Where we're going, when, and what we're carrying will be strictly off limits.'

'And Liverpool? Where you're docked, where you sail from?'

'Have it your own way, Jessica. Even if you think the idea's such a duff one, the Merchant Navy doesn't. No one knows better than you that Liverpool's at the centre right now. God damn it, you spend your life mapping it all.'

She fell into a sulky silence. Eventually: 'I'd thought of going to the flicks.'

'Go with Babs. What's on, anyway?'
'*In Which We Serve*. It's a big hit.'
'Talk about coals to Newcastle!'

Cynthia Maitland struck a match to the gas ring and tightened the silky cord of her dressing-gown. As she refilled the tin kettle under the tap, she looked out into the back garden, smiling softly at the evidence of spring. The clutches of snowdrops under the apple tree had been and gone with the February rain, and now the daffodils, in ranks along the borders, were stiffly in bud. Soon the apple blossom would be out, so much more subtle than that of the blowsy cherry trees that fronted the school. Cherry blossom at school, where she came into her own, displaying leadership and character that would be unwelcome to her timid mother. Apple blossom at home, subdued and subtle as the temperament she revealed there. She lived in two worlds and held them in balance. It had become second nature.

She knotted the dressing-gown cord tighter and stroked the fleecy cherry-red wool across her stomach with a sense of approval. She was keeping her figure well and took pride in it. No one commented, of course, but she cared about her appearance: it was one of the many little efforts that made up her life. She patted the Dinkie curlers in her hair and reached for the tea caddy. She knew she was a little vain, but where was the harm in that?

Cynthia took her mother a cup of tea and a slice of buttered toast each morning in bed. Butter, not margarine, a good part of their weekly ration. Her father, Arnold, had begun the habit long ago as a treat for his shy wife. It had hardened into an expected routine, compensation for the demeaning requirements of the married state. Cynthia had sometimes speculated about their marriage, wondering why it had seemed so chilly. Beryl, she thought, must have yielded with the sense of doing Arnold a favour for which she felt entitled to a reward. And nothing in the book of sex advice she knew her father kept wrapped in brown paper at the back of the bookcase could have helped.

Cynthia's birth had come as a further shock. Beryl had once hinted about it to her – 'Women go through so much!' It seemed that no one had warned her of the wrenching agony or explained that the baby would arrive between her legs, a place of secrecy and shame. She took home what she called 'our precious bundle' swaddled in hand-knitted shawls and the next month ordered twin beds. Cynthia was an only child.

Beryl woke slowly and accepted the proffered tray with its embroidered cloth, fresh each week and wilting now from several days' use. It would go into the wash on Monday and a new one, freshly ironed, would take its place. A drawer in the sideboard was packed with tray cloths along with ivory serviette rings, and place-setting cards that had never been used – a mistaken present from remote cousins who misunderstood the family's social standing. There wasn't much that was new around the place. There wasn't much that was new about Cynthia's mother.

When Arnold died Beryl had wept copiously, then promptly transferred the emotional hold she had exercised over him to the local church where, through her wheedling prayers, she urged Jesus to do her bidding. St Saviour's was only a short walk away, and the Reverend George Potter must have been surprised to find her there almost daily. With the deftness of his calling, he offered her duty rather than friendship, integrating her among his most useful parishioners. Beryl was soon on the flower rota and even took on the challenge of embroidering a hassock.

Cynthia stood in front of her wardrobe mirror and accepted that it was she who did the coping. As well as her job, there were medical appointments to arrange, her mother's favourite mint imperials to buy, the coal to bring in and the blackout to check. Beryl could have insisted she give up her work, as many daughters did, but there was an unspoken understanding between them that neither wanted to lose the headmistress's wage. She must be grateful for that – but her mother could simply not expect her to dance attendance at every minute. Today would be a big day so she would need to take extra care how she dressed.

If he was honest with himself, Josh would have had to admit he was out to impress. He had a Scots regard for the chalk and the taws, and a grammar school was a prestigious institution. Jessica might have gone to an exclusive school, but he reserved his real admiration for places that taught Latin and sent people to university. The headmistress of such a place must surely be something of a Gorgon. He would establish the terms of their encounter by taking her to tea at Manchester's Midland Hotel.

The Midland – like its Liverpool rival, the Adelphi – expressed the grand civic pride of its city's mercantile classes. It had once housed a theatre, where the legendary Miss Horniman had created the first repertory company. Manchester's businessmen, entrepreneurs and investors had made the Midland their temple. It was where Rolls had met Royce. Everyone knew it was the best, and it would be where Captain Percival met Miss Maitland.

Wartime had muted its style. The entrance now had a concrete canopy, and sandbags protected its glazed terracotta exterior. Inside, the airy, arching atrium was hidden behind lower, more serviceable ceilings. But the spacious lounge remained, dotted with tables and flimsy chairs, where waitresses in black dresses with frilled pinafores served afternoon tea. There were limits to what and how much food could be served, but you could still, in the interest of elegance, cut crusts off sandwiches.

Josh arrived early, chose a place where he could watch the door, then waited for the drama to begin. First came the cast, a trickle of hungry people, those in uniform given priority. In the Midland that meant officers' uniform; two GIs and a squadron leader had settled themselves already. Josh was wearing his uniform, too, something he would never do on shore in the usual run of things, but he hadn't known how else Miss Maitland would recognize him.

He began to scrutinize the newcomers. He was looking for someone who had the eccentricity and *sangfroid* of the actress Dame May Whitty: he had seen her in *The Lady Vanishes* at Liverpool's Futurist Cinema in the months before the war. She was how he expected a headmistress to be. And, sure enough, there she was, striding through the doors, authoritative and robust, white hair drawn back severely in a bun, and marching purposefully across the carpet, peering unashamedly into every face.

In a moment she was upon him, her strident voice informing everyone of her presence. 'Ah, you're waiting for me. I can tell. You're not quite staring, but you *are* looking. Am I right?' He stood up thinking he'd been correct about Dame May Whitty.

From the corner of his eye he noticed that others were pausing to observe their noisy encounter, among them a neat, slender woman clasping a handbag, a little hat sitting fetchingly on her head. He felt self-conscious suddenly, and wished that whoever she was expecting would turn up and distract her.

'Yes, you are – right, I mean. I'm Josh Percival – Captain Josh Percival.'

'Oh, no. I'm not right, then – you're not who I thought you were.' The tweed bulk took in the significance of his uniform, that of the Merchant Navy, and recoiled as though she had been insulted, which, in a way, she had. 'And now I perceive my regrettable mistake. I'm expecting to meet a captain of our gallant *Royal Navy*, sir, not, not—'

The 'sir' had been expressed with a disdain that sent Josh into a sulphurous rage. 'And I, ma'am, was expecting to meet a lady.'

He turned away, cut to the quick that those with whom he served at sea, albeit in a different service, should be regarded as so far superior to himself.

He found the bar and ordered a large pink gin, a confusion of anger and embarrassment boiling within him. A few minutes later he was ordering a second when he realized that, if Dame May Whitty wasn't the headmistress, the real one might be stranded, waiting somewhere to have the tea she had been promised. He swallowed the drink and turned to leave. The neat, slender woman who had earlier caught his attention was at the entrance. Alone and self-possessed, she was watching him with calm pale eyes. She made no move to speak or approach, simply waited.

'Er, it isn't Miss Maitland, is it?' The drink had softened his unease. 'I hope I'm not mistaken.'

'I am Miss Maitland.'

'Oh, good. I'm pleased.'

She smiled at that. 'I saw what happened, Captain Percival. How do you do?' She held out a gloved hand. Wary, not bold.

'Yes, a frightful mix-up. You can see why I thought . . .'

'Oh, I can. And . . .' a slight hesitancy '. . . I can't say I found it flattering.' She was looking him in the eye.

'Ha . . . no, well . . .' He floundered, disarmed by her poise and steady gaze. He shrugged helplessly. 'Who is the old dragon, I wonder?'

'She's Mrs Murgatroyd, in charge of evacuee children in the north-west. She's also a governor of my school, a little forceful, perhaps.' Cynthia was not to be drawn into criticism of other women, who were asserting themselves in different ways in this war. It wasn't for her to judge how they did it. Nevertheless she felt a certain quiet satisfaction.

'It wasn't a very good start to our meeting, I'm afraid. I thought you might like tea.'

'Does it go with gin?' She was smiling, but it had sounded like a reproof – she must be a stickler for correct behaviour. He mustn't forget that.

'Tea would be perfect.'

And so it was. The Midland had the correct china, starched napkins, a flowered teapot and, on a white doily, some little rock buns, meagre rations dressed up to echo luxuries long gone.

They had much to discuss. The ship: four thousand tons, a crew of forty-five. The school: four hundred girls, a staff of thirty.

'We're not far from Manchester, in a suburban road. They've been planting trees there, so in a few years it'll be very leafy. We have a beautiful building, dating from the turn of the century. Of course, the war means we've had to dig up the lawns for air-raid shelters, and put supporting timbers along the corridors, but I love it. And I'm very proud of it.'

'Well the ship wasn't built for style. It belongs to a shipping company in the West Country, and is on charter to the government as Ministry of War Transport. So we come and go but, of course, I can't say where. Can't risk chattering schoolgirls blabbing about where we're sailing.'

'My girls don't blab, Captain Percival.' Another reproof. Damn. 'But I fully understand and will insist on the utmost discretion about any contact between ship and school.'

Yes, he thought, she's clearly been a schoolmistress for

40

a long time. It's embedded in her manner, her way of thinking. Same as me, I suppose. I've been at sea getting on for twenty years now so I talk and think like my own kind. Can't hold that against her. In fact, he didn't want to find any fault with her.

She was relieved he was so at ease. No doubt the drink had helped. She wondered fleetingly whether he was often drunk. Sailors were notorious for it. But his ease of manner suited her. Once the civilities were over she stayed longer than she had intended.

His long limbs stretched out as he relaxed. She leaned towards him as they talked animatedly of the war, though he noticed restraint even in her eagerness. They parted in the gloom of the evening, each feeling they had exchanged more than plans for the school and his ship.

Leave

Robert had known that a great welcome awaited him. His family, the Warburtons – sturdy farming stock – had run Blazebrook Farm in Cheshire for many generations. He had grown up among its green fields and muddy ditches, scabbing his knees on trees and five-barred gates, roaming the banks and meadows that fed his father's Friesian herd. He strode along the lane in which celandines dotted the grass. The driving mist had cleared and left the fields, pasture, trees, grasses and bare, twisted brambles with droplets on budding leaves and stems.

He turned the corner and paused to enjoy the view of the half-timbered house. Within its walls his emotions would be more complicated. Theirs was an ancient Catholic family, proud of its piety – there was even a priest's hole tucked behind the timbers. With the farming tradition, their faith was what gave the family its identity. Robert had fled to sea long before the war to escape its smothering expectations. And it was only to his sea-going friend that he could talk now.

Tim slipped into the Slaughter House as a gale of laughter burst over his head. The place was full of smoke and men, and across the bar he spotted Robert's raised hand, calling him over.

'What the heck was that all about?'

'Oh, a lorry skidded and overturned on Water Street. Spilled its load on the cobbles – cartons of Brylcreem, would you believe?'

'What's it doing here? This is a dock, not a bloody airfield. How's the RAF going to get its hands on it?'

'It's not. There's been a rush. They were handing it out before you got here. It's not too late if you fancy a jar.'

'Get away! You'll not see me with a straight parting and my hair slicked down. Who d'you think I am? Robert Donat?'

They ordered pints of the thin watered beer, and drank with long greedy gulps.

'So – then – how was it?' It was Robert who asked.

'Well, good to see them, of course, but, I dunno, I can't really talk to them. The folks want you back, naturally, but they don't really want to hear about what's going on. And you?'

'Oh, terrific . . . and not.' Robert searched for generalizations. It was disloyal to speak of family quarrels too explicitly. And yet . . . 'You remember how we once talked about POWs in England, how we felt?'

'We said we'd better not meet them anywhere or else.'

43

'Yes, I agree, but I've been wondering.' He looked up, concerned that Tim might think him a sissy. 'I've been wondering – they've just been called up, given no option, poor blighters. They're probably no different from our lads.'

'The working classes fight the wars, and that's the truth, but we've got to stop the other side killing us. That's clear enough, isn't it?' Tim called to the barmaid for more beer.

She was coping well with orders, and much cheek, from the sweating, swearing crowd – 'Oy, darlin', a pint and a squeeze, please,' and 'Give us another, Mother!' She rattled Tim's money with a 'Ta, love,' and a flying kiss from bright red lips.

Robert was still following his thoughts: 'I can't think of the man I've met as an enemy. They're two different things.'

'You've actually met one? What happened?'

'Yes, that's what I'm trying to tell you.' Robert pulled a packet of Park Drive out of his pocket and lit up distractedly, cupping the glowing tip in his palm.

'Pass 'em round, Rob.'

'Sorry.'

'He's an Eyetie, Angelo, and he's working on our farm. Pa needed the labour, because our men have been called up. The Min of Ag is letting POWs work on farms.'

'How's he doing? You'd best watch out – he'll be poisoning the milk.'

'He could do that – he helps with the milking and churns the butter. But he's rather soft. Big and strong, but soft . . .'

A silence fell between them.

'He sings Italian songs all the time.'

'You like him?'

'Well, not exactly. We had a big row, Dad and I, before I'd met him. I shouted a bit and slammed about: one of the enemy in my own home . . . it riled me. You know how it is.'

Tim who had never quarrelled with his father pretended to agree. 'That's families for you.'

'They just don't know what it's like, do they? How can they? You want your leave to be perfect. You dream of being home. Then this gulf opens up. You've left them behind.'

'True.' Tim could identify easily enough with this. 'Dad was going on at me about politics again. He always does. Of course I agree that things have got to change, but I don't want to talk about it all the time. I just want some quiet.'

Tim's arrival always unleashed a cascade of talk from his father. At the family home in a small terrace below Staveley station Sam, primed with books from the Mechanics Institute, would hold forth on labour matters, the workers' struggle, the iniquities of employers. Tim's mother, in the armchair and absorbed in her knitting, would look suitably stern when he spoke disparagingly of his employer, Mr Sykes, but she didn't usually comment. Women were fine and loyal but their nature was different from a man's. Getting no response from her, Sam would tap his pipe and fall silent, saving his arguments for Tim.

45

'You see, our lad, old Sykes is doing fine by the war. Corruption – the country's riddled with it.'

Tim made an effort. 'Is there enough coal, then?' His father took the cart out daily, delivering from house to house. 'I'd have thought the factories would get it all.' He was familiar with his father's trick of trying to rouse him to a goodly argument. Since his early teens they'd shadow-boxed amiably over their political ideas. 'The lad and I've been giving the politicos a good thrashing,' Sam would tell his wife, when they gathered for their tea around the gate-legged table.

'Aye, for the moment,' Sam said now. 'Though some folk's greedy, but I make sure there's fair dos all round. The pits are going all out. Nationalization'll come after the war, mark my words. There's no doubt about it. Even Churchill's having to bow to the inevitable.'

Despite himself Tim was caught up in the older man's fervour. He lit a Capstan and fetched a brass ashtray from the mantelpiece. Sam was off. 'All these government rules and such, rationing, conscription, no one dares bat an eyelid. It's for the good of the country, you see. That's how to soften them up for what's to come.'

'Well, it had better be victory first.' Tim had heard the talk in Britain's ports: how much worse could it get? Surely some kind of negotiated peace must be possible. In pubs, hostels and quayside offices the mood was of defeat. But he couldn't share that with his father. Or with anyone else. Well, there was just one . . .

Next morning, he went up the street to the phone box, put in the two pennies, and dialled a number he'd scribbled on a scrap of paper. When a strange voice

46

answered, he pressed button A. The money clattered down and he asked for Robert.

'That's it, just as you said. Let things rest and give us some peace, for God's sake, not all this talk.'

They were silent until two girls, bright and gaudy as parrots, started to chat. They bought them drinks, joined the inane babble. One, Jessie she called herself 'after Jessie Matthews', pressed persistently against Tim till the hard button of the suspender below her tight skirt aroused him.

Robert winked and turned away. If Tim was interested, it was up to him. He carried on smoking and struggling with fretful thoughts.

Tim escorted her back to her digs in a dingy back-street. Jessie, a trainee nurse, she said, rented a room from a Chinese landlady whose five sons were stokers signing up regularly on the merchant ships that used the port. She filled their absence and their rooms by letting them to the untidy flotsam of young people dislocated by the war. 'Goodnight, Ma Chow,' Jessie called. Not many landladies were so indulgent.

Her matchbox was running low, so she bent down carefully, wanting to light the gas fire at the first strike. It popped into life, throwing a meagre warmth on to the rag hearth-rug. Tim watched the scarlet skirt ride up round her haunches as she knelt there. Unselfconsciously she reached to loosen the suspenders on her laddered stockings, and with a deft hand rolled them down to her ankles and off the neat pink toes.

Suddenly Tim adored the sight of her. His eyes drank in every curve.

'Take your shoes off, why don't you? Clumsy things.'

Tim complied. He would have kept his socks on, but the lumpy darning at heel and toe looked so woebegone that he snatched them off too.

'I'll put the kettle on. D'you like Bovril?' She stood and moved to the greasy gas ring by the corner sink. 'I suppose your friend'll be all right?' She was winding up a small black gramophone, which yielded a scratchy sound: Gracie Fields singing, 'Sally, Sally, pride of our alley . . .'

'What?'

'Your friend. He went off – looked lonely to me.'

'Robert? . . . Oh, he's OK. Likes his own company. We sail together on the same ship. Some people think he's moody, but he's a great bloke.'

'He's good-looking, too, blond and handsome.'

'Is he? Don't you like them dark, then?' He was standing behind her as she waited for the kettle to boil and slid his hands under the woollen sweater and up to hold the fullness of her breasts.

She waited, enjoying the moment, then turned, smiling, to face him. 'Well, I like you, don't I?'

'I'm glad you do.'

'What did you say your name was?'

'Tim . . . I told you. Tim.'

'Yes, you must have. Tim, then. Let's have that Bovril first, shall we?'

Jessie left the gas ring burning, but it, and the fire, did little to warm the drab little room. So, in their clothes, they climbed under the green eiderdown and sat hunched against stained pillows, sipping the dark drink. Tim hadn't felt this good for a long time.

They made love in a jumble of clothes and blankets, their bodies still aware of the chill around. When they lay huddled side by side, he reached for the eiderdown from where it had fallen on the floor and tucked it tenderly round Jessie's pink and quivering body.

'I liked that,' she said, staring at the ceiling. 'Yes, I really liked that.' She turned and smiled, pulling a strand of golden hair across her mouth.

Tim felt like a god. The few girls he'd known had usually been more practical, glad to get it over with, always a let-down. Perhaps Jessie was different.

'I like it every time,' she mused. 'I do it for all the boys. After all, they could be dead tomorrow – who knows? I think of it as my bit for the war effort.'

Tim reached for his darned socks. He dressed with a sense of sweet melancholy. The world always disappoints. At the door she offered him a scruffy bit of paper with the landlady's telephone number on it. No name. 'You never know,' she said, and shut the door quietly behind him.

Searching

2003

The taxi turns into a long avenue of beech trees hinting at the fresh green leaf to come. The branches meet overhead, cutting out the sky but winnowing the light into a thousand refracted points of brightness. She stops the driver and pays him off. She has one of the Ashworth Grammar School magazines in her bag.

While Millie waits for the specialist's results, she has decided to follow up the strange rag-bag of things left in the old wicker basket by her mother. There is a febrile excitement about waiting. There is a febrile excitement about the country, too. The public talk is all of ways to avoid war, the demanding of concessions, voices raised in contradiction. You can't appease a tyrant, they say, but there is no evident threat to this country. Yet war will come, everyone knows that. Millie has stopped listening. She hears Kate rail against the politicians but sees only her exhausted face and slender damaged arm which the dialysis leaves scarred. She has been told the tests will be ready any day now.

Terraces of substantial red-brick houses with the taint of industrial smoke are set back from wide pavements, where the trunks of beech trees, grey and stately as elephants, set the distances and equilibrium of the space. Last year's beech mast crunches beneath her feet. Sedate gardens unburden drifts of snowdrops on to the path.

The school is halfway down the avenue: a large pillared gateway opens on to a long two-storey building. 'Glenfield School', proclaims a weathered black notice-board. 'Headmaster: Julian Hathersage.' Well, at least it's still a school. It might have become an outpost of Scientology or a health spa and beauty hydro.

A small girl in a grey skirt and cardigan with a maroon tie and a maroon-trimmed blazer takes her to the headmaster. She is shown into a study that, with its panelled walls and long windows, must once have had dignity and authority. Large metal filing cabinets stand everywhere, drawers open spilling papers, while the oak bookshelves are stacked with stationery, a DVD player and a small bulky television. The single row of books includes the *AA Handbook*, *The Time Out Guide to Film*, a dictionary of medical symptoms and *Harry Potter and the Goblet of Fire*.

'Mr Hathersage?'

He stands to greet her as though he has nothing to do but wait for her arrival to break the boredom that seems to have shaped his appearance. He is thick around the ankles, with clumping shoes and trousers that bunch there as though they are a size too large. His tweed jacket has leather patches at the elbows. Its pockets bulge and he reaches for a grey handkerchief, honks into it, then returns it whence it came. His shoulders are narrow, his bald head even more so. His demeanour suggests the discouragement of years has taken its toll.

'Mr Hathersage?' He appeared not to have heard her the first time.

'Oh, yes, that's me all right.' He offers a flabby grey hand. It has the feel of cold pastry.

Millie takes it reluctantly. 'I must have made a mistake. I was looking for the Ashworth Grammar School for Girls.'

A dull smile breaks the thin line of his lips. 'Oh, dear. You're thirty years too late, I'm afraid. Oh, yes. Ashworth went the way of so many grammars.' Her disappointment gives him the most pleasure he's had all day.

'And this is now Glenfield School. A private school?'

'Yes. Parents want their children in smart uniforms, with hatbands and elastic under the chin. We try to keep up old-fashioned values, you see. Are you here to consider putting down the name of a child, perhaps?'

'Oh, no. That's not why I'm here at all. I came on a whim . . .'

'Oh, I could say the same myself. Frankly, where we fetch up in life is usually so far from where we intended. I would have been much happier in the diplomatic corps.' He sighs wistfully. 'But this place suits me well enough. Nothing too ambitious. I know their names. I imagine they're nothing like as bright as the girls who came when it was a grammar school. But times were different then. They were keen as mustard, eager to get on, create the new Jerusalem. At least, that's what an old teacher told me. Miss Jessop taught them French. It was wartime so hardly anyone wanted to do German. From the way she told it, they'd have been too lively for me, assertive young women always defying the strict discipline. Apparently the place was alive with drama productions, house competitions, gym displays, top marks on speech days. Not my style at all.'

'Is Miss Jessop still alive?'

'No, she died last year after falling downstairs. Till then she was a spry old thing. She lived opposite – she liked to call in and walk round the corridors. "Conjuring the ghosts" she called it. I think her time here was the happiest of her life. She taught at Ashworth for thirty-odd years. Teachers did in those days. Wouldn't dream of it now, of course. There'd been some scandal at the school. She never told me what it was.'

'I don't suppose there's any archive left of the old Ashworth Grammar is there? Daily registers and books, perhaps?'

'No. All that sort of stuff was dumped long ago, I believe. I did find an old noticeboard. A list of head-mistresses. I suppose I imagined my own name ought to go on it one day. Fanciful, I'll grant you, but it's handsome with gold lettering. Used to be displayed in the grand hall. Though it's not such a grand hall now. I'll show you round if you like.'

They took off as a skirmish of noisy children surged along the corridors moving from lesson to lesson.

The old assembly hall had indeed been rather grand, but was now used as storage for tubular chairs with torn canvas seating. At one end a series of plywood screens displayed an array of blotchy art. Elsewhere a bookcase was stacked with prayer and hymn books, old and unused. Millie had seen enough.

She made for the avenue of tall beech trees as if the headmaster had contaminated her day. She had forgotten the noticeboard on which the names were painted in gold.

Dancing

1942

Jen was going to try out her ballroom-dancing skills. She and Polly had been attending the Morton-Grantley School of Dancing where a stick-insect woman called Miss Sharp led them through steps marked out on the lino with the outline of large male shoes opposite smaller feminine ones. Dancing had become Jen's passion. She fumbled at swimming and was hopeless at netball, but dancing came naturally. She had swooning thoughts of the dancing she saw in films – Betty Grable and Ann Miller – the boys she partnered at the classes held her at arms' length, their sweaty palms made stickier by the touch of a girl's loose dress and the feel of her brassière strap beneath it.

The town-hall dance would be different. Her mother had run up a dirndl skirt on the sewing-machine made from a Lewis's remnant with a modern design of bright splodges. With it she'd wear a peasant blouse like Deanna Durbin's, with a red drawstring tassel, flowers embroidered on the front and puff sleeves. She paused at

Polly's garden gate. Which door to use: the lowlier familiar one used for friendship and trade; or did being dressed up for the dance deserve the shiny front door, with its lozenges of coloured glass? On seeing the brass knocker and the plate with 'P. G. Grimshaw: Dentist', she opted for the door round the back and rapped on its chipped green paint.

Polly's mother welcomed her into the large, shambling kitchen and offered her the broken-down leather chair in the corner. 'Polly's upstairs, just putting the finishing touches.'

Jen's parents would have been shocked at how a better class of person like Daphne Grimshaw could let her home fall into such casual disrepair, leave it so unashamedly untidy. She knew Mrs Grimshaw was busy, caught up in the WEA and planning a branch of the WVS. What was more, she and her husband were rumoured to be dangerously free-thinking. Jen spotted copies of *Picture Post*, the *Statesman* and *Nation* flung on the table beside a bottle of Milk of Magnesia (how indelicate) and knitting left halfway through a row, with a pattern for a Fair Isle pullover lying beside it. Jen's mother, Ruby, would have tutted at the mess.

'I should tell you, Jen, that I've had a little talk with Polly and explained to her how nice it would be if you'd take Hans – I mean Harry – with you to the dance. We all call him Harry now. He's growing to be quite English, these days, but he's still finding it hard to make friends. It's not his fault and he'd love to go with you, I know.'

'Of course, Mrs Grimshaw. Hans – er, Harry,' she gave an apologetic laugh, 'will be fine with us.'

Jen gushed her reply, needing to be polite, but was privately upset that the talk she and Polly would have shared was now impossible. She mustn't let it show. 'And I'll be happy to dance with him.' She plunged further and further in. 'If he doesn't know the steps I can teach him.' Stop it!

Mrs Grimshaw beamed.

When Polly swept in, she saw at once how the land lay. 'Oh, Mother's told you she's foisting Hans on us, has she? It is a pig. Means we can't talk.'

'Polly, he so admires you, and you know—'

'I know, I know, but, heck, Ma, I want to be with Jen. We have things to talk about.' She turned to her friend for support. 'Jen, have you just agreed to this?'

'Well, yes. I thought . . .' Jen had caught on late to Mrs Grimshaw's ploy. At the same time she was shocked that Polly could so openly defy her mother. 'I said I'd dance with him. I don't mind . . .' Jen trailed off, realizing she was trapped. 'Polly, that dress!'

'C and A, seven coupons in one fell swoop. Like it?' Polly twirled and the bright rayon billowed out. Jen felt crazy with delight and disappointment: Polly, her friend, so lovely and eye-catching. She'd be the belle of the ball while Jen lumbered with the hapless Hans/Harry round the edges of the floor.

He joined them in the kitchen. It was immediately clear to Jen why he wanted to be called Harry: he looked as English as they did. When he had first arrived everything about him had been vividly German. His clothes had had a Germanic neatness, a different cloth and cut, smoother, close fitting. His hair was slicked rigidly to his

head at either side of a knife-edge parting. When intro-
duced, he held out his hand and gave a neat little nod as
he shook yours. Jen could almost imagine he'd clicked
his heels, as the wicked German soldiers did in so many
films. Like them, too, he had round spectacles with wire
rims.

His parents had sent him to Britain three years ago,
and he was entirely used to his new world: Polly had
related how he had come down one morning declaring
triumphantly, 'Tonight already I have a dream which
is in English.' He was getting to be like them, he was
used to the scratchy flannel of school uniform and the way
English men did their ties. Now he was going to a Saturday-
night dance with two older girls.

The town hall stood at the top of the town. Its pillared
clock tower topped a series of colonnades of figured
alabaster, and inside, sumptuous marble halls and curving stairs of wrought ironwork bore witness to the
imperial bombast of one of the north's proud industrial
towns. Young people were swarming through the doors,
chattering like chicks as they shook rain from macs and
umbrellas. Girls made for the ladies', to rescue curls
fallen suddenly flat in the drizzle. Harry waited dutifully,
standing aside from the rush.

The spectacle in the ballroom was something to
behold. A great swarm of young people was circling
clockwise, like some great cosmic cloud, moving in pairs,
each held together, arms raised to shoulder height, every
girl's head looking to the left above her partner's shoulder, a flock of birds moving as one, turning, circling, each
sensitive to the impulses of the next, wheeling round the

room as the throb of the music kept them on course. There were exceptions: lovers, eyes fixed on each other, bumped into other dancers. Jen and Polly watched and kept watching. Lovers . . . people who had found a kindred spirit. What must it feel like? They didn't smile much, caught in some trance that locked them away from the rest even as they swayed within the crowd. Would it be their turn one day?

The notice on the door declared 'Those in Uniform, Entrance Free,' so there was a goodly sprinkling of young men. They came in ones and twos, joshing and joking together, at the sides; they, too, were watching and being watched. Uniforms spelled glamour, the eyes of the town's girls flicked and flashed; each appraised the looks and promise on display, whispering to a friend behind a hand, catching and holding a gaze deliberately a moment too long until the stranger, nudging his friends for courage, walked across and asked, 'May I have this dance?' Soon, stranger with stranger, the room was warming to new friendships and excitements.

Jen and Polly felt giddy. It was enough at the start to stand with Hans – Harry – and observe the throng. They had rarely seen so many of their own generation together, boys and girls mixing with such familiarity and pleasure. There was but one mood among them: that of the moment, the music, the dancing, young bodies greedy for life and for one another.

There were, of course, far more girls than boys. The war had seen to that. Those boys not in uniform had jobs in factories, mines and government offices, tough jobs that mostly left them with dirty hands. They weren't sure

59

that dancing was right for them. Wasn't there something soppy about it? Yet the rhythm and the bold sound had them tapping their feet. Above them all, a huge ball, covered with a million glass prisms, revolved slowly, catching the light. It was the ultimate in glamour, casting interesting shadows around the room. Among those who lined the walls, there grew an eagerness to join in, to plunge in with those already launched on the heaving tide. Girls waited to be asked.

'Look, Harry, you'll be all right if Jen and I dance, won't you? We'll look out for you as we come round.' Hans had no option. He sloped off to fetch a glass of dandelion and burdock from the bar.

'This is a quickstep, isn't it?' Polly wasn't sure as she took the lead and propelled Jen among the dancers. They danced silently, concentrating on remembering the footsteps on Miss Sharp's lino. But while Polly was capable and serene, something more lively was bubbling inside Jen.

The band was big and brassy, men with thinning hair in draped grey jackets with maroon lapels, blasting away at the tunes of the moment. 'It's A Lovely Day Tomorrow', 'Yes, My Darling Daughter', and 'You Are My Sunshine'. They knew them from the wireless and hummed along. Four or five sailors in Royal Navy bell-bottomed trousers and the wide blue collars it was considered lucky to touch, sauntered across the open floor, purposefully targeting a bevy of red-lipped girls, legs painted with gravy browning. The band saw them and segued into 'The Sailor With The Navy Blue Eyes'. There was a murmur of recognition. A while later the band leader spotted a clutch of young men in the light blue uniforms of the RAF, and led his players into 'Comin' In On A Wing And A Prayer'. More approval. People were relaxing and talking more than ever.

There was a flurry of excitement by the entrance. Half a dozen young men, tall, blond, confident, broke through the crowds and came laughing into the hall. The Yanks had arrived, golden gods, so recently become their allies. Everyone had been relieved when they had joined the war. And here they were, good health radiating from them. Heads turned. Necks craned. They must be from the station at Burtonwood. Their uniforms were exquisite, the finest cloth tailored to fit close over rippling torsos. The locals looked shrunken and grey by comparison. The band burst at once into 'Deep In The Heart Of Texas', and the dancers sent up a welcoming cheer. On an instant the tallest and blondest had snatched a girl from among the bystanders, wrapped an arm round her waist and swung her across the floor. Couples parted appreciatively, allowing space for the American way of dancing. Everyone was laughing now. The band struck up 'Ma, I Miss Your Apple Pie' and more young people flocked on to the crowded floor.

Hans had been sipping his drink at the side, where Polly and Jen had joined him. 'I'd better be fair,' said Polly, nudging Jen. 'Come on, Harry!' They disappeared into the mêlée, trying hard not to step on each other's toes.

Jen stood alone, refusing to look or feel left out. The dancers swirled past. One of the sailors was with Peggy, the girl who sold tickets at the cinema. An airman with his RAF hat folded flat and tucked into the shoulder flap of his tunic was making solemn progress with a chunky woman in slacks. Fancy a woman coming to a dance in trousers! She must be working in the local munitions factory but, still, not to find time to change for a Saturday night out marked her as either eccentric or poor or both. Jen felt pleased with her dirndl skirt and embroidered blouse, but then felt noticed. 'The girl in the dirndl skirt isn't dancing,' they must be saying.

She was considering a strategic retreat to the ladies', when someone tapped her on the shoulder. 'Dance?' He was about her height and in some sort of naval uniform, navy with gold stripes on his sleeves. He had dark hair, too thick to be tidy, and a direct, open gaze.

'All right . . . yes.' She stepped out and placed herself within his arms.

The pressure of his hand on the small of her back made her feel safe. He knew what he was doing, steering and guiding her, turning with precise, easy movements through the foxtrot. Suddenly those awkward lessons made sense.

'I've not been here before.'

'Do you come here often?'

They spoke together, then laughed at the obviousness of what they'd said.

'I'm Tim.'

'I'm Jen. Hello, Tim.'

'Hello, Jen.'

All too soon the music came to an end. The couples stood around, rather than dispersing, and called for more. Jen wasn't sure of the etiquette and turned away, searching for Polly, as the band struck up in an altogether different mood.

Tim caught her hand. 'Stay!'

'In The Mood' broke around them, and the crowd hit the floor like a hailstorm, swinging and jumping to the hot sound. Tentatively at first, but then with gathering strength, they began to dance in different styles, moving together, then apart, bouncing away from each other, backing on to their heels, then tense against each other, and Jen was spinning under Tim's arm. This was swing – she'd seen it at the pictures. Or was it jitterbugging? There hadn't been footsteps for this on Miss Sharp's lino.

Tim grinned and pulled her hand. 'Come on – you're really good – let's go!'

And Jen went. Suddenly she felt like blown gossamer, her weight landing exactly where she wanted it, each foot bouncing with the rhythm as Tim grasped her hand, let it go, caught her up again and spun her round. Was this dancing? No – it was more like ecstasy. She twisted and spun. The laughter fled from her throat as she gasped for breath, arms wide, elbows pulsing with the beat, meeting his grip, and was flung away again. She sensed other couples smiling at them in the blurred beyond. Somewhere across the room the Americans were actually throwing their partners into the air. Once, their path crossed that of Polly and Hans, blithely swinging their arms between them with beginners' enthusiasm. Polly's eyes widened as Jen sped past, cornering briskly, then spinning back into Tim's embrace. The music changed, crescendoed and died to a roar of approval.

'More!' the crowd bellowed.

'OK to go on?'

'Oh, yes, please!' Jen wasn't shy any more, and didn't want the dancing to end – ever.

Meanwhile Polly was working hard, urging spontaneity from Hans, and he was working hard, too, not knowing what was expected or allowed. They held hands, jogging up and down, Hans's eyes on other couples. If he could just analyse what it was they were doing he would be fine. But there seemed no set routine. How much easier it had all been with the waltz and the polka. This American stuff was so confusing, loud and jazzy, not leaving you space to collect your thoughts. But it was thrilling, no doubt about that.

Polly smiled encouragingly as he bounced and turned. He failed to catch her as she came back from a spin, then made a grab, more clumsy than graceful, still clearly determined to keep with the rhythm. Polly felt a little shy: his antics were making them conspicuous. She wanted him to calm down. 'You OK?'

He grinned and nodded, lips clenched in a rictus of concentration.

Unwisely and wrongly believing he was getting the hang of it, Hans's style became ever more expansive. The arc he and Polly made among the dancers grew wider. They were skidding and skirting now to avoid collisions. When it came, the crash was considerable, the pair of them cannoning from one couple to another as Hans dragged the wretched Polly with him into the turmoil.

'Agh! *Vergeben Sie mir! Es tut mir Leid!*'

Polly, trying to stop him being heard, let out a long cry.

'Aaaaaaaaah, no, Harry! No!' And more emphatically, 'Harry!'

But the damage was done.

'He's a Jerry – did you hear him? That bloke's a bloody Jerry!' A finger prodded Hans's chest. 'Say, that again, chum. Just say that again.'

A woman's voice asked threateningly, 'Why isn't he interned? I thought they'd all been interned for the duration.'

'Exactly – ex-*act*ly. We don't want the enemy in our midst, do we?'

'He's probably a spy – a spy on his night off, eh?' There was bitter, unkind laughter.

'Oh, no. They never have a night off. The enemy never sleeps. Yes, we're on the lookout for folks like you.'

'Or should it be *Volk*, eh?' a wit added.

Polly had placed herself protectively in front of Hans, but she was helpless when a large red face thrust its chin at her: 'Out of the way, missy, or we'll have you down as a collaborator.' His fist would have landed hard on Hans's cheek, had she not raised her arm to stop it. By now others were muscling in. And those further off were stopping to look.

'It's nothing. He's sorry. We're both very sorry.' Polly stood her full height and gripped Hans's hand until it hurt. 'He's a friend – a friend of my family.'

'But he's a German, isn't he? Are you German, too, then? Answer me that!'

'Well, yes, he is German born, but he's a refugee. He's on our side.'

'Oh, is he? Is he, really? Then he is a traitor, isn't he? A traitor to his own side. How d'you explain that, eh?'

Hans stepped out from Polly's shadow to make an ill-advised intervention. 'I am already coming here for to be with the English.'

Polly shut him up. 'He's German, yes, but he's Jewish, a German Jew.'

'Oh, *is* he? Is that supposed to be an excuse? A dirty little Yid, and that makes it all right?'

Out of the crowds an unidentified man's voice spoke up: 'Lay off, there. Can't you see he's just a kid?'

The intervention wasn't soon enough to stay the blow that Red Face landed on Hans's cheek. He reeled away, backing into Polly, who collapsed into the owner of the voice that had just spoken. 'Come on,' it said. 'Don't stay here to be insulted.' He grabbed their arms and thrust them through the crowds.

They didn't stop until they were in the marble foyer outside the ballroom, where groups of people talking, smoking, and couples kissing hadn't seen what had been going on.

'Oh, thank you. You're so kind.' Their rescuer was a sailor in some kind of officer's uniform. 'What a beastly bully he was.'

'Yes, well, plenty like that. You both OK now?' As he made to leave, he said, 'I've a friend in there somewhere.'

'So have we, but we'll wait outside. Thanks again.'

He was lanky and blond, with droopy hair that fell over a broad brow. Polly liked the look of him, even had a fleeting image of herself gliding round the room in his arms. Some hope. He disappeared into the crowd, and she and Hans sat on a bench to recover.

'I'm sorry, Hans, so sorry. Don't let it worry you.'

The boy was silent and thoughtful. He stared down at his hands with the pale pink nails, like soft-shelled crustaceans, then at his shoes, polished and neat even after the scuffle on the dance-floor. 'Why dirty? Why did he say dirty? I am clean, Polly, aren't I?'

'Oh, that. Well, I'd have thought what else he said was more insulting.'

'Being unclean is awful. I promised Mutti I would be always clean in my person.'

'But he called you a Yid, Hans. I don't even like to say it.'

'But I am, Polly. I'm a Jew. That's what I am. You told him that yourself.'

'Yes but Yid – well, Ma and Pa always said it was rude.'

'Here I am not understanding your English. I am sorry more he called me dirty. Please look and tell me. Am I dirty?'

'Oh, Hans, of *course* not.' Polly laughed in relief and bewilderment. What a tricky thing language was. She recalled Miss Johnson's English lesson about synonyms. 'I'd say, Hans, that you're immaculate, fastidious, pernickety, faultless almost . . . innocent, certainly.'

'I am all these things, am I? Is that good?'

'Oh, very good, Hans.'

'Yes? Then I am happy. But remember, "Harry", please.'

He had a point there.

Suddenly a flustered Jen rushed out of the ballroom. 'What on earth happened? What's been going on?'

'Oh, some lout was rude to us but it's over, Jen, really it is. We were rescued by a sailor.'

'Yes, I know. That's how I know. I've been dancing with his friend, who's called Tim and we've really clicked. Dancing, I mean. I've been having such a good time.'

'We noticed, didn't we, Harry? In fact, it was when we started to copy you, or tried to copy you, that we got into such a mess.'

'Anyway, it's nearly half past ten. Dad said he'd come to collect me – didn't want me alone on the late bus. I bet he's fretting on the steps outside.'

'But what happened to this Tim? Where is he?'

'Oh, they've gone. Both of them. They've got to get back.'

'Where to?'

'Dunno.'

The thought saddened them. It felt as though silver coins had slipped away into the gutter.

Finding Out

2003

'Mr Hathersage was such a decayed old buffer, I thought he might crumble away before my eyes. I fled as soon as I could. Anyway, according to him all the records are gone. Just some noticeboard left, but he didn't say where it was.'

'So, why did you go? What made you? What's so interesting about Grandma's stuff?'

Kate has flung down her canvas bag and slumped into the leather chair. She's tired; her failing kidneys mean she is often tired. She doesn't speak of her mother's visit to Mr Charles. She knows not to trespass too often on her mother's time. Millie, after all, is a scholar, writing learned books that command respect and take her full concentration. Kate seeks her help sparingly.

But these days she comes home for comfort. There are cushions and chairs to sink into, rugs and shawls, patchwork quilts and Indian-silk hangings. The house speaks for her mother more than she speaks for herself, a rich and elaborate nest cradling a medley of exotic tastes.

Now this sudden concern about the contents of a hamper. Odd.

She begins a game to distract the chattering Freya, building brightly coloured rings into intricate patterns.

'Well, I was in Manchester anyway, looking at paintings. It's near Staveley. And, honestly, I'm intrigued. What are these things? What might they be telling us?'

'Such as?' Kate can't imagine ferreting around among dead people's bits and pieces. Who knows? They might be full of germs. Her illness makes her susceptible.

'Oh, you know, mothers and daughters . . . Gran always found it hard to say what she was really thinking.'

Kate lets the remark go, then after a pause announces: 'I've got a job. You'll never guess.'

'Good. What is it? I hope it lasts longer than the others.'

That's exactly what she'd expected her mother to say. She knows that Millie disapproves of Kate's drifting lifestyle; a job here and there, even briefly at a McDonald's. Nothing with any point to it. Kate won't rise to the barb. 'Oh, this is worth making a go of. It's arranging and conducting funerals!'

'Kate, are you talking sense? Are you saying this is a real job?'

'It is! I am. I've been doing the training for just over a month. I didn't want to tell you until I'd done the dummy run. And I have! Bit of a hoot, eh?'

'Oh, do be sensible. I never know whether you're serious or not.'

But Kate is suddenly too tired to tease her. 'Ma, I am serious. It's for a secular society. They want someone to take their funerals. More and more people don't want that religious mumbo-jumbo any more. They want poems and songs, things meaningful to them.'

'I just wonder *why* you want to do it, that's all.'

'Well, it's work I can fit round my dialysis, for one thing.' Kate hesitates, then decides to be honest. 'But it's close to people, isn't it, people who want you to be kind? I want to be kind.' Kate plucks at the lace edge of her cardigan as though the thought is embarrassing. 'Besides, I remember Gran dying and how awful it was: the service drawn up by that nutty group of hers. So formal and stuffy. People don't want God stuff any more.'

'Oh, I can see that, but—'

'I always thought Pa got it right. He never had doubts, did he? He knew what mattered – things like beauty and friendship, loyalty and truth. "To hell with superstition", he used to say. "And while we're at it, to hell with money and promotion." I hope I take after him, a bit.'

Any mention of Dominic mellows Millie. Kate reflects so much of what she loved in him – directness, idealism – and stubbornness too. Kate has always gone her own way.

'Well, Kate dear, it's all very worth doing. But isn't it rather . . . gruesome?' She can't help herself. The word she actually has in mind is 'perverse'.

'Considering what?' Kate's voice is suddenly sharp. 'I'm not dying, Mother, if that's what you mean. I have a kidney condition, that's all. I'm not going to die, not for a long while yet.' Freya catches the tone of her mother's words, if not their meaning. She looks up, startled.

'Of course you're not. I know you're not. Who knows

that better than I do?' Millie takes a deep breath and hurries on. 'That's not what I meant.'

Kate reaches out and strokes Freya's hair, soothing them both. But she is not appeased.

'Well, what did you mean? Say what you mean, for God's sake.'

The First Visit

1942

Grace Bunting stirred under the blue blankets with the satin edging. What a day in prospect. In a moment she would be up and doing, but first her morning prayers. She hesitated because of the cold. Would God mind if she said them from the warmth where she lay or did He need her to feel the cold? She knew the answer, leaped out with a girlish shiver and, clasping her hands together, knelt beside her bed, winceyette elbows perched on the crumpled sheets. Suddenly she was not feeling the cold, so absorbed was she in her devotions. A little miracle in itself. Who said God didn't watch our every movement? She rose joyously to confront the day.

Grace was at school early. She'd known there would be lots to do and she was keen that everything should be in order. She took pride in her responsibility to ensure that all ran smoothly. Miss Maitland had drawn up the plans herself, having called an exceptional meeting in the staff-room the previous week. Grace felt privately it had been a little too informal: teachers were allowed to smoke and the room was quickly thick with blue grey clouds. And to perch on top of the desks like that – some, even, with their knees folded beneath them, for all the world as if they were wielding a toasting fork in front of the fire!

It was Miss Maitland's way of bringing them together, she could see that. They sat in ways they had as students, ruffling skirts and stockings and sending up a faint whiff of Yardley's cologne. She noticed how, off-duty, they were surprisingly like other people.

'Why don't you gather closer? Then we can share our ideas more easily,' Miss Maitland had said.

There had been a rumble of desks and chairs scraping and gentle laughter, as mistresses of maths and biology, history and French had crowded forward like overgrown versions of the children they taught.

'Quite clearly the school is at the start of a new relationship, between us and the outside world. I hope you think it's a good idea. I certainly do. I also hope you don't think it's too risky – but there is a war on, after all.' There was a good-humoured ripple of agreement. Quite what was Miss Maitland suggesting? She smiled too.

A knock on the door heralded the arrival of Mrs Clayton with the tea trolley. She barged into the room, intent on delivering the large enamel urn with a stack of cups and saucers at the correct time. 'Oh, I beg your pardon, I hadn't noticed.' She began to put her wagon into clumsy reverse.

'No, Maggie. Come in, why don't you, and stay with us? This may affect you too. We're discussing next week's visit of the ship's crew.'

Mrs Clayton parked the trolley and reached into the pocket of her overall for a Park Drive.

'Captain Percival will be bringing with him his first and second mates and a young apprentice. I think we should begin their day by asking them to join our assembly.'

'Will they sit on the platform?'

'Why not ask the captain to read the lesson?'

'They might like to choose the hymns.'

'What about "For Those In Peril On The Sea"?' This last from Mrs Clayton, who was as familiar as they were with *Hymns Ancient and Modern*.

Grace Bunting, poised to take notes – not because she needed to but for the chance to flourish the sapphire and diamond engagement ring – winced at the slack reference. Its correct title is 'Eternal Father Strong To Save', she thought to herself.

'They may be sick of hearing it, you know.'

'Well, they can like it or lump it.'

'Are you suggesting "Roll Out The Barrel"?'

'Oh, I don't think so!'

The mood was getting frisky.

'Then I thought I'd ask some of the sixth form to escort them round the school. Lorna, do you think you could mount a gymnastics display?'

A small mousy woman, in a silken sports tunic over black stockings, nodded silently.

'And, Marie, perhaps when they call in at the lab you could be overseeing a dissection.'

'Frogs, it'll have to be. The butchers get all the rabbits now.'

'Then after lunch in the dining room, I thought I'd offer them a break in my study.'

'Coffee and cigars?' muttered History to Biology, and was overheard.

'I shall leave them to decide that for themselves! In the afternoon I'd like the whole school to attend a display of folk-dancing in the main hall. What do you think?'

And so Miss Maitland's plans were finalized, giving everyone the illusion they had contributed.

Lime Street station was full of noise and steam, the air a pungent mix of smoke from toiling engines, the misty rain blowing in off the Mersey and more smoke from the surrounding chimneys, big and small. It had the rich identity of industrial well-being, and the busy crowds breathed it with confidence and pride.

Beneath the station's blackened glass dome, Robert offered to stand in the queue at the ticket kiosk while Tim went in search of a morning paper. 'The *Daily Mirror*, before the government bans it,' Robert called after him.

Tim understood what he meant. Just a few weeks before there'd been an almighty row about a cartoon that Tim and his dad, Sam, had thought was right on the mark. It showed a merchant seaman clinging to a raft in a storm-tossed sea, alone under a brooding sky, desperate and beleaguered. The caption had read, 'The price of petrol has been increased by one penny.'

There had been protests from the war cabinet, but its message seemed true enough to those who passed it from hand to hand in the Slaughter House pub, and along the quays of Liverpool and Manchester. It was a vivid way to remind people that merchant seamen were risking their lives and that no one should be wasteful with petrol. Many a merchant seaman had torn it out and shown it around to others.

Tim's dad would have liked the *Daily Worker* to have published it, but it had been closed down the previous year, part of the government's attempt to stop working people criticizing the war effort, he claimed. The BBC had been pressured to take J. B. Priestley off the air. Censorship was rampant. It was making everyone suspicious.

The MPs who had huffed and puffed over the cartoon were right, Sam thought. 'Too bloody right they are – and it's not just the oil companies boosting their profits!' The *Daily Mirror* went on reporting inefficiencies, cock-ups, mistakes. Everyone felt they might be losing the war.

Tim and Robert heaved their holdalls on to the luggage rack of the third-class compartment, having left the Old Man in first, courtesy of a warrant from the shipping company. Apprentice Rawlings was hitching a lift. All four would meet up at Staveley before they went to the school. Josh Percival had asked them to take a day's leave to help launch the ship-adoption scheme. They'd gone along with it because they'd had no choice. But they didn't know what to make of it. Still, the Old Man wanted to do it, so it was all right by them. Hadn't he made a special effort to keep them with him on the *Treverran*? It had been easy enough for Robert because he was signed up with the same shipping company, but Tim had been 'on the pool', seamen who became available at the end of each voyage to go wherever the Board of Trade sent them. That meant Josh had had to fix things.

'No point in being a bloody ship's master if I can't pull a string or two,' he'd said. 'Come back from your leave early so I can keep you out of the shipping master's clutches.' And he had.

From Staveley station they would make their way to Ashworth Grammar School for Girls: Josh had a neat white card, a bit dog-eared from being thrust in his pocket – with a trim little diagram, precisely drawn in black ink and tidily labelled street by street. It had been a project for the school's fourth form, and this was the winning effort.

Together the four men strode along the cobbled streets, past the library, then the public swimming baths where scruffy lads were lined up, each hugging a roll of ragged towel. Finally they turned into a road of young beech trees, their slender branches reaching into the mist, not yet an arch, but holding the promise of green beauty. Beyond, they could see the mellow red brick of a formidable establishment. 'We've faced worse!' Josh grinned.

'I'm not so sure, sir,' and with a laugh they followed him bravely into the fray.

'They're here! They're here!' A whisper of excitement ran through the classrooms. Those whose desks were next to the windows had sounded the alert.

Grace Bunting smoothed her hair, checked that her stocking seams were straight, then went to greet the seamen and lead them to the headmistress's study.

Cynthia Maitland rose with obvious pleasure and moved, hand outstretched, to greet them. Oh! thought Josh. So this is what she's like in her own territory. He recalled her reticence at their first encounter, which had warmed only slowly into gentle confidence. Here, she was clearly the queen bee in a buzzing hive. The four men had picked up the hum of curiosity that had passed along the corridors at their arrival. Women cut off from men in an establishment such as this were a mystery to Josh. Tim and Robert were clearly bemused as well, but Charlie Rawlings was clearly awkward. He shuffled his feet and kept pulling at his left earlobe.

Morning assembly was far from normal. The four sailors were the object of obsessive scrutiny. Necks were craned, girls pushed and nudged each other, shamelessly appraising the uniforms and demeanour of the young men. Captain Percival turned to his officers and Rawlings with a raised eyebrow that urged them to hold fast. Deciphering their ranks by the gold rings on their sleeves, the girls were muttering: four stripes captain – obviously; next one three, then two. The fourth and youngest, had no sleeve braiding but tabs on his lapels. What did they all mean?

Melanie Grout, of the fourth form, stepped forward to declaim a welcoming poem: John Masefield's 'Cargoes', which every girl knew by heart. It was a well-intended choice. But when she came to 'Dirty British coaster with a salt-caked smoke stack, Butting through the Channel in the mad March days', Josh winced. After all, he was the proud captain of an ocean-going merchant ship, not a humble coaster. He pointed to himself with a grin and a vigorous shake of the head: 'No, not me.' There was a murmur of laughter from the girls. Would Miss Maitland smile? She did, and the ice was broken.

*

At the back of the hall something else was going on. When the sailors had arrived on the platform and removed their caps, a cry of recognition went up among the lower sixth. 'That's him. That's Tim! Oh, golly! It can't be!' Jen was convulsed as giggles fought with surprise and both were sabotaged by shock. Who could she tell? Polly was at the other end of the row. She had to reach her – it couldn't wait. The school was now singing 'Eternal Father Strong To Save'.

Jen tore a page from the back of her prayer book, and, with a stub of pencil from her pocket, wrote to Polly, 'That's the boy at the town hall dance.'

The message was passed along the row, each girl reading it, then craning to see the platform, wondering which one Jen meant. Impatient for the answer they, too, tore blank pages from their prayer books and sent back, 'Which one?' 'You mean the dark one?' Their tittering, like a hedgeful of linnets, alerted Miss Hartley, who confiscated the note intended for Polly, read it and was appalled not only by the information but by the page having been torn from a religious book. Under normal circumstances Jen would have faced detention. But this giddy day was like nothing she had known. And the message hadn't even reached Polly. Well, now it would have to wait.

Back in the classroom, Jen and Polly whispered together while other girls watched jealously, with feigned contempt.

Oh, golly gosh! How would they cope? They felt self-conscious in their uniform and neat white ankle socks.

Things got worse when Jen was assigned by Miss Maitland to take Tim and Robert on a guided tour of the school. Brenda Alsop, designated to chaperone the captain and Apprentice Rawlings, bore them off with a flourish.

'I'd so much rather be going to the flicks with them,' hissed Polly, as Jen went to fulfil her duties. 'What on earth will they make of all those idiotic gymnastics? They'll think we're stupid.'

But the sailors didn't find the girls stupid. In classroom after classroom they basked in adoration and curiosity. Girls stood politely as Brenda's group entered, then settled at their desks to listen with growing interest as Josh Percival talked about the life of a cargo ship. The maps on classroom walls showed large pink areas across the world, and Josh took a pointer from beside the blackboard and explained how world trade took the school's ship to different and exotic cities all within the British Empire. Here was Gibraltar, gateway to the Mediterranean and a British dependency, and there the Crown colony of Malta, which had recently survived intense German bombardment.

The girls knew most of this – the story of the Empire had been taught since they were in kindergarten – but they were glued to his performance, weighing his words and style in readiness for the judgements of the playground.

Further east, he was saying, was Egypt, a British protectorate, with the British-owned Suez Canal, Palestine, currently under a British mandate, and in the Far East, the Crown colonies of Hong Kong, Singapore, India, Ceylon, the Malay states, and then, most distant of all, the dominion of Australia.

Charlie Rawlings continued to be embarrassed. He

scuffed one shoe against the other, bit his nails and was thankful to be offered a chair.

The captain was well into his stride: across the Atlantic, Britain's merchant fleet traded with the British West Indies, British Honduras, British Guiana and the great ports of Canada – Halifax and St John's. At the mention of Halifax Josh gave no indication of how well he knew it, and how hazardous his visits there had become.

Then came questions, and Apprentice Rawlings suddenly found his courage: in a thin, clear voice he talked about cotton, how it came from Egypt, America and India to keep the mills of Lancashire thriving. All this was heard with the awed pride the girls felt at belonging to the greatest nation on earth. And the ship they had adopted was their emissary to all the far-flung places in which, they were told, they had a stake. Surely this was what they were fighting for.

Meanwhile Jen was putting on a good performance, showing off the school's different rooms and talking about their functions. All the time she was wondering what kind of impression she was making. She didn't want Tim to think of her as a child. He hadn't when they had been dancing together. She must speak to him alone. But what would she say? It took an effort to remain correct and formal, but gradually she found she could do it. Neither man criticized, just listened. She grew confident in her task. Tim was listening and smiling. Eventually, as they moved along the corridor between classrooms, Robert feigned a need to look out of a window – and Tim seized the moment.

'You! I can't believe it!'

'It's just as surprising for me. I had no idea.'

'I didn't realize you were still at school.'

'Does it make a difference?'

'To what? What d'you mean?'

Oh, God, what did she mean? 'Well, I'm sixteen. I'm not a child.'

He bellowed a laugh. 'Course you're not. I know that. I've seen you dance, haven't I? Dancing like a woman, I'd say.' Jen grinned with relief.

Then a voice spoiled it. 'Jennifer!' It was the gym mistress, summoning them. The others were already there.

'One thing. Quickly. Can I have your address?'

There was something unnerving for the salt-hardened merchant seamen in the sight of so many naked teenage thighs. Charlie Rawlings was overcome: a crimson blush rose to his face and spread to his hairline while the rest of him broke into a hot sweat. His eyes never blinked.

Off went the school's gymnasts, clad in black knickers and crisp white blouses, vaulting the horse, climbing ropes, swinging from bars and somersaulting in all directions. The pungent smell of young sweat and rampant hormones soon clouded the air. A single girl sat at the side, watching. She had a heavy period and her mother had sent a note. Only when Enid Carter misjudged the horse, fell clumsily on to the mat and burst into tears did the youthful euphoria dissipate. 'Up you get!' cried the teacher in the silk tunic. 'Try again. Don't snivel!' She jabbed at the girl with her elbow.

When the display finished, the thankful seamen gave a

hearty round of applause, picking out Enid for special congratulations on account of her pluck and hurt feelings. Everyone was touched by that, except Silk Tunic, who marvelled that failure could be so rewarded.

Next they were to visit the labs where finally Robert was thrown within Polly's reach. She had been put in charge of the frogs. He grabbed her arm as she edged to the cubby-hole to fetch more, and Polly froze.

'Hello . . . er . . .' Robert was casual, easy-going, expecting the same of her. 'I don't know your name, but I wonder if you remember . . . ?'

Polly wished they were anywhere but among a gaggle of nosy fifth-formers. 'I do, actually. Yes, I do.' She had spoken as though to drop a portcullis on their conversation, but added, 'My name's Polly.'

'Well, the fight you were in that night at the dance . . .' Robert sailed on. Several pupils nudged each other and rolled their eyes.

'Oh, yes, of course. You were such a help. I never had the chance to thank you properly.'

'Well, you can thank me now.'

'Thank you . . . er . . .'

'Robert – Robert Warburton.' Suddenly they smiled and the science class gawped. 'I'm glad it's your school we're joined up with.'

'Good. So am I . . . Robert. But I'm afraid you've got to see some frogs being dissected now. I hope it won't put you off.'

Miss Hayter, gaunt and harassed, had already demonstrated to the class how the dissection was to be done. A frog's torso lay open on the top table, with pins and tiny

84

labels indicating the different organs. Girls were dispersed round the room, each one with her own dead frog on which to copy what she had just seen. In the event, they fell short of Miss Hayter's immaculate example. Frogs' bodies were stabbed and torn, several fingers were bleeding and expressions of horror – 'Urgh!' 'Agh!' 'Oooh!' – echoed round the lab. While the more studious among them were earnestly querying whether this pink bit was the liver or the stomach, two at the far end were throwing frogs' legs at each other, while Madge Prendergast was challenging Muriel Grainger to 'Eat one, go on, the French do!'

'Not raw, you dope. Stop it, stop it!' The unfortunate Muriel scrabbled to retrieve the slimy flesh from the neck of her blouse.

'I hope you found that interesting.' Cynthia Maitland met them in her study, among murmurs of appreciation and quiet laughter.

'We're having a very good time, I can assure you!' Captain Percival was laughing more than she had expected, but no more than gave her a warm sense of success. And when he laughed the furrows of his face fell into friendly lines round his mouth. He was, she realized, what they called handsome.

For his part Josh noticed the girlish colour in her cheeks and the flying wisps of blonde hair that gave her the prettiness of a younger woman. He saw, too, the photograph on her desk of the young soldier and, as the others were shepherded away to school dinner, hung back to ask, 'Not this war?'

'No, the last. We were planning to become engaged.'

'I'm sorry.'

'Oh, I was very young, little more than a schoolgirl, and it was long ago. But thank you.' She held his gaze. He had been presumptuous, but she didn't mind.

At dinner time the high table had been laid for the visitors, with glass and silver Cynthia had brought in from her mother's unused hoard. She presided, smiling and nodding, to hide a certain apprehension about the meal. The kitchen had done the best it could: boiled cod with parsley sauce, boiled potatoes and peas, followed by tapioca pudding – known universally as frogspawn.

Afterwards the party retired to the headmistress's study where Grace Bunting brought in a tray of coffee for them all.

Coffee was not something Grace was used to. It was what the French drank, she knew. But she did what she could with a teaspoon of Camp coffee in each cup, cream in a silver jug, and tongs for the sugar lumps. The jug and tongs were a little tarnished: they had come with the serviette rings on a rare outing.

To crown such excess Cynthia offered not only the usual Senior Service cigarettes but cigars in a fragrant wooden box that Miss Hayter's brother had brought back from Jamaica. As each man lit this exotic treat, and the coils of smoke filled the room, they knew the visit had been a triumph and that the bond between ship and school was soundly established.

Grace, in her sentry-box next door, heard the murmured conversation and gave herself credit and the reward of a single Rich Tea biscuit.

*

The afternoon concert confirmed the school's aspirations. Four flautists sent the haunting sounds of Telemann's 'The Hunt' into the hall's vaulted spaces; next, a clarinettist, with a teacher on the piano, tackled Brahms's Sonata for Clarinet and Piano with muscular, rather than musical, instinct. The school choir let fling with a powerful rendering of 'Linden Lea', and then came the folk-dancing. Quite which 'folk' had been the source of such steps it was hard to gauge: there were no nationalistic clues by way of Spanish flounces or Dutch bonnets. The dancers had to take the costumes on trust: no one, thanks to the war, had been across the Channel. Skirts encircled with coloured ribbons, little waistcoats made of black velvet, and plenty of jangling beaded necklaces gave an air of improvised exoticism – Bulgaria, perhaps, or Romania (they had found such places on the map and they weren't pink). The girls from the junior-school classes made charming mistakes that evoked smiles and nods. The older ones suffered the embarrassment of ungainly limbs and large, unanchored breasts. Brassières were judged by several mothers as too precocious for daughters who, they insisted, were still children.

When all was over, Josh Percival stepped up to the platform and made an impromptu speech of thanks that crowned the day. He extolled the staff, mentioning the nimbleness of the gym display (was Enid Carter quite recovered from her fall?), the international flavour of the dancing, the scientific value of the dissection. His audience found his lilting Scottish accent wonderful, whatever he said. Josh himself began to enjoy the sound of it too. He went on to speak of winning the war. Like many adults addressing children he tended to get carried away whenever the subject came up. Faces grew solemn as he declared that they were all in it together. He told them how, whenever they were at sea, he and his men would remember the kindness and enthusiasm of Ashworth Grammar School, and what they were fighting for. Two teachers reached into their pockets for handkerchiefs. He mentioned that times were often grim at sea, but that their ship visited exotic places and foreign peoples with strange customs.

He and his crew would write to them regularly. They must be strong and brave in the face of the enemy, as his crew was in the face of German U-boats. It was good to know they now had such friends. Thank you.

Suddenly the teacher in the silk tunic stepped from the shadows and called, 'Three cheers for our ship!'

The hoorays rang out, and not one voice was silent.

'Just wait a mo, will you? I've forgotten something. Won't be a tick.' The four men had said their goodbyes and were striding towards the school gate and the avenue of budding trees. Seized by a sudden impulse and keen not to let it go, Josh Percival dashed back into the school, sped along the corridor, across the tiled vestibule, past Grace Bunting's office, took a deep breath and knocked on the headmistress's door.

'Yes? Is that you, Grace? Oh, no, it isn't.'

Josh stood on the threshold. Cynthia had been winding down. It had been an exhilarating day and she was flushed and excited by its success. She rose from her chair. 'Oh, do come in, Captain. Did you forget something?'

'I did. Nothing to do with the school as such. Or the teachers and girls. Something more personal.' The wind of opportunism that had gusted him into the room was dropping. He hesitated. Was he making a fool of himself? 'I forgot to tell you – you personally – how much this has meant.'

Her eyes widened. She sat down abruptly behind her desk, leaving him marooned on a colourful Indian rug. 'Well, you all did that. But it's kind of you to—'

'No. I meant something else. I meant meeting you . . .' he paused. 'Miss Maitland.'

'Oh, I see.' She took a deep breath. 'Well, we'd met already, hadn't we . . . at the Midland Hotel? I'm sure you remember.' She was playing for time. Forward or back. Which way to go? 'And . . . er . . . Cynthia. My name's Cynthia.'

'I'm Josh . . . Good. It's Cynthia, then . . .' He left for a second time.

Sailing

The prospect of the *Treverran* sailing into predictable dangers heightened tensions for everyone.

Tim spent his last night of leave in a good old argument with his dad. It was a show of mutual affection. His mother, Ida, had served braised lamb's hearts for their dinner – Tim's favourite. Then as they settled back in their armchairs, Sam rested his head on the antimacassar and launched his assault.

'The Jews are really profiting from this lot.'

'Churchill will have to go.'

'The country would really prefer Stafford Cripps.'

He watched warily, pulling on his pipe, which hid from his son the pleasure he took in seeing Tim rise to the bait: 'Oh, Dad, you're talking damned daft.'

'The press are saying as much. You've been away. So go on, then, how am I talking daft? You tell me!' He waved the stem of his pipe good-humouredly towards his son.

'Well, from what I hear Churchill's holding the country

together. All sorts agree on that – the girls in the Naafi, the blokes at sea, even the GIs over here.'

'That's nowt but gossip – and Churchill's grand style of speaking. He'd better get a move on, I say. There's grumbling everywhere.'

Ida recognized that Sam was getting into his stride. When he got excited, things could get nasty. But she knew the remedy. With womanly familiarity she lifted his leg on to her lap, unlaced his boot, pulled off the thick woollen sock and set about scratching the sole of his foot. He paused to murmur his delight. It was a pleasure he'd enjoyed all their married life.

Tim lit a Capstan with a flourish of his Zippo lighter.

Only his mother noticed: 'That's American, isn't it?'

'Yes. I'm glad you like it.' Then he turned back to his father. 'One of the lads says Churchill's mother was American. That can't be true, can it? And, if so, why'd they take so long to come into the war?'

'Tha' might well ask. Waiting to see us run down and desperate, that's what I say. They'll see this war destroy us, end of empire, and they'll be smiling, that's why. Churchill's own family, eh? It's a bloody disgrace.'

'Language, Dad!' Ida admonished him gently. They both ignored her.

'Look, we owe them a lot. I can vouch for that. I'm telling you, we're bringing plenty back from the US – bacon, beans, dried egg, evaporated milk, canned meat. That's what we're carrying. Where'd we be without it, for God's sake?'

'Language, son.' Ida reached for Sam's other foot and another boot clattered on to the lino.

'And that destroyer of theirs that got sunk back in October, well, she was on convoy duty. Hush hush, it was. Word only got out when she was hit by a U-boat. Not much neutral about that on either side was there, eh?'

'Aye, but they didn't half dither.'

'Anyway, they're in now – and great blokes. They're tall, too, give us six inches, I'll swear.' Tim, who was short and sturdy, felt the challenge personally.

He hadn't read the political stuff his father had but he knew what he knew. He didn't like men at home in civilian jobs having a go. 'Anyway, where do these writers get their stuff from?' Tim looked round the close little room. The two bookshelves held at least fifty books. He didn't know anyone else who had as many.

'The book to read, son, is H. G. Wells's *New World Order*. It's what'll happen after the war. There'll have to be universal socialism, Mr Wells says. The government'll take over the mines, you mark my words.'

Ida had now finished with his feet and reached for her knitting. As they talked, she took out a fresh skein of wool and gestured to Tim to help her. He unfolded the skein and spread it wide across his hands, holding it in place with his thumbs. Ida took the single thread and began to wind it into a ball, not too tightly so that the ball was hard, or so loosely that it lost its shape. She knew the tension instinctively. In harmony with her, Tim moved his hands back and forth at exactly the right speed for the wool to unspool. It brought them close.

'Oh, by the way, Mum, there's a lass I met at a dance in the town hall.' Ida didn't pause in her winding but she looked up at her son. His eyes were on the skein. 'Yes, she's nice,' he went on. 'She's called Jen. You'll like her.'

Sam was tamping down the tobacco in his pipe and holding a series of Swan Vestas to the strands that spilled from the top. The 'Pah, pah, pah' of satisfaction as he pulled on the stem stopped. 'We're going to meet her, are we?'

'I asked her to call round and see you, yes.' Ida and Sam looked at each other. Ida gave a pleased smile.

Sam stirred in his chair. 'What does her father do, then?'

'He's station master over Greenley way. Very keen on the trains, by all accounts.'

'He'll be in the NUR, then, that's my guess.'

'Oh, I don't think he's political, Dad, not like you. Certainly not like you.' Tim laughed, and patted his father's shoulder.

'You can't be on the railways and not be political, son. They'll be nationalized, too, like the mines, you can bet on it.'

'There, thanks, lad,' was all Ida said when the ball was complete. Then she added shyly, 'She'll be very welcome.'

But Sam hadn't finished yet. He needed more argument to stoke his thinking: the failings of Lord Beaverbrook, the treachery of France, the scandal of Oswald Mosley. Tim ran out of energy before he did.

On the way to bed, Sam tapped his son's back with the cooling pipe. A final salvo as he stooped to stoke the overnight fire with damp coal dust. 'But watch them Yanks, that's all I say.'

'G'night, Dad. I will, I will.' Tim went to bed smiling, loving the old man.

Josh knew time was short if he was to contact Cynthia before he left. They were sailing within forty-eight hours: he had his orders. Their convoy was even now assembling in the Western Approaches, some from the Clyde, many from Liverpool: some forty-six merchant ships in all. After crossing to America together they would disperse, the *Treverran* heading for St John's and Halifax, where she would load timber and steel. She could expect to be away eight weeks or more. It was too long to wait.

His was a different kind of war from his wife's: he knew it in the raw, not from charts in fusty basements full of smoke and noise but out on the tilting deck with the salty wind in his face, his binoculars scanning the horizon until his eyes ached. It was a man's world. He couldn't talk of it with Jessica. He didn't have the words to convey how it felt. He felt it viscerally, on his skin, in his bones. There was no sharing such things. And now there was something else he couldn't share.

Jessica buried her growing anxieties in her work. She had been moved from her first-floor office with windows on to the street to the bunker underground and the Naval Teleprinter Station where more than a hundred machines rattled and clattered, disgorging a stream of messages. Each day she battled appalling headaches to keep up with the pace. But that was what she must do: others had tougher ordeals to endure. This was hers, and a matter of pride.

The mood in Derby House infected her with its almost fevered sense of secrecy: what happened in one office was unknown in the next. There were notices everywhere: 'Operations Room B61. No Admission. To go through without authorization is punishable by imprisonment.' The cipher operator was locked into his tiny room with an armed guard posted outside, and another stood over the phone line that went directly to the war-cabinet office. No one had walk-through rights of the entire complex. The solemnity that went with secrecy made Jessica all the more alert to whispered gossip. 'They're in a blue funk about something,' a girl from the teleprinter room had hinted, back in February.

A sailor agreed: 'By heck, when this comes out there'll be what-for.'

And there was: Germany's two mighty battleships, the *Gneisenau* and the *Scharnhorst*, had slipped past naval defences and raced up the Channel to their home ports. The country was appalled.

Then at the end of March came the triumphant news of a British commando raid on St Nazaire, destroying the German submarine base. Optimism surged. With two of her family serving at sea, Jessica's spirits were in turmoil, periods of euphoria dashed into gloom and silence. The word in Derby House was 'If we lose the war at sea, we lose the war.' She knew things were serious and grew ever more intense. She and Josh never discussed such matters, though by coded references they could infer what the other knew. It made them distant and jumpy.

*

Cynthia woke to the knowledge that something unexpected had happened. It was no more than the tiniest perception, and as the day went on there was no denying it. She would be caught by it unawares. As she told Grace of the day's duties, drew up the agenda for the governors' meeting, took the bus home to her forlorn mother . . . there it was. At first it was fleeting: an image of a kind face, eyes looking into hers, a lilting voice that said things that were not normally voiced. She allowed herself a pause in the day's routine while she mused on what it meant. Grace was intrigued to see her smiling without reason, just smiling to herself.

The end of term was in sight and, with it, the usual flurry of activities. All of Staveley was alert to the coming concert to be given by the Gaia Choir. A local philanthropist, who'd made his money in brass curtain rings and loved music, had set up a scheme to give voice training to the town's best. Over the years these assorted talents had built into one of the most celebrated choirs in the north of England. Polly was one such talent. Each Monday evening she turned up with singers from other schools across the town to rehearse in the draughty Jubilee Hall, and each week took home music by Purcell, Handel, Elgar, Vaughan Williams and Edward German. Her mother stabbed out the notes of the accompaniment for Polly's practice. Miss Maitland, as her headmistress, would attend the concert.

It was Grace who told Captain Percival. He had telephoned the school, but Miss Maitland had been in the governors' meeting at the time, and she would not be available that evening, Grace explained, because of the

Gaia concert in Manchester. No, not the Free Trade Hall –
that had been bombed. He winkled the address of the
venue from her.

Cynthia was accompanied by Lorna, the gym mistress,
who had changed from the silk tunic into a curious knitted garment to attend the concert. She had a passion for
Vaughan Williams, and friends in the choir. The tap on
Cynthia's shoulder came as she was reaching into her
bag for the tickets.

She jumped, turned and recognized an eagerness as
powerful as her own.

'I thought when the concert's over we might go for a
drink,' he said.

'Well, the last bus goes . . . Yes, I suppose we could.'

'I'll meet you here.'

'Perhaps at the corner?'

He was not in uniform. Lorna was peering myopically
through her thick lenses, trying to identify the intruder.
'Don't I know that face?'

'Probably not.' Cynthia was amazed at how easy it
was to lie. She settled to the Purcell and Vaughan
Williams with a heightened sense of appreciation.

Later he took her elbow to steer her through the maze
of streets. She felt the touch on her arm and, just fleetingly, as he opened the door of the pub for her, he laid his
hand on her back and left it there for a moment. Her skin
shivered like scratched silk.

They sat sipping their drinks, looking at each other
and smiling.

'So, how was it?'

'Er?'

'The music.'

'Oh, that . . . very good. Yes, really very good.'

'I've been walking the streets thinking of you sitting in the concert, listening to the music . . .'

'The choir is exceptional.'

He paused. 'It's grand . . . being with you.'

'Well, . . . thank you . . . I'm . . . for me too.'

The talk was casual but their eyes were intimate.

Cynthia glanced at her watch. 'I have to catch the bus.'

They swallowed the last of their drinks and ran down the dark streets to where late crowds were converging. He caught her arm. 'Just a moment, while we're on our own . . .'

'Oh, Josh.' She blushed but her eyes shone. 'I simply have to get the bus.' And she hurried away, without looking back.

When he returned late to the flat Jessica was in her knickers ironing her uniform skirt while Babs was perched at the kitchen table, darning stockings.

'Oh, don't mind me. I'll take myself off to my room.' Babs bunched her mending into a sewing basket.

Jessica wriggled into her skirt, still warm from the iron. 'Hmm, that feels cosy.'

He wondered again whether she knew and was keeping from him some information concerning his next crossing. He, after all, was keeping things from her.

'Have you had any supper, Josh?' Practical but curt.

'No. Thought I'd eat with you – the last night before we sail. Any news of Peter?'

Jessica shook her head. 'Not a bally thing.'

He raised an eyebrow. Was he right? *Did* she know something?

'Pilchards be OK? You can have them with fried bread and HP sauce. That do?'

He was back on board by midnight.

It was a good night for sailing. The three men were together for a moment in the darkened wheelhouse before going on stand-by at their harbour stations. It was a chance to catch up on personal matters.

'Good few days, then?' Josh asked.

'Yes, sir. Very good. Thanks.'

They were in formal mode.

'Get over the school trip, eh? What did you make of it?'

'Oh, good, I reckon. Very good. They're all so nice and neat. Cheerful, too, those schoolgirls.'

'Shall you be writing, then?'

'Oh, I think we'd better, sir, don't you? They'll expect it. You'll expect it. We're probably under orders.'

'Oh, yes, certainly.'

'In fact, do we have any say in which ones we write to?' This was from Robert.

'Oh, I dare say. That's the whole point of this ship adoption. I think we might all have our choices.'

Moments later, down in the captain's cabin, Josh gave his orders. First the chief engineer, Lofty Clarke, put his head round the door to announce that the engine was ready to move. He'd spent his leave visiting his ailing mother in Wallasey and worried about her being alone. He paused on his way out. 'It'll be Easter in three days.

The folks at home'll all be going to church on Sunday. Funny sort of Easter for us, sir.'

'I doubt it'll be the last, Chief.' Josh liked Lofty and approved of his concern for his mother.

'D'you think this war will last as long as the other, sir?'

'Probably longer, since you ask.' He rang the bell to the bridge. He must remember to look out his *Seaman's Prayer Book*. Typical of Lofty to remind him. For some it was little more than superstition, though no less powerful for that. For others, like Robert, it was a close personal faith. Josh had to conduct a special service on Easter Sunday. The men looked to some Divine Presence to see them through.

Next the ship's leading signalman, the senior apprentice, chubby young Charlie Rawlings, presented himself at the cabin, cap tucked neatly under his arm, signal pad and pencil at the ready. The visit to the school had been a rite of passage for the seventeen-year-old. He'd never before had permission to stare unashamedly at the shape and movement of girls' bodies. The women he met in ports were raucous and after his money. His mother had warned him to keep away from them. But she would surely approve of the school. He waited for his captain to speak. They discussed the signals going downriver.

'Pendant-numbers, pilot-flag and under-tow signal.'

'I'll see to all that, sir.' And Charlie Rawlings went about his work with a man's stride.

Finally Robert came to report: 'Ready to move, sir.'

'Thanks, Mr Warburton.' Josh seized his cap and binoculars, left the cabin and climbed the ladder to the bridge. There was a full moon and a drift of cloud across the sky. The light fell on the sea with glittering precision, like a diamond catching and reflecting its radiance. Easter coming and such moonlight. It should have been perfect.

The mooring cables were cast off, splashing into the water before they were reeled in, and the SS *Treverran* pulled away from her berth in Princes Dock. The minimum of dim blue light gave guidance where it was necessary. As she moved out along the Mersey they could see the debris of destruction still not cleared from where the SS *Malakand*, loaded with bombs, had blown up in Huskisson Dock almost twelve months ago, killing four and causing terrible devastation. The Blitz had been heavy in May that year, and ruined buildings – the Customs House, the Cotton Exchange, Lewis's department store – were now part of the landscape. Since January, fingers crossed, there had been no further raids on the city, which took nothing for granted. Sandbags and scaffolding shored up buildings. Dock gates were impassable without permission. But the people, dragged down by strain, could still enjoy a laugh. After all, wasn't the nation's favourite funny man, Tommy Handley, from Liverpool?

A steady line of ships was moving slowly towards the mouth of the Mersey. There was a stateliness about the procession that suggested confidence and power. The men felt it, and this was a moment to enjoy, setting out with the tang of salt air in their nostrils, hearing the slap-slap of water that would be with them across oceans, with the regular creaks and groans of the ship. Some twenty or so vessels navigated in and out each day. Each crew was alert, watchful, avoiding half-sunk ships: the SS *Silver Sandal* and SS *Duke of Rothesay*, hit in enemy raids and now lying across the channel. They headed past the Formby Lightship, then the Bar Lightship, where the escort was waiting. Their eyes grown used to darkness, the *Treverran*'s crew could mark the shapes and identities of other ships. It was a fine sight.

Suddenly a sound burst upon the chill air, sharp and alarming, blaring out, carried far across the waters.

'God! That bugger Walker's up to his tricks again. Will you listen?' Grins and muttered jokes broke across the bridge. Word was passed below, and those who were free of immediate duty climbed on deck to hear. The strains of 'A-hunting We Will Go!' were being tannoyed across the moonlit sea, a braying defiance: it was the signature tune of Captain Johnnie Walker.

He had brought an aggressive engagement to his posting in Liverpool: he went out intending to kill and so he did. The song said as much, and so did his naval record. Convoys were beginning to realize the benefit of having him with them while U-boat commanders weren't yet alert to his targeting skills. It did everyone good to hear him. The convoy and its escorts sailed steadily into the night.

Later on, after the second dog-watch, three of the crew, back in their familiar routines, took time for personal pleasures and began letters, each to his own.

Dear Jen . . .

Dear Polly . . .

And Dear School . . . The latter a missive of forced

chattiness, an account of the ship's activities from its captain, harmless details such as the hours of watch, the disposition of quarters, and correcting misconceptions: 'The officers' mess in the Merchant Navy is known as the saloon.' Then, satisfied that he had discharged his obligations as captain of an adopted ship, Josh took a fresh piece of paper. 'Dear Cynthia . . .'

Finding Out More

2003

The school magazines yield little. Millie kicks off her shoes, folds herself into the sofa cushions and addresses their pages with a scholar's attentiveness. She stays up late. Her mother must have kept them for some reason.

Solid paragraphs of print, relieved only by occasional poems, 'To a Primrose', 'Dream Ponies'. No pictures or photographs. It was wartime, after all, when paper and rolls of film must have been in short supply. But that didn't seem to have inhibited the school's activities – 'Climbing the mountain: the school's youth hostellers tackle Coniston's Old Man'; school debates, 'This house believes that Britain is declining in political, moral and intellectual force and cannot continue to be a first-rate power', defeated by an overwhelming majority; high-minded lectures, 'The Coloured People and the New World'; and notes from the Old Girls' Association, 'I spent three years at a school of dancing . . . Terpsichore is a zealous muse.'

After the war the school had collected money and

goods and sent six pounds five shillings to the Save Europe Now fund. There is plenty to give a flavour of this busy, worthy community, but Millie scours the names without success. Nowhere is there a complete list of pupils or teachers, simply references to netball captains, heads of houses, those who had led visits to silk mills and small factories. There is no sign that her mother had passed that way.

Something called Ship Adoption attracts a paragraph each year:

Through the good offices of the British Ship Adoption Society and the Staveley Education Committee we have had the good fortune to adopt one of Britain's merchant ships. Her birthplace was the Clyde, and although her name was whispered to some of us, for her own safety we are never to use it. We know her as MS 898/S34. Her comings and goings are a secret which no one is allowed to share, but in imagination we always accompany her wherever she sails. We brave the icy wastes of the convoys to Russia, battling through snowstorms, submarine packs and dive bombing. We have confronted the dangers of crossing the Atlantic to a royal welcome from our American friends before loading our holds with much-needed supplies for British larders, then turn round to face the perils of those 3000 miles of treacherous seas before reaching safe haven in one of Britain's great and welcoming ports.

There it was: a reference to the inscription on the model boat, MS 898/S34.

There are later references to visits by the still-anonymous captain, and 'his good lady, the Admiral'. Millie's hopes rise that there will be something about terrapin or turtle shells, but there is nothing. And, anyway, what on earth has any of it to do with her mother? The ship-adoption angle is intriguing, though.

Scholarship is really detective work, she muses, as she parks her precious red Karmann Ghia in the space that the National Maritime Museum authorities have allotted her.

The gaunt branches of the trees give as yet little promise of spring. There is a bright sun and a stiff little breeze, enough to puff meringues of white cloud across the translucent blue sky. She has grown conscious of clouds, writing about them, studying them in oil and watercolour. She knows how fine a day this would be at sea, how the sails of the mighty tea-clippers would have swelled and driven forward, how Drake and later Nelson would have given chase, how today the jib of the sprightliest dinghy would dance, and the wake of ferries and liners spread foaming white. She is thinking of ships and the sea, the sea and the sky, as she turns her mind to Turner and Constable, who loved them, too.

She is there as a scholar, of course, serious about Constable and Turner, intent on marine painting and clouds. That is her legitimate business. But it is also a cover for her personal search: the ship-adoption files are waiting.

She spends the morning on the business of her book, completing footnotes, adding attributions and provenances, then breaks for lunch, a sandwich of mozzarella and tomato at the museum café, where a Croatian waitress has scarcely enough English to complete the transaction. But the girl, with a ponytail and bold lipstick, is eager and willing. They have a fruitless exchange of mutual incomprehension. Nonetheless Millie thanks God for the European influx that is restoring courtesy to the catering trade.

Afterwards she climbs the broad mahogany stairs, stows her jacket and handbag in a tinny little cupboard, then enters the uniquely settling silence of the library. This is her world, where she is most fully herself, undistracted by others' lives and needs. She is at once in her element, a place where knowledge is compacted, held in readiness for the unfolding fingers, the searching eyes of those seized by intellectual curiosity.

The British Ship Adoption Society was not, as she imagined, a wartime project conceived to boost morale. It was first mooted as long ago as 1935 as a way to help teach geography in schools – about the Empire primarily. The Steamship Owners Associations all pledged their support as more and more schools were invited to apply. At the beginning they had looked to the BBC for publicity – there had been two brief talks on the radio, and a mention in the *Listener* – but within a year there were problems: Mr Wilson of the Mercantile Marine Association complained that his officer members were already overworked and underpaid; they'd not liked the scheme. There was also concern that the country's disaffected seamen would use their letters to spread political propaganda and indoctrinate the children, the Seamen's Union being strongly left wing with plenty of communist sympathizers. If any such thing were to happen, he stressed, 'The officers would lose the support of the nation.' Another argued that such letters 'would be of the nature that would pass between father and son'. Others agreed that, as they were forwarded through teachers, 'any improper matter was hardly likely to reach the children'. The scheme continued.

By 1936 some five hundred schools had enrolled, and a year later seven hundred. Applications came from abroad – St George's School in Jerusalem even sent a cheque – but it was decided that only dominion schools could have associate membership and the money was returned. The outbreak of war brought opportunities and problems: the chance to boost morale and cheer the troops, of course, but also disruptions. Schools were evacuated, ships were sunk. The master of a ship sunk by the *Graf Spee* was allowed to transfer his school to his next command. Pupils across Britain were knitting; the goods piled up.

Education and shipping authorities began to doubt that the scheme could carry on: it was hard for captains and crew to travel to their schools; it was only rarely that children could visit busy docks. But letters came in pleading otherwise: captains spoke of their pleasure at receiving school letters in the middle of war and battle, 'taking the dark edge off a gloomy day'; hand-knitted cardigans and jerseys, however erratic and shapeless, were welcome to sailors plucked from sinking ships. The scheme stayed in place.

But where was her mother in all this? Could she have been secretary to one of the contributing organizations? Millie tries to imagine her precisely pinned hair, her trim body in the milky shades of dull clothes. Her dedication to her abstemious way of life had rendered her almost colourless. Her mother had seemingly passed without trace through these pages, connected but disconnected. As she had been with Millie.

Writing

1942

Dear School

Here I am in my cabin beginning the first of what I know will be many letters to you. We certainly enjoyed our visit to what we now call 'our school', we often talk about how kind you all were, and remember so many little incidents, especially the frogs!

Because of the war there are many things I can't talk about but there are some things that might interest you. It is six bells in the forenoon now and this is when I have a little time to myself.

Our day is divided into watches of four hours each, six altogether. In the days when watchkeepers worked four hours on and four hours off, alternately, this meant that the men were on at the same time each day. To remedy this, the four p.m. to eight p.m. watch is divided into two watches of two hours each: the first dog-watch and the second dog-watch. These are the other names: midnight to four a.m., the middle watch; four a.m. to eight a.m., the morning watch; eight a.m. to noon, the forenoon watch (where we are now!); noon to four p.m., the afternoon watch; four p.m. to six p.m., the first dog-watch; six p.m. to eight p.m., the second dog-watch; eight p.m. to midnight, the first watch. So far, so good.

But it gets more complicated. There's the matter of the bells. Each watch is divided into half-hourly periods by the striking of a bell: one stroke of the bell at the end of the first half-hour of the watch, and an additional stroke of the bell at the end of each subsequent half-hour. Thus, when the watch starts at eight o'clock, one bell is at half past eight, two bells at nine o'clock, three bells at half past nine and so on until twelve o'clock, which is eight bells. Then we begin all over again with one bell. There is an exception. Remember the two dog-watches, each of two hours? Bells are struck in the ordinary way up to four bells at six p.m. Then a new watch begins so we start again with one bell at six thirty, then through to three bells at seven thirty. But eight bells at eight o'clock. I suppose a ship is rather like school and each watch a series of lessons. You have bells between lessons, don't you, each rung after the same length of time? We just have a lot more bells! Remember when your bell rings that the same thing may be happening on board your ship.

But I've not finished about bells yet! Ships' bells are always struck in pairs. For example, four bells go – ding-ding, ding-ding – with a second's break between each pair of strokes. And finally, a quarter of an hour before eight bells in each watch, a single bell is struck. This calls the next watch to duty.

I think I've gone on long enough about bells so I'd better ring off!

All good wishes,

Your captain,

Josh Percival

He took another sheet of paper and set it on the cabin table, then sat back wondering how to begin. She was constantly in his mind . . . and it was nice holding her in his imagination. He felt momentarily guilty that he wasn't thinking of Jessica, but she was part of the stale familiarity of his own world. Besides, she was very odd, these days. The war had unsettled her. Those new friends of hers weren't a good influence, either. He was more serene, happier, thinking of Cynthia.

'My dear Cynthia,' he wrote. Well, she'd given him her Christian name quite willingly. She would expect him to use it. But 'My'? Perhaps that was too familiar. He'd have to waste the page and start again. Before he did so, he let his fountain pen experiment . . . 'Dearest Cynthia' . . . 'Darling Cynthia' . . . 'My darling Cynthia'— Christ! He tore up the page and screwed it into a tiny ball. Then, unsure how to dispose of it, he slipped it into his pocket.

'Dear Cynthia, There is a lot I can't tell you – about the ship, I mean. You will know that where we travel, and what we carry, has to be a wartime secret so perhaps I can tell you about myself . . .' He knew it was an excuse. He yearned to tell her about himself. 'I was born in the tougher part of Glasgow – Dad worked in the shipyards, as had his dad before him. It was a hard life, but he was a strong, big man. When he carried me on his shoulders, I was always higher than all the other boys. I liked school and was Miss Mackenzie's favourite – but the other boys ragged me so I wanted to leave and go to sea . . .'

The pen paused. Miss Mackenzie had urged him to do well, lending him books, which he had returned unread: he was happier outside, in the sharp air, down by the water. His mother had pleaded, but he'd had no time for her feebleness. He regretted that now. One day, perhaps, he would tell Cynthia . . . Instead he spun a yarn about a bold boy loving the sea and left it at that.

He sat back in his chair and considered the two letters he had written. The first made him smile. Perhaps it wasn't the way to write to young girls but he'd done his best. And he remembered the rows of eager faces in the assembly hall, hanging on his words. He had always loved children.

It was a long time since Peter had been small: he was eighteen now and Josh's equal in height. He had the same craggy face, without the deep clefts that experience and weather had etched into his father's cheeks. He, too, had a crown of curly black hair, although Josh's was growing wiry as it turned grey. He wasn't Peter's guiding light any more, neither his hero nor his rock. They were adults together, respectful, fond, but grown men. How touched he had been by the younger people's company; they were so trusting and open-hearted. Even their silliness was comforting. Out at sea, the school's presence came to stand for all that was innocent and good about his home country.

And then there was Cynthia. He wondered if she ever

lost control, ever stepped out of line ... She seemed so fastidious and exact. But he sensed something within her that wasn't afraid of his friendship.

The letter arrived wrapped inside the other letters to the school, the package opened by the censors, then put back tidily together. The ship-adoption transaction was conducted through a clearing house in London, the only body allowed to know where the different ships were calling, and in possession of the code numbers by which the schools knew their ships. Because they were sorting and sending out shoals of letters, to and from some seven hundred English schools, hurried censors took in their stride poems, drawings (as long as they were not of ships) and recipes (wartime shortages made people inventive with cabbage and flavoured breadcrumbs). Expressions of patriotism could never be too strong. Some smiled at flirtatious comments, but took the heavy ink to anything that overstepped the mark to schoolchildren. The adults, they reckoned, could look after themselves. Which was what Cynthia thought.

'Grace, do take these letters to the forms. There'll be one for each, and some individual ones, too. No lesson must be interrupted. Go when the bell rings. They're to be read only at break.'

Her own letter lay open on the roll-top desk. She had read it quietly and steadily, then sat and looked at it. Its tone was of hesitant cheeriness. She liked that. But was there something else? Josh, as she would now allow herself to call him, had written about his younger days, straightforward information clearly set out. Her teacher's eye had been alert to the awkward grammar and occasional spelling mistakes, but as she reread it – it was only two pages long – her woman's eye was teasing out any significance that might lurk behind the words. It wasn't clear to her whether she did this from curiosity or in the hope of discovering a lurking intimacy.

When Brian had been killed she was seventeen and her world had ended. They had been giddily in love, a new and engulfing feeling; she had been breathless with excitement simply to be with him. He had scarcely been able to stop himself holding her, stroking her . . . her hair, her neat little waist, her long legs. They had done a lot of touching, he always the bolder, she tentative but devoted. Oh, they had been young, of course, and inexperienced, with plenty of years ahead.

His loss was as dramatic to her as their love had been romantic. She would treasure all the little happinesses they had had together, and made up her mind to turn her life, sacrificially, to other satisfactions. She would become a dedicated teacher.

Over the years she had come to know many like herself. When the war had ended, the men had not come home. There was desert where there should have been fields of golden youth. Without any prospect of marrying, armies of young women had become teachers. Miss Hayter, in the biology lab, had lost a sailor boyfriend at Jutland. Lorna, the gym mistress, had been engaged to an army captain who fell at the Somme; grief had damaged her spirits and she had retired into a life of few words and eccentric clothing. Individual pain had been subsumed into the shared purpose of the school.

Cynthia looked up at the photograph in its silver frame: Brian in officer's uniform, home on leave, smiling, outlined against the sky with a briar pipe in his hand. It had been taken in the orchard at his parents' home. It was September and they had just picnicked under the laden trees; ripe fruit had fallen into her lap. He was going back to the front the following day. She had been no older than the girls now in her sixth form.

Cynthia sighed. She reached out, picked up the silver frame in both hands and held it in her lap. She smiled at Brian's face, shaking her head, acknowledging what she had long ignored. That it had not been perfect.

Brian had asked and she had said no. She had refused him, turned aside from his urgent embrace. She was little more than a child, he had known that, but he also knew he might be killed and wanted to be loved before he died. Cynthia had been confused. Her body was a mystery to her, flushed and eager, her pulse racing, her mouth ready for his, but the rest unknown. 'No, no . . . please, no.' She could hardly bear to remember it: her refusal clanged in her ears, sounded increasingly self-righteous, prim. What failure of the heart, what freezing of the body had denied him what he wanted? She had sobbed and tossed in her empty bed as the years had passed.

Josh was unsettling all those ancient hurts and choices. And she was glad it was so.

Dear Jen,

We're all writing our letters to the school. I'm so pleased it's you. Wasn't it odd how we met up again after the town hall dance? You're a great girl on the dance floor, Jen. My mate thought that too. Perhaps we can go again, another time, when we're in Liverpool. Though even we don't know when that will be. I wish I could tell you more about life here: it's pretty ████████ [several lines had been blacked out]. Tell me more about your life, please. There's not much to say about mine.

My dad works delivering bags of coal from a cart. It's pulled by a great horse called Chance. She's a Clydesdale, I think. Some of the coal men are wanting lorries but they're all needed for the war. But my dad doesn't mind. He likes her, and she likes him. He's wondering whether there's going to be coal rationing. Seems there's quite a fuss going on. He thinks there should be. He's all for people being treated equal. He takes it very serious, always lecturing me about how they'll have to nationalize the mines. No reason why all the profits should go to the owners when men risk their lives. I agree with him. We'll be seeing great changes when this war's done, I expect. And they're sure to be for the better. We can't have the bad days back again. My dad was unemployed for years. It got him down. It was only my mother being so good that saw him through. It's great to have a good mum, like I do.

I hope you'll write and tell me all about yourself. Have you been dancing again? Oh, I'm jealous!

With good wishes from your friend at sea,

Tim

My dear Polly,

At least, I've made a start! We used to have pen-pals at school, and I wasn't a very good one. Now the Old Man (that's the man you call our captain. In the Merchant Navy he's officially called the master) wants us to write. I asked if I could write to you, rather than any of the others, because at least I know what you look like. The rest of the crew are being handed names from a hat, and there's some rough talk I wouldn't like you to hear about what the owners of the names might look like.

I know what you look like, but that's all I know. We didn't have any time to chat, what with the row over your Jewish friend. How is he? Hans, I think you called him, though your friend said Harry. Which is it?

Have you read any books by Richard Jefferies? He writes about the countryside and I admire him very much. I'd like to know whether you agree with me. I love the fields and trees and spend what time I have free out on our farm. I thought of being a priest when I was younger, but I've got over that now. At least, I think I have. My family are Catholics, which isn't such an important matter to me but they go on about it. It bores me silly. It shouldn't matter so much to people what religion you are, but apparently it does. So I usually shut up about it.

But here I am telling you. So you must have made a good impression.

Anyway I prefer the Young Liberals. Have you heard about them? You have to subscribe, then you

can go to their parties. I could take you, if you'd like.
Usually I take Brenda Foster because my parents
know her. But I'm not keen. I'm keen on you.

Yours very sincerely
Robert (First Mate)

'Dear Josh, I was really pleased to have your letter. It was
thoughtful of you to write me my own letter as well as
one to the school.' She felt, shyly, that this was almost too
forward. 'I have read it a number of times, because I am
interested in what you tell me about your early life . . .'
This was becoming very obvious so she added, '. . . as I
would be in any of the crew's.' That wouldn't do: it
sounded forced and condescending. Untrue, too. Perhaps
the best way to respond was to copy Josh. She began the
letter again, guilty at the reckless waste of paper. When it
came to the point, she continued, 'so let me respond by
telling you something of my life.' She posted the letter
without rereading it to avoid any second thoughts.

Josh's reply began, 'My dear Cynthia . . .'

Holidaying

During the Easter holidays Cynthia took her mother, Beryl, to Lytham St Anne's for a week. They stayed in a guest-house, one of the red-brick villas on a back-street near the station. It smelled of cabbage and Mansion polish, and bottles of HP Sauce were set permanently in the middle of its six dining tables.

Their routine was rigid, dictated by Beryl. Each morning they walked down to the front, hired deck-chairs and set them up bleakly on the windy foreshore where Beryl read the *Daily Express* and Cynthia didn't. Cynthia would have liked a pursuit of her own to break the boredom of the uneventful seafront and the long, slow crawl of the tide across the flat sands. There was little sunshine and the threat of rain was constantly upon them. Everywhere bore the same grey, sandy colouring, even the passers-by. It was a place devoid of stimulus, empty, neutral. That was how Beryl liked it. She demanded that Cynthia should like it, too.

'You have all that school time to yourself, to serve your

own needs. Now it's time I had a little attention.' Beryl's gnarled arthritic fingers grasped the broad pages of the newspaper flapping in the wind. Irritably she complained, 'Can't you help, girl? Show a little Christian consideration.' Dutifully Cynthia folded the paper so that her mother could tussle with its bland crossword.

Sitting in the sagging canvas of the deck-chair, with nothing to distract her except her mother's rasping demands for humbugs and Pontefract cakes, Cynthia's mind was free to wander where it would.

A busy and well-regulated brain with little to feed on tips into a maelstrom of random thoughts and sensations. At first her own ideas tumbled without focus, odd notions and curiosities – she must remember to plant the lettuce seedlings . . . How old was Bette Davis? . . . Was that a boy or a girl running in wellingtons across the distant sand dunes? . . . And that dowdy young woman who sat each mealtime at the table next to theirs, what job did she do? Her pink angora cable-stitch jumper was very nice, though the fluff must come off on anyone she touched. Who would she touch, she wondered, at her age? A man. She might touch a man, a man wearing a dark suit, and the angora wool would give it away. Everyone would know he and she had touched, which wasn't allowed.

She herself had been touched quite recently. What did it mean? Who did anyone she knew touch? Who touched them? What touching was allowed and not allowed, and where? No one had touched her for many years until the evening of the concert. Even Mother, who regarded displays of affection with distaste. Sometimes she yearned to be touched. Sometimes she lay on her back in bed and ran her hands up and down below her Viyella pyjamas, touching.

How would it feel if a man were to do that – to do more than that? Josh had shaken her hand and held on to it. He was a man who touched women, she sensed, and was at ease doing so. What was wrong with it? Would she let him touch her again? Would he even ask? She'd prefer it if he didn't. Then she could tell herself she wasn't complicit. But she imagined she would like it to happen.

Her mother dropped her bag of sweets. Cynthia snatched up the bag in a show of almost authentic concern, dusted the sand from the sticky wrapper, eager to get back to her thoughts and the images that went with them. Where was she? What exactly was she ... Touching, and letting it happen. That's where she was. But the sweetness had gone. Face the facts: he was a married man and she was an ageing spinster – they all were, all her colleagues. Who had touched any of them? Miss Hayter – no; Miss Fletcher, possibly; Lorna, poor sad Lorna, alas, never; Miss Jessop, almost certainly – after all, she taught French and had been abroad; Miss Franklin and Miss Johnson, well, they lived together; Grace Bunting, with her flaunted engagement ring, imminently and the Bible permitting. Other than Grace, they were a sad and disappointed lot, surely.

And yet they weren't, were they? That wasn't the only truth about them, if indeed it was true at all. These were women she knew and admired. They were buoyant and full of goodness, funny sometimes, always reliable. No self-pity, little introspection. They were her school. And the girls. It was her job to see they saved themselves for married life, which would come soon enough. Until then they had freedom of mind and spirit, a brief whirl of ideas and nonsense, laughter and friendship, before the routines of marriage closed round them. She was happy for them, and suddenly happy for herself. Life was full of possibilities – she must never forget that. Even for a spinster teacher dumped in a deck-chair on a windy Lancashire beach. She hauled her mother back to the guest-house midday meal with more genuine affection than Beryl deserved.

By the afternoon the tide had completed its crawl towards the promenade, and Cynthia's mind was still roaming free. Mother and daughter stationed themselves on one of the park benches among the formal gardens, near the old windmill, careful to choose one apart from the others. They would dislike being engaged in conversation by complete strangers. After all, they scarcely spoke to each other. But Cynthia had upset their routine by buying a copy of the *Manchester Guardian* that afternoon. In her mother's eyes it was a wayward and disjointed thing to do. Newspapers were a morning thing, discarded by noon, used to light the fire the following day.

Suddenly her mind quickened: a new idea began to take shape. It involved something called current affairs, a subject beyond the school's curriculum but she'd noticed it cropping up in youth groups and conferences for young people organized by national newspapers.

Cynthia would found the Tea Club. It would be for

123

sixth-formers only, and they would be invited to take tea in her study after school on Friday. A local worthy – a librarian, the mayor – would come to discuss matters in the news. She turned the pages of the *Manchester Guardian*, looking for topics.

The war was not going well. Somehow she had not realized how bad things were. Busy with daily life, her mother, the school, their various projects, and now the ship adoption, she had assumed that the effort everyone was making must be paying off. It was such a grand effort: everyone was part of it. It united the country and felt exhilarating, even triumphant. But assembled together, the news – from Africa, Malta, Tokyo, Burma – was mostly of loss, struggle and defeat. She wasn't sure how the Tea Club might benefit from that.

At half past four they gathered up their things: Beryl's knitting bag; the discarded newspapers; what remained of the sweets, twisted into the corner of a grey paper bag to be saved for later. A thin drizzle had swallowed the horizon and was closing in for a drab evening in the residents' lounge, with other grey couples and the girl in the angora jumper. Resolute to break the boredom, Cynthia insisted she and her mother go to the cinema. And there it was again: the bad news, carefully contained within a show of buoyant hopefulness. Until now Cynthia had unquestioningly shared it.

She thought of their ship battling through rough seas and enemy attacks, men she knew facing storms and the blaze of guns. How much of a relief was it to know that, as part of the war effort, the Archbishop of Canterbury now allowed women to go to church without hats, or that the government had banned embroidery on their underwear?

Beryl, who rarely revealed her feelings and would certainly think it inappropriate to convey them to her daughter, had had a wonderful holiday. She told the vicar as much. Most particularly she boasted of the care Cynthia had lavished upon her. 'She really is a wonderful daughter, you know. I scarcely ever have to complain. Not many mothers can say as much.' The Reverend George Potter agreed. For a woman who hadn't managed to find a husband Miss Maitland had done well. Beryl allowed herself a smug smile as she returned to the flower rota and plans for a display of daffodils at next weekend's wedding.

The wedding in question was that of Grace Bunting: the flashing engagement ring was soon to be tamed with a slim gold band. Cynthia cultivated a restrained response to weddings. For years she couldn't help but imagine her own, the shadow image of what would never be superimposed on the flutter of dresses, bridesmaids and music. But those days were gone, regrets now dusted away. For Grace, with her fiancé away fighting in another war, she had had special concern. It was why she put up with the girl's fussing attention and all its irritations.

And then Roderick had been invalided out of the war after a night attack in the western desert. His injuries put him out of the fighting for good, and he was growing restless in the routine desk job he now had. At first he was overcome by episodes of black depression, but he found solace in the growing intensity of his religious life.

The idea of marrying the gentle, capable Grace lit up his dull days. They had met at a church youth club, years before, and shared a shyness of people and an intimacy with God. 'Do you understand what it's all about?' Grace had asked him, of the vicar's account of the Trinity while they were being prepared for confirmation.

'Not yet, but we will in time.'

Cynthia, as Grace's boss, was a conspicuous guest, and Beryl, proud pillar of the church, was happy to bask in the attention. Wartime scarcities made it a modest affair. The bride wore a short crêpe dress and coat bought with coupons hoarded for months by family and friends. The organist being away in the navy, a family acquaintance fumbled through the notes but was cheerily forgiven – people simply sang louder to cover the mistakes. At the altar steps Mr Potter smiled benignly at the trim, unshowy pair, the wounded groom wearing his one medal on his RAF uniform.

The reception was held under the corrugated roof of the church hall next door. They had eked out the rations, saving enough dried fruit and fresh eggs for a sturdy little cake, set inside a cardboard copy of an idealized wedding cake, all shining white cardboard decked with swirls of glitterwax flowers. Regular use had made it a little shabby.

The best man, Roderick's brother on leave from the RAF, made fulsome reference to Grace's role in the running of Ashworth Grammar School for Girls, a job she would continue even though she had become a wife. She was, after all, indispensable. Cynthia smiled behind the little spotted veil of her elegant green hat. And a whisper went round the company that, give it a year or so, Grace was sure to be more than a wife.

Cynthia's first Tea Club of the summer term got off to a tumultuous start. Several sixth-formers grumbled, some rebelled and had to be fetched from hiding in the lavatories, while a few worried that they might dry up when asked their opinion and look foolish in front of the others. Finally, at Cynthia's insistence, they sat in an arc round her desk and the red unused sofa was brought out from below the window to seat their first guest, Mr Crouch, the curator of the local museum. The subject: the Baedeker raids, a series of German bombing attacks on Britain's most historic cities. Exeter had been hit in March and Bath a couple of days later. Norwich followed, then York. None of these places had any strategic importance. Mr Crouch had been brooding at the barbarity of attacking our cultural heritage.

Once cups of tea had been handed round he had his moment. 'We get the measure of Hitler's brutality from such attacks, don't we, girls? Can you see how absolutely without a shred of human decency the Germans are? We can expect Liverpool to be bombed, and Manchester. Think of the docks. You could say these are legitimate targets. They're helping us to defeat the enemy. But war has nothing to do with our quiet and beautiful cathedral cities, has it? Why would they attack them? Well, they're trying to break our morale, you see, attacking us where it hurts, damaging things we care for in the hope we might surrender.' Mr Crouch was leaning earnestly forward, his hands clasped between his knees.

'Oh, we'll never do that. Never, never.' Several voices were raised in passionate declaration.

'We've got to win, that's the first thing.' Tall, gangling Angela was captain of netball. 'We've got to be sure of that at any price!' There was laughter at the obviousness of the remark.

'Presumably the Germans want to win too, though.' The reedy voice was Jen's, its pitch higher than usual because she was nervous. 'So they'll want to be sure of just the same thing.'

'Oh, my God, she's a Quisling!' A guffaw from a couple of feebler spirits.

'No, she has a point.' Cynthia steered them towards logic and away from xenophobia. 'Polly, you're being very quiet. What do you think?' She had spotted Polly studying her fingernails, probably planning the colour she'd paint them when she grew up.

'Oh, yes. Well, perhaps we shouldn't torture people, not even Germans. Not the good ones, at least.'

'Torture? The British would never do that. Who said we did?'

'Are you saying we don't?'

'And *good* Germans? Name one!'

'Well, they're ruled by a dictator so they have to do what Hitler says, whether they approve or not.' Jen had taken courage from Polly's contribution. Both had tacitly agreed not to mention Hans, even as Harry. 'Some may be just like us.'

'That's truly insulting! Germans are barbaric, and you're siding with them, Jennifer . . .' It was widely known that Brenda Alsop envied Jen her friendship

128

with Polly, and Brenda Alsop was fuelled by perpetual anger.

Cynthia, who was keen to encourage differences of view, was alarmed that the debate was turning personal. She looked at Mr Crouch, now folded even more towards his knees. Wearily he braced himself to help.

'Well, the Germans did vote Hitler into power. They made a choice.'

There was a general gasp. For most it was welcome confirmation that the Germans were demons; for Jen, the sheepish realization that she hadn't known Hitler had been elected by the people.

Mr Crouch shook the dust from his limp suit and seized the lull in the conversation. 'We are, after all, dealing with a race descended from the warring tribes of Central Europe. Think of Attila the Hun, and how he marauded across Europe. Hitler is in the same league. He is set on devastating even our quiet and peaceful cities. The beauty of centuries is under attack, which it should not be.'

Voices clamoured.

'We certainly wouldn't do it, would we?'

'Not our forces. I can't believe we would.'

'Er, can I say something?' This from Elsie Dawson, a colourless girl who, to give herself some colour, had chosen to learn German rather than French.

'Yes, Elsie, speak up, dear.'

'What about Beethoven and Goethe?'

'Who's Goethe when he's at home?' This was whispered between the two who had called Jen a Quisling. Neither knew the answer.

Mr Crouch did. 'Ah, Beethoven and Goethe. Good Germans, I agree. But dead.'

There was a mild titter.

It was hard to think dispassionately about the war, and it had been clear that her girls weren't prepared to do so. Nonetheless Cynthia judged the first meeting of the Tea Club a success.

It was Jen on whom the outcome fell hardest. Arriving at school the following Monday she found her cloakroom locker had 'Hun Lover' chalked on it. She rubbed it off with spit on her handkerchief and said nothing.

Talking

'I'm surprised you haven't thrown the whole lot out by now. That's what I expected you to do.' Kate has noticed the school magazines stacked beside the glass bowl on the coffee table.

'Well, I haven't. Not yet, anyway. I'm getting quite involved . . .'

Kate has brought Freya round from her morning playgroup to be with Millie for the afternoon. She waddles in wearing a green corduroy pinafore dress, her arms outstretched for her grandmother's embrace.

Kate wears a black linen trouser suit and a bright red T-shirt splashed with letters and gold paint. She moves without haste. Her eyes are thoughtful. The illness is making her slender and pale.

'Goodness! You do look smart.'

'Don't I just. They're my funeral clothes: I've been conducting my first. I told you I'd done the training and the dry run. This was for real.' Kate struggles to conceal her pride.

'And how was it?'

131

'Well, I did all right: no fluffs or awkward moments. A small family and a few friends. They were very quiet and pleased. They wanted Christina Rossetti – that's always a favourite, apparently, and very moving.'

'And how do you feel now you've done it?' Millie is amazed that Kate is proving so resilient.

'Rather serene, actually. Quiet and peaceful. Other people's sadness makes you think about things.' Kate averts her eyes and unpacks a bag of bright toys, some soft and cuddly, others made of shapes to fit together, and begins to play with Freya.

'It doesn't upset you at all, then?' Millie persists, waking to a new sense of her daughter.

'Oh, no. Not at all. The fact that I'm ill and not getting better does something to my head. I'm not depressed . . . more resigned . . . I can understand their grief a bit more.'

Millie doesn't answer, leaving the thought hanging in the air. She has been back to see Mr Charles. He was as precise as ever, neat little hands like a badger's, and this time his tie was flecked with seabirds.

He rubbed his hands together, pleased with himself and Millie. 'I'm delighted to tell you the tests are just as we hoped: your kidney will be completely compatible with your daughter's.' Compatible? Strange word. Kate is her own flesh and blood, and yet such different temperaments. Millie looks at him steadily, waits to collect her thoughts then speaks with deliberation.

'I'd be grateful,' she had told him, 'if, while I make my decision, you'd not tell Kate about it. I want time . . .' The enormity of what she has said appals her.

*

Now she looks sorrowfully at Kate who, sensing her mother's unease, takes up one of the school magazines from the table.

'Perhaps Gran was at school there?'

'Well, I thought of that, but the years don't match.'

There is interesting news to report, however, and Millie brightens up. ' I was at the Maritime Museum in Greenwich last week, checking out some of the art references for my book. I looked up the records of something called the Ship Adoption Society. It gets a mention in all those magazines. Ashworth Grammar School did it, girls and sailors writing to each other.'

'Wow, how risky was that!'

'Oh, it all seems to have been terribly decorous: formal visits by the captain, educational visits by the girls. They write girlish accounts, full of gee-whizz excitement. It's all wonderfully dated, like something out of Angela Brazil: innocent pigtailed girls leading innocent lives, and all those sailors. Away at sea, rough lives, rough weather . . . and full-scale war, too, of course.'

'Who'd get schools now writing to our troops – specially if they're being sent to Iraq. "The nation is behind you." It just couldn't happen. Perhaps Gran was a teacher at the school?'

'That occurred to me, but I'd have known if she'd been a teacher. She would have said. I don't remember her ever talking about herself much at all.' Millie pauses thoughtfully. 'I just couldn't get on with my mother . . .'

She has grown steely and remote. The long shadow of hurt and loss looms in the bright room. Why do we know so little about each other, parents and children? From generation to generation everything shifts and nobody tells. And here is Kate, open and needing her. They move to the table where poached salmon and raw vegetables meet the needs of Kate's diet. She helps Freya climb on to her special cushion, plain and sturdy to catch any spills. Millie stirs an unsalted dressing into the rocket and spinach salad.

'There were good reasons. Both Mummy and Daddy were in that very strict Christian group. It was virtually house-arrest: prayers at breakfast, Bible-reading at bed-time. Plenty of people were repressed in those days but none as fiercely as they were. I kept my life separate and private from theirs. Never came close. I know it sounds terrible but, you know . . . I sometimes think I hated her.'

Battling

1942

Josh surveyed the noisy, busy quay where they'd just tied up, standing on deck in the tropical sunshine. The *Treverran* had been calling at ports down the eastern seaboard of America and by now Europe and its preoccupations seemed a great distance away. He felt the sun strike through his open-necked shirt and warm the bare skin above his uniform-issue white socks, and knew there was another way of feeling and living. As they came into port they had seen along the shoreline the straw huts of the natives, their nifty boats trading fruit and cloth along the coast, and on the hillsides behind, the startling white of comfortable villas nestling behind dense green palms. Men and boys had laughed and waved to the ship as it passed. Was there, behind this jolly charade, something they knew that he didn't, some secret about living in the sun and heat that didn't belong in a mind that had grown up with strict Scottish values, bound tight from child-hood to ideas of duty and obedience? It was good to be in the sunshine, strolling the palm-fringed shore with no more immediate task than to search the local markets for treasures to take home.

'You can't take them back to Britain, sir.' Robert had been wandering the dusty roads that straggled away from the deep-sea port and now he stood beside Josh as they contemplated a market stall loaded with animals and fish, all alive and moving. A miasma of strange smells hung in the air, pungent but not repellent.

Robert disliked seeing the creatures penned in cramped dirty cages and overcrowded tanks, and thought suddenly of how much love his father showed his cows, the warm comfort of their stalls, the scent of hay, the crackle of straw. All a world and a war away.

Josh was negotiating the purchase of six terrapins from a small, wizened man in a filthy shirt. The notion had occurred to him out of the blue. How would those giggling girls and their serene headmistress react to such a gift?

'Perhaps we could eat them, sir,' Robert suggested.

'Certainly we will not. They're going home to the school.'

'Hang on, sir, they won't survive the journey. Anything could happen.'

'Oh, anything almost certainly will. We'll gamble on it.'

'Where'll they go? Not in the hold?'

'This man' – the stall-holder was grinning helplessly – 'is selling me a brand-new tank, and we'll find somewhere to put it. The school will love them.'

The tank proved less than new but the man offered to deliver it, with the terrapins, to the dock gate. The rest of the crew laughed at the idea, joking among themselves that the Old Man had gone soft. But secretly they liked the idea: there was something wayward and crazy in its daftness that cheered them up. 'What next?' they muttered. 'And what's the school going to make of them?'

They were to join an Atlantic convoy home. There was never any time to be other than alert, but making their way to the rendezvous, Josh was less apprehensive than usual. He could snatch some privacy in his cabin, a tight fit of bunk and wardrobe, basin and desk, but his own. He could close the door on the world if he wished, though in the tropics it remained constantly open on its brass hook, with the curtain wafting gently in the light breeze. It was as private as you could get.

The small space made him neat in his movements, and tidy in his habits, lest the photographs of Jessica and Peter crashed from the desk and things piled up on the narrow day-bed. He never let that happen: his possessions were stowed below the high bunk with its polished mahogany lee boards. He did any relaxing on the dusty drab green of the day-bed, with its wretched unyielding cushion. There was just enough shelf space above his desk for a few books, his pipe and tobacco, with a trinket or two. The tiny bathroom next door held his shaving kit above the basin. His living quarters had been honed to meet minimum needs. No excess, no indulgence. But however confined, it was still his space: his flask of whisky was here, his family photographs. It was where he collected his thoughts and, when the going was rough, where he tamed his fears and became familiar with his courage. And it was where he read his letters.

He had joined the mercantile marine in peacetime, a

civilian body of men trading goods around the world. His work was rich in small pleasures. He'd been at sea for more than twenty years and knew the satisfactions of running your own vessel, choosing your own route, contacting agents in each port, reporting to the owners, all on your own responsibility. What he hadn't reckoned on knowing was U-boats and how they operated, torpedoes, magnetic mines and depth charges. Now he found himself hooked up to the Royal Navy as, together, they battled the enemy's blockade. The convoys made it explicit: he was dependent on the protection of wartime recruits to the RN, raw young lads fresh from school and college who didn't know their way round a bathtub. Their convoys safeguarded his cargoes; their courage saved his life. He didn't like it. He didn't like it at all. It diminished his sense of independence.

They sailed north in a small convoy of some eleven ships, merchantmen joining them from all points of the compass: from Australia and New Zealand with wool and frozen lamb, two tankers from Maracaibo full of Venezuelan crude oil. They would be stationed in the centre, he reckoned, and wondered which column would be his. Not on the outside, he hoped, with a cargo of bauxite.

The Atlantic convoy then gathering around St John's would be as large as any to make that crossing. The system was well into its stride, a more slick and efficient operation than Josh's earlier experiences. More ships were being built to purpose all the time, a whole class of corvettes and one or two of the new frigates, coming off the slipways of the Tyne and the Clyde with men from the Royal Naval Reserve called up to command and man them.

Josh, Robert and Tim stood on the bridge and tried to take in the scale of the spectacle. Round them some forty-two ships were assembling in nine columns, each ship less than half a nautical mile behind another. What they had in common was the bright flutter of signal flags and the reassuring sight of the white ensign. The red, yellow and black of Belgium, flying from a corvette, was just one of many exiled by war – Danes, Norwegians, Free French. As they watched, a signal from an Aldis lamp warned them they were getting out of station.

'Work to do, gentlemen. We can't stand here all day.'

'No, but quite a sight to write home about, sir.'

'You'd better get on with it then, Tim, when you've an idle watch below.' They grinned, going their separate ways.

Josh stood a moment longer. Faced with such united purpose, his tetchy resentment of the Royal Navy mellowed, one mood giving way suddenly to another. He was comfortable now, feeling part of it. He raised his binoculars and smiled at what he saw, nodding with a sudden grim pride. He would lead his ship and his crew as he knew how, careful of discipline and obedience, neither too rigorous nor too indulgent. He had good men with him: Robert and Tim had grown, under his guidance, into the best of officers. This was as good a convoy as you could get, a tough challenge to any pack of German U-boats.

And such a pack was gathering even now to scour the seas in what was uncharacteristically mild Atlantic weather, the wind a moderate south-westerly with only a little cloud cover, and an almost full moon expected. Ideal hunting weather. The enemy would be feeling confident.

On the third night the sound came, unmistakable, the deep, heavy boom that held its resonance for several seconds, like some great cathedral organ. Everyone heard it, with resignation. It was not the *Treverran* that was hit, but very close. They heard it in the smoke-room where Tim, just off middle watch, was making tea. They heard it in the radio office, in the galley, below decks. They heard it in the engine-room and the stoke-hold where it came like a great hammer blow to the hull. Those in their bunks, catching some kip against the prospect of a disturbed night, heard it; the naval gunners heard it, and knew it was their call. Apprentice Rawlings heard it and muttered a prayer. Six small terrapins, stowed away between decks, must have heard it too, and thought, perhaps, of whales and sharks, rocks and the sea.

Action stations! Action stations! Whistles blew, men ran. Josh, who liked to prowl the bridge when it wasn't his watch, had just gone down to his cabin to stretch his legs and smoke a pipe. His sea boots lay on the floor. He reached for them and, in seconds, was out through the door and up the steps. The clang of boots on metal, the scratch of slept-in wool sweaters, the choke of cigarette and pipe fumes, and the stale smell of bodies released into the sweet tang of sea air – all vivid sensations. Fear was exhilarating yet exhausting. They felt a savage power.

Josh was the man they looked to: standing four-square

on the bridge he focused his years of experience on the moment. His strength drew to him the cares of the crew. His words were calm and exact. 'Starboard easy,' he said quietly, and was glad when the helmsman's tone echoed his own.

'Starboard easy, sir.' The *Treverran*'s bow swung out of line.

''Midships . . . stead-eee . . .'

''Midships steady, sir.'

The ship just ahead had taken a direct hit amidships, and the explosion was sudden: clouds of black smoke billowed dense and poisonous against the deep dark of the night sky. Flames followed almost instantaneously, throwing into the air sheets of yellow, gold and red so bright they plunged whatever was beyond into further blackness. The oil was escaping fast, shooting slivers of fire across the surface of the sea. Against all this, silhouetted figures were moving fast.

Josh brought the *Treverran* back on a parallel course, but offset a little so they could pass the crippled tanker. They watched. It wasn't their job to help.

'Fuck, oh, fuck, oh, fuck . . .' someone was saying, as they drew ahead of the blazing tanker.

'Stop that,' Josh snapped. No time for anger or despair. Simple action, that was all.

Somehow the tanker's crew managed to swing two of the starboard lifeboats over the side, but the ship's heel was already preventing the skids riding down. One cleared and made it to the surface. Men scrambled after it. Others jumped into the ocean. From the bridge Tim saw, through his binoculars, the outline of greasers, in nothing more than their thin cotton trousers and grimy cotton singlets, leaping, limbs flailing, into the chaos beneath. The tanker was sinking fast, her bows already plunging, the huge screw astern rising out of the water, its downward thrust gathering momentum. The men in the single lifeboat made frantic efforts to avoid the deadly suck of its final plunge.

Many had witnessed it before, but there was always something awesome in a ship's last moments. The tanker's foundering extinguished the wall of flame in a great hiss of sound, but it was the gentle settling of the ocean's waters over what had been, but seconds before, a hive of human activity that hushed the watching mariners.

Across the convoy there were mutterings.

'Bastards!'

'Poor buggers.'

'Jesus, help them!'

Everywhere hearts were struck with awe and terror.

This was the opening salvo of the U-boat attack. Men on the *Treverran*'s bridge could see, way out to port, explosions among the convoy as two merchantmen were hit. They heard rattling gunfire from an escort ship that had spotted the conning tower of a surfaced U-boat. Star shells showered balls of fire and dissolved into nothing. White parachute flares hovered a little longer, hanging below the gathering clouds, casting light on the small boats of survivors, overcrowded, some waving, others not.

The *Treverran*'s concern was local. Where was the U-boat that had torpedoed the tanker? New radar systems had recently been installed on Royal Navy ships, but somehow the U-boats had penetrated their shield and were now loose among the merchant shipping.

As destroyers raced pell-mell to scenes of action, dropping their depth charges, guns barking whenever a damaged submarine surfaced, the merchant ships, the body and purpose of the convoy, sailed on, their pattern now awry but their captains unflinchingly obeying orders to leave the battle and the rescue to others. Josh was doing the same when the lookout shouted, 'Light ahead! Christ, it's a U-boat. No, it's a bloke in the water.' Tim, currently officer of the watch, ran out to the bridge wing.

'A single survivor, sir, almost immediately ahead.'

Where the hell's he come from? Josh wondered.

Another voice: 'He's very close, sir. No one else will spot him. He's a goner if we don't act.' Josh leaped to the engine-room telegraph and swung the handle to STOP, then gave a double ring for 'full astern'. This was reckless, against orders, fucking madness. But it could be any one of them, single, alone, one of his own, himself – Peter.

'Permission to lower a ladder, sir.' Tim was urging him. Josh could do without this – just for one sailor, his ship and maybe the whole convoy in jeopardy. The *Treverran* was already shuddering to the reversed engines, her head falling off as she lost way. Those on the bridge knew why but those at action stations elsewhere would wonder what on earth was going on.

'What the—'

'We'll cop it!'

'He'll not do it,' Robert muttered to himself, as he

143

leaned over the bridge wing to catch sight of Tim. 'He'll need help.'

Josh's hand shot out and prevented him going. 'Stand by that telegraph,' he said quietly, 'and when I order "full ahead", I want you . . . Well, you know what to do.'

Josh was playing for time. Tim would need all his strength if he was to clamber down the pilot ladder, then reach down and haul the poor bastard up. But he was single-minded, his small frame broad and sturdy, his tattooed forearms muscled. For minutes, silent, dark minutes, there was nothing but a distant grappling in the churning water.

And then the miracle happened. A wayward wave, larger than most, lifted the survivor towards Tim, who made an extra lunge and had him in his grasp. The man, sticky with oil, had not been long in the water and was conscious enough to help himself a little. Both clung to the ladder as a rope snaked down from the deck. The boatswain had arrived and taken in the situation at a glance. He watched as Tim got the looped bowline round the other and the climb began.

'Got him, sir,' Tim called up, into the darkness.

Josh chuckled almost with glee, a satisfaction that came from nerves stretched taut.

The man was hauled up, gasping.

'Full ahead,' called Josh, surprised by the snarl in his voice. The *Treverran* moved forward again, as ships coming up astern were passing him. 'I expect the convoy commodore will give us a bollocking at daylight,' he said, to no one in particular.

'Where the hell did that bloke come from?' It was

Robert, relieved but mystified. 'You don't think he's a German, do you?'

Josh glared at him. 'Better not be.' He waited for the *Treverran* to reach full speed. He needed to dodge in astern of the three ships that had overtaken him. That would put him at the tail end of his column but not too far, he hoped, for the corvette acting as tail-end Charlie to spot them. She'd be busy picking up the tanker's crew. 'You'd better go and have a look,' he said, as Robert dropped down the bridge ladder.

He found Tim, the boatswain and a couple of able seamen struggling to get the survivor into the mess-room, stumbling over the sea-step in the dark. His oil-soaked clothing made him hard to hold – the problem Tim had grappled with at the bottom of the ladder. For a moment Tim had feared that the man might bring him down too and the rescue end in disaster, but he had pulled it off. Together they shook their new shipmate back to life. Yes, he would survive despite the gasping and gurgling.

Robert reached down to open the man's clothing. A large bottle of whisky, half empty, fell from his pocket. He leaned forward into the man's wretched face and smelled his breath. Christ, the bastard was drunk. He tossed him impatiently back to the deck where he lay. It happened, he knew that. In the terror and confusion of sinking, a sailor would make for a cache of drink and gulp down whatever he could in the blind hope of courage or, at least, insensibility. It was why this man had missed the lifeboat, and drifted away from the reach of helping hands.

Tim took the bottle, shaking his head.

'We could do with a swig o' that,' one of the seamen said, 'after what we saw back there, like.'

'Shut up,' said the boatswain, 'and chuck it over the wall. Then get this poor sod cleaned up and then chuck him in a bunk.'

'OK, boss.'

'You did bloody well, sir,' he said to Tim.

Tim went back up to the bridge, suddenly weary. It took him a moment to adjust to the darkness again and then he spotted the master's bulk.

The Old Man had already seen him. 'Well,' he said, 'I hope he's not a bloody German.'

Tim smiled. 'No, sir. He's definitely one of ours.'

Questioning

Her mother had provided a nice macaroni cheese for Jen's tea. They had eaten it together when Father had come in from work, listening to the six o'clock news as they did so. The news was not good. The announcer's voice was serious, without any trace of encouragement. Bert was preoccupied with filling in his pools coupons, not heeding the reports from North Africa where the British Eighth Army was taking a hammering. Jen helped wash up in silence.

'You OK?'

Ruby liked to see her smile, but she only said, 'Fine, yes, homework to do,' and went up to her bedroom, pulled on an extra cardigan against the evening chill in the unheated room and began her algebra.

Bert Wainwright had had a busy day at the station. What with all the coal and iron trucks coming through for Liverpool, the tracks could barely keep up. He was a carthorse of a man, broad of shoulder and girth, massive rather than tall, with ruddy cheeks made more so with the help of alcohol. He had been undernourished as a child and lived in a smoky city so rickets had kept him out of the forces but secure in his cherished job as station master on a small branch line of the LNWR. Here his quick wits rendered him master of timetables, junction points, signal boxes, sidings, freight yards, ticket options, excursion specials and all the by-laws governing the carriage of animals, pigeons, bicycles, cabin trunks and horticultural produce. Since the war had begun the platforms had never seen a moment's quiet; the smoke never cleared.

Now he coughed hard, put away the pools and pulled the scruffy copy of the timetable out of his uniform pocket to consider how the system could be improved. He loved numbers and was naturally adept with them. Everyone was welcome to come up with ideas.

And then there was Jen's algebra. After she'd won the scholarship to Ashworth Grammar School, he'd resolved to learn too. When she went to bed she would hand over the books from her satchel and leave him to teach himself. He flourished, loving algebra with its mix of letters and numbers. It hadn't seemed right, a daughter knowing more than her father, and him earning a family wage.

Jen seemed to be a long time shut away tonight, he thought. He went upstairs and tapped on her bedroom door. No reply. Ruby had warned him against barging in. The old-fashioned look she gave him hinted at strange female rituals best avoided. He tapped again. No reply but a shuffling noise, and . . . sniffling, was it?

Jen opened the door slowly, not inviting him in. Her

eyes were red and she had a crushed handkerchief in her fist. He looked past her, seeking clues. 'Jen, lass, what's the . . . I'll fetch your mother.' A girl's tears were women's stuff.

'No, no. Don't do that. Come in, Dad. Do you want the algebra book?' Bert shook his head and lumbered into the tiny room, lowering his splayed limbs into the one chair; he was conscious of taking up more than his share of her tiny space. There was a rich red Welsh coverlet on the single bed, and Jen had framed a large reproduction of Ford Madox Brown's painting *Work*, bought on a school visit to Manchester City Art Gallery. Bert could see she was getting to be quite a lady.

He sat and watched her. She was no longer his little girl so there was no question of him hugging her. He could only wait, awkward, clumsy man that he was, and let her take her time. She sat on the dark red coverlet, and let the algebra books slide away.

'Oh, Dad, it's so awful, isn't it? So awful . . . I can't bear it.' Had there been bad news, then? He frowned. Ruby had said nothing. Surely she'd have mentioned any family upset.

'Oh, Dad . . . are we . . . could we . . . might we lose the war?' The tears stopped, and a sort of juddering courage shook her jaw. 'It's so terrible, everything . . . We're losing, aren't we? Aren't we?'

Well, this was a facer and no mistake. No one talked like that, not out loud. There were mutterings among men of his own age, but they had fallen silent as the bad news piled in. The rumours from Liverpool, the gossip among the railway lads, was that losses to U-boats were heavier than ever. Bert had assumed Jen's tears were for small distresses, family and girls at school, that sort of thing. But this!

'They say it's at a place called Tobruk, somewhere in North Africa. Just imagine – thirty-five thousand prisoners taken. Tim has a brother out there. He could be one of them. But how will we know? How will his family know?'

'Tim? Who's this Tim all of a sudden?'

'I told you. I met him at the dance – when you collected me. His brother's in North Africa and Tim's on the Atlantic convoys.' Now the tears came.

Bert reached out a meaty hand and held her shoulder. She went on weeping. Another meaty hand to the other shoulder and he pulled her to face him. 'Now look here, my girl. We're going to win. *We're going to win.* WE'RE GOING TO WIN. Do you get that, eh? Say it after me. We're going to win.'

Jen's tears were dribbling down her cheeks and into her mouth. She spoke through them, holding her father's gaze. 'We're going to win.'

It was a sad little sound, not enough for Bert. 'Again, Jennifer.'

'We're going to win . . . we're going to win.'

'Attagirl, that's the stuff. And we mean it, don't we?'

She nodded briskly, reassuring them both. 'But, Dad, it's going to be terrible, isn't it?'

'It already is, lass. It already is. Now, you get on with your algebra and help the war effort.'

Downstairs he reported to Ruby: 'Seems the war's bad. It's upsetting her. She's got the idea we could lose.'

'But we won't, will we? We will win in the end, won't we?'

'I really don't know, love. Your guess is as good as mine.' And he went back to the pools and his railway timetables.

Jen hadn't told her father everything. On their way home from school, she had walked with Polly, who travelled the same route. As they waited together for the bus, Polly had drawn her aside from the gaggle of other girls. 'There's some terrible news that Daddy's heard. It's about what's going on in Germany. He sent Hans – Harry – up to bed before he told Mummy and me. I don't know if it's more than a rumour but it's terrible.'

'Is it a family secret?'

'It is, sort of . . . I just don't know. And I don't know who to ask.'

'Well, tell me. I won't split.'

Polly's eyes widened with sudden trust in her friend. 'Yes, just you, Jen. No one else. You mustn't tell anyone. It's about the Jews. The Germans are killing lots of Jews. Lots of them.'

'Why would they do that? Many Germans are Jews, after all. Think of Hans. It doesn't make sense.' But Jen remembered the scuffle at the town hall and began to wonder.

Polly spoke her thoughts. 'And some people hate Jews, don't they? Even round here. They're not allowed to be members of the golf club, I know that much, but not why.'

'What else did your father say?'

'Oh, awful things. Ever since Hitler came, they've been smashing Jewish shops and stopping Jews voting and travelling. It's been going on a long time.'

'But Hans came here.'

'His parents sent him, even though they guessed they wouldn't be able to follow. Jen, it's terrible. They've killed simply loads.'

'Well, why aren't they fighting back? Why don't they get together to fight back? Can't we help?' By 'we' she meant the mighty British Empire.

'We're doing everything we can, I'm sure of it.'

'Yes, me too. I'm sure we would. That's what we do, isn't it?'

The guest for Friday's Tea Club was Mr Pierce, agent for the local MP, a weasely little man who rushed round doing the bidding of his master, rubbing his hands with satisfaction at every task fulfilled. He sat now on the red sofa in Miss Maitland's room, eager to discharge yet another constituency duty. He could scarcely wait for the headmistress to effect the introduction.

'Yes, yes, girls. Miss Maitland has invited me to give you an insight into how our system of democracy works, and as part of that system myself, I am eminently placed to do so.'

Frank Pierce's job didn't amount to much. He presided over much drinking at the Conservative Club, which reddened its members' faces and that of their jovial leader, Sir Christopher Chandler MP. There was always much talk of how Winston was doing a grand job, though never quite to be trusted. Frank usually had a cigarette lolling from his lower lip, stuck there by its thin paper. His fingertips were the colour of piccalilli. The girls, sitting upright in the arc of chairs, gave him their full attention. They had important questions to ask.

'Why are we losing the war in Africa, Mr Pierce? My uncle's out there.'

'So's my dad.'

'And my cousin.'

A tally of relations, all of whom might be missing, was paraded before him.

'Whoa, now. Whoa, it isn't all bad news.'

Cynthia Maitland suspected it was, but believed in being polite to a visitor.

'Oh, it's wonderful to hear that. Tell us some good news, Mr Pierce.'

'Well, we've had a setback, that's all. This fellow Rommel, he likes to put on a bit of a show. But our country has never been more resolute, more determined to defeat the foe. We'll soon be turning the corner of this awful war and racing towards victory by pulling together – all those fathers and brothers and cousins are sure to triumph in the long run. What could be better news than that?'

'But how long is the long run exactly?'

Cynthia, nervous of the impending attack, fidgeted with her three fountain pens. Was she allowing her girls too much freedom? And, a tiny afterthought, herself, perhaps.

'Ah, my dear young lady,' he was addressing the sturdy figure of Brenda Alsop, whose jaw was clenched, 'er, yes, well, you credit me with powers I don't possess,

153

powers beyond my station. But I'm sure Winston knows. He's doing a fine job.' Mr Pierce was getting more than he'd bargained for. He ran a finger round his collar where his neck was growing red with suppressed indignation.

'Excuse me, can I ask about Parliament, Mr Pierce?' This was from Jen, who piped up from her seat at the end of the row.

Things were changing. Jen was becoming her own woman. Despite their close friendship she was beginning to have ideas that were alien to Polly. There was other evidence of their separateness: halfway through their first year in the lower sixth, Jen was steadily getting better marks. 'Swot-pot!' Polly had called her. But every beauty likes a clever sidekick and she didn't press the point.

The better marks told a further story: Jen was more and more engrossed in the books they were told to read. More than that, in the footnotes she found references to other books, books they weren't expected to read. The whole set-up came as a revelation to her. It seemed knowledge was one long chain of connections, each leading further into different, even remote fields of study. What a prospect. Would she ever gorge herself to the full on all there was out there? Now it gave her courage to confront Mr Pierce about politics.

'Ah, that's more like it. My own subject. Fire away.'

'Well, what is a motion of censure, and why has one been made against Mr Churchill?'

Mr Pierce gave a wintry smile in the direction of Miss Maitland who showed no sign of coming to his rescue. He ploughed on gamely. 'Oh, that's just a handful of trouble-makers. You always get them on the fringes of parliamentary life. Don't worry your little head about it.'

Brenda Alsop sneered, then hissed to her neighbour, 'Trust Jen. She's such a show-off. And she's on the side of the Germans, too, remember.'

But Jen persisted: 'But what exactly is a motion of censure?' She was beginning to relish argument wherever she found it. Mr Pierce had offered her a chance to practise.

'Yes, well, it's also called a vote of confidence, a better term altogether, which is perhaps what you're referring to. It's a vote taken in the House of Commons when a group of awkward-squad MPs who don't like the government try to knock it off its perch. If the vote goes against the government, it has to resign. That's all. It happened just recently but, of course, Mr Churchill got an overwhelming majority. We were sure he would. Only a measly twenty-five votes against, and a whopping four hundred and seventy-seven votes in favour.'

'Mr Churchill's a great debater, isn't he?'

Cynthia sensed the arrival of a pincer movement and sat back to let it happen.

'Oh, I'm glad to hear you say that, young lady. I thought when you raised it, you were in favour of the censure – er, confidence vote.' His smile was getting desperate.

Jen leaned forward, pressing the attack, enjoying the encounter. 'In the debate Mr Bevan said, "The Prime Minister wins debate after debate and loses battle after battle." That's true, isn't it? When did we last win a battle? Not for years. The only one we might be winning is the battle of the Atlantic, but we just don't know, do we? It's awful.'

There was a collective intake of breath at the insolence of Jen's challenge. The girls knew they were expected to respect their guest's wisdom and experience.

Mr Pierce glowered and reached into his tin cigarette case for another crumpled cigarette. Defiance hung in the air. Brenda Alsop, stunned into silence by the outrage, couldn't help feeling jealous of its impact. Even Polly looked up from contemplating her nails.

Cynthia was startled and impressed by Jen's stand. It was going much further than she had intended for the Tea Club. But then . . . but then . . .

'Oh, that jumped-up character with the fancy Welsh name.' Mr Pierce took refuge in parliamentary mockery. 'Aneurin Bevan, Aneeuurin Bevan, a wheedling Welshman who likes the sound of his own voice. As all the Welsh do.'

There was a squeal from the girls.

Miss Maitland chose to soothe the hurt she could handle rather than the one she couldn't. 'Oh, watch what you say, Mr Pierce.' She gave a choking little laugh that she hoped might rescue the mood. 'Mona's Welsh, and very proud of it, Mona Rowlands.'

'Sorry, Miss Rowlands, no offence, but your country-man shouldn't insult our great leader, eh?'

Mona giggled. Like the rest of them, except Jen, she hadn't heard of Aneurin Bevan.

When Mr Pierce had been seen from the premises, huddled in his sweat-stained trilby and camel-hair coat, and the girls had packed up for the day, Miss Maitland held Jen back and invited her to sit down. 'That was really very

156

interesting, Jennifer. Very interesting.' Jen waited. It didn't sound like a reprimand. 'I must admit you know more about this vote of censure than I do.' She was in unknown territory. Teachers were expected to know more than their charges, and if they didn't, then not to admit it.

Jen was intrigued. She was being treated like an adult.

'But, tell me, where did you learn all this? About what was said in the debate. It is accurate, I take it?'

'Well, Miss Maitland, you see, ever since we had the visit from the ship, I've been . . .' She paused. What was the discreet way to phrase this, adult to adult? . . . 'I've been in touch with the second mate, Tim Beesley. We've been dancing together. And we write. He asked me to keep an eye on his mum and dad so I've been round to see them.'

'Ah, I see. Good.' It was the whole point of the adoption, after all. But the idea seemed to be galloping off in directions Cynthia hadn't intended. Her own impulses, after all, were beyond what was correct. She had been writing to Josh with ideas in her head that she could only acknowledge as wayward.

Jen was warming to her story. 'They miss him far more than I do.' She realized she'd given something away, without quite knowing what, and hurried on: 'Well, of course they would, wouldn't they? Anyway, Mr Beesley knows a lot about politics.'

'And do your parents approve?'

'Oh, yes. Well, my mother does. I mentioned it to her.'

'That's good, Jennifer. I'm pleased to know that. But if I may say something about the style of debate? Being so direct, so, well, forceful, isn't quite seemly for girls such as yourself. And, believe me, it will make you unpopular with your classmates.'

Jen was thoughtful for a moment, 'Oh, it has already. Nothing much. They call me names, that's all. But I don't care. Polly's still my friend. That's all that matters.' And with that consolation ringing in her head, Jen went to fetch her coat. Brenda Alsop had tied the sleeves in knots.

At home Cynthia walked late in the garden, her arms folded, enjoying the colour and fragrance of the few remaining flowerbeds. Had she gone too far in encouraging her girls to question everything? Were some things best left unchallenged, at least while the war was on? How guilty might she feel if it all went wrong? Well, she concluded, life brings change, and if it's unavoidable, we must simply face up to it. Her decision made, she went meekly indoors to prepare her mother's bedtime Ovaltine.

At the Conservative Club Frank Pierce chewed angrily on an unlit cigarette as he asked the telephone operator to put him through. He was irked, irritated. It was happening all over: women taking jobs in factories and disrupting canteens with their loud, lewd laughter; women in the Land Army striding around in trousers with no sense of decency. And now a school was actually encouraging young harridans to insult their elders and betters.

'Mrs Murgatroyd? . . . Yes, I'd like to speak to her personally, please, on behalf of our MP. It concerns a school matter.' He waited, picturing with male contempt the battleship of a woman he knew pulled so many strings in the constituency.

Mrs Murgatroyd, though eager to keep on amiable terms with the MP himself, lent only half an ear to what his agent had to say.

'About Ashworth Grammar School. I understand, Mrs Murgatroyd, you're a governor . . . Well, I want to be sure they're giving full support to the war effort . . .' She began to read a council paper on her desk as he droned on. 'Winston is, after all, doing a terrific job, and we must all be behind him. Every one of us. And that includes schoolgirls . . .'

Frank Pierce rang off with quiet satisfaction. Girls were getting too uppity, these days, and Miss Maitland was encouraging them. He lit the cigarette then coughed long and hard into a grey handkerchief. Not to worry: the advertisements said, 'Craven A will not affect your throat.'

Protesting

2003

'Did you see it on the television? Did you? It was huge.'
Kate is scarcely through the door before she is exploding
with excitement.

Millie has spent the weekend coiled up within her
dilemma and has scarcely noticed public events.
Saturday morning she set out the pots of hyacinth bulbs
in the conservatory, anticipating the time of year when
they break out into their luscious bloom and fill the house
with their giddying scent. But that time is not yet. She
spends Sunday quietly, almost obsessively reviewing
Kate's illness. She makes a half-hearted attempt to search
the internet, knowing as she does so that there is no cure
on the horizon, no new drug bringing imminent promise.
She scans, with weary familiarity, an online discussion
about whether donor cards are the best way to find
organs or whether a system in which people had to opt
out rather than in might get government backing.
Always her search comes back to herself and her fears,
her fear of medical interventions going wrong.

'I was there. I went on the march!' Kate looks triumphant, grinning with a sense of success at having been there. 'It was fantastic. There was such a sense of unity and purpose.'

'Oh, Kate, you're not strong enough for that kind of thing!'

'Well, I went. OK? Not very far. Josie and I joined the marchers as they turned from Pall Mall up Haymarket. Honestly, Ma, the pictures on TV didn't give any idea. The crowd covered the entire road and both pavements. And it was moving so slowly, one step, then another, slower than you'd ever dream of walking, so it was ideal for me. We got to the top of Haymarket and joined another great stream of people from Shaftesbury Avenue. Then we all went down Piccadilly together. We filled it.'

'I hope you think it did some good.' Millie smiles indulgently at the optimism of the young.

'Well, it had one very good result. We stopped for a coffee and met this nice family and got talking. They're Quakers. One of the sons turns out to be a set designer, works on all sorts of plays and shows. Really very attractive – jeans and Amnesty T-shirt – easy-going and full of smiles. When we rejoined the march he and I walked together, talked about a lot of things. Then swapped numbers.' Kate hasn't been this animated for months. How lovely she is with her bright, bobbing curls and blue eyes. She wears a flimsy scarf round her neck. It covers the scar where the tube entered. But, thinks Millie, you'd hardly notice. You wouldn't guess.

'He's called Baz. I never expected to hear from him again but he rang that night and asked if I'd like to go to the National Film Theatre. They were showing an old war movie. Well, I didn't care about the movie. But I liked him.'

'What was the film?'

'*In Which We Serve*, a really soppy story of our brave lads at sea winning the war and gaining glory. My God, it was so dated and sentimental. I thought it was odd a Quaker wanting to see a war movie but he loved it.' Kate laughs.

Millie has never known Kate so talkative about a boyfriend before. Laszlo, Freya's father, whom she'd met at a Radiohead concert, had seemed dour and silent. He'd said he was an accountant and always had plenty of money. He'd been pleased when Freya was born, but when Kate got ill and became tired all the time, he was off. It turned out his stay in the UK hadn't been legal, so he'd gone back to Budapest. Perhaps this new one, Baz, will be kinder.

'Does he know about the dialysis?'

'Of course. How else could I explain why I was sucking slices of lemon and ice cubes while he knocked back the beer?'

'You could have kept your illness to yourself. Or told him later. You might have waited a little.'

'It won't scare him off, Ma, if that's what you're getting at. I think we really like each other. I really do. Anyway, you know I hate secrets.'

Millie feels only a little uneasy. She isn't keeping the test results secret exactly. She's on the way to making a decision. Surely she's allowed to do that.

The Second Visit

1942

It was unusual for the phone to ring in the evening, which had its predictable routine and telephone calls were no part of it. Once a month Beryl would ring her sister, Nancy, whom she didn't like, to check that she was still alive. So the phone, when it rang as late as eight thirty, gave them both a start. Perhaps Nancy had died, after all.

Cynthia answered. Beryl was settled in the living room, its windows closed against the summer air, and listening to *ITMA* on the Home Service. Cynthia was in the hall rather a long time. *ITMA* was just signing off when she came back. She was shivering. Even in summer the dim little hall was draughty and chill. But there was a shiver of excitement too. She waited to be quizzed.

'You were a long time.'

'Oh, was I?'

'Course you were. You missed Mrs Mopp.'

'Ah, yes.' Mrs Mopp, the *ITMA* charlady, whose catch-phrase was 'Can I do you now, sir?' It had the nation in stitches. Cynthia smiled wanly. 'Sorry to miss her.'

'So,' Beryl hated being forced to ask, 'who was it?'

Cynthia enjoyed making her wait. 'It was Captain Percival, from the school ship, to say they're back. They've docked in Liverpool.'

'The captain himself ringing here? How on earth did he have our phone number?'

Cynthia sighed. 'I gave it to him, Mother. I live here.'

'But it's rather presumptuous of him to ring in the evening. Couldn't it have waited until tomorrow, when you're at school attending to school affairs?'

'Yes, it could. But why not now? He's been at sea for weeks. Why not ring straight away?' Cynthia was taking delight in it, a woman's delight. He was keen to speak to her. He had said as much. Her cheeks burned. 'It's wartime, Mother, and people don't have time to waste. Get things done, there may be no tomorrow. That's how they feel.' It was how she felt.

'He must have thought it was very urgent to get in touch. What's he like, this Captain Percival?'

'Well, he's tall, rather good-looking, craggy face, hawk-ish nose, greying curly hair, rather athletic type. Not like Dad at all.'

'I was thinking more what kind of person.'

'A sea captain, as you know. Strong-minded, patri-otic, of course, brave. A good leader, from what I've seen.'

'Is he a churchgoer like us?'

'Well, I'm not actually . . .' Cynthia thought better of trying to disabuse her mother. 'He's a Scot, lovely lilting voice. From somewhere in Dumfries, I think. I imagine that makes him a Presbyterian, doesn't it?'

'I'm glad to hear it. They're sticklers for morality, the Presbyterians.'

Cynthia went to her bed, smiling to herself.

The last thing Jessica could cope with was a tankful of live terrapins. 'Not for us, surely. Are you mad?'

'Hang on, old girl, they're for the school.' Josh advanced into the flat to deposit the tank on the rug in front of the fireplace. 'Just let me get my breath and I'll explain.'

'It had better be good, hadn't it, Babs?' She winked conspiratorially at her horrified flatmate. 'They can't stay here for long. You'll get us thrown out. Mrs Scragg's used to the odd sailor and bottle of gin, but no other wild creatures.' She grinned broadly.

Josh looked from one to the other. Neither seemed entirely sober, and there were full ashtrays of cigarette stubs. Had they taken to giving parties? He wasn't sure whether to disapprove or join in. There was a hectic gaiety about shore life, these days. 'It was a moment of recklessness. Robert tried to dissuade me. But it was so sunny and lovely, so relaxed and happy. I'd forgotten what that felt like. That's when I bought them. They're jolly little chaps.'

'They're livestock,' said the unrelenting Babs. 'Who the hell's going to feed them?' She took the toasting fork from beside the empty fireplace and poked around in the tank.

'Stop that! They're my responsibility. That's why I've got to get over to the school as soon as possible.'

'But you've only just arrived.'

'Well, yes, but . . .' It was awkward. Josh made a thought-less concession. 'You can come too, Jess. You'll enjoy it.'

'But you haven't heard the news. Peter may come for the weekend. He's hoping to come down from Rosyth.'

'Really?' His heart lifted. Seeing Peter. There was so much to say, so much to share. For a moment his eager-ness to see Cynthia felt flimsy and unreal. Shameful.

'Well, no. It's what he hopes.' Jessica was willing it to be so. 'He's having to sweet-talk his captain. You know the drill.'

Peter loved the sea as Josh did. When they were together they talked nonstop.

'Well, I'd better cancel the visit to the school, then.'

'You go right ahead, shipmate.' This from Babs, arms akimbo above the tank. 'Got to shift these monsters from the deep.'

'Hardly monsters, Babs. Can't they stay here?' Jessica pleaded.

Josh began to hope the bossy Babs would prevail.

'Sweetie, imagine if Nellie Scragg found out, and we know she goes snooping. We'd be out on our ears, and herded in with the merry mob at the hostel. We'd lose our precious privacy.'

Josh wondered what such precious privacy amounted to. They were just two Wrens, even if one was his wife.

But Babs persisted. 'Look, Jess sweetheart, I'm happy to slave for you here, washing and ironing all your inti-mate little things, even buying sweet nonsenses of lace and parachute silk when I get the chance, but I draw the line at wildlife.' She gave a sly grin. 'Your husband's wildlife, I mean, not ours!'

Josh was amazed. How had his wife fallen into the hands of such a ghastly woman? Babs had been perfectly civil when he'd met her before, though he'd not had much to go on. She was a wartime flatmate at a time when people took pot luck. Jessica was a bright spark, everyone knew that and liked her for it. Giddy, too, but steady underneath. Besides, she was a wife and mother, not some larky girl-about-town. What was going on? He remembered the jokes on the ship when anything went wrong. It was a cliché they would all chorus: 'I blame the war.' Well, what was the war doing to Jessica?

Jessica looked from one to the other, eager to please both. She was used to jollying people into doing what she wanted. But between Josh and Babs she wasn't sure what that was. 'Look, Josh, couldn't we make a very quick visit to the school? There and back in an afternoon? We could dump the tank and explain we have to be back to see Peter. Then we wouldn't have to burden Babs.'

Sod bloody Babs, he thought, but did not say. Instead he saw the chance he needed. 'Well, if we do that we'll need a car. I was going to scout round and try to borrow one. I suppose you couldn't spare yours, Babs, just for a day, could you?' Quick to soothe the approaching frown, he added, 'I'll drive slowly so we don't spill the tank.'

'They'll ban private motoring any minute now. You know that, I suppose?'

'No, I didn't. I've been at sea, remember? Does it apply yet?'

'Not quite, but you'll be one of the last to go for a spin just for the pleasure of it. Make the most of it, that's all.'

'Oh, thanks, Babs.' And Jessica gave her a bear-hug,

which seemed fine, then a splonking great kiss on the lips, which didn't.

'Tell me about Babs,' Josh said as they drove out of Liverpool.

'Oh, she's a classic, isn't she? Quite mad, really. Drinks like a fish. How she got her commission I'll never know, except that she's aces bright. She's in some sort of arty set in Chelsea, poses for artists when they're not all having parties and having sex. She's right out of her cage up here. But she's sweet to me, says I've got to visit when this bag of stuff is all over.'

The main road snaked across the Lancashire plain. White clouds hung low but unthreatening in the blue sky, the horizon broad in the brittle heat. The Riley made steady progress until they found themselves stuck behind convoys of lorries slowing the few private cars that still had petrol. There were horse-drawn carts too, heaped with goods in coarse hessian sacks. There was no point in trying to hurry. But Josh was enjoying the car: he'd never driven one of these.

'She's not quite your type, though, is she, Jess?'

'Oh, don't be so prissy, Josh. I like her. She's not stodgy and dull. She livens me up.'

'And she's a lot younger. After all, it's only the war that's thrown you together.'

'Yes – wasn't I lucky to meet her? But it makes me realize what I missed in marrying so young. Oh, that's nothing against you, Josh. It's just that I seem to have missed out on such a lot. I wish I'd made more of a go of it those months I spent in Paris after school.'

Josh became quiet and thoughtful. He was aware that

there were things he'd missed, too. He drove carefully so as not to spill the fish tank. There were thoughts he didn't want to spill either.

Grace ran forward to greet them, fussing around the old Riley, giving little cries of delight and getting in the way.

'Look what we've brought for you.' For the first time Josh had doubts about his gift. It had been a happy whim back in the sunshine of the Caribbean, but in the cloudy skies of a northern July it seemed suddenly sad and silly.

Grace dispelled any doubts. 'Oh, the school will adore them, I promise you.'

Marriage had changed Grace. Being Mrs Boyd, and addressed as such in church and at school, in shops and at the doctor's, gave her new status. She had joined the universal club of those who had reached the destiny for which biology and their upbringing had readied them. Roderick had wooed and won her, but in a sense it hardly mattered. It might have been any other. She was in love with marriage itself and what it had brought her. She had gone through the ritual before the altar and been initiated into the secrets of the bed, which hadn't been as strange or as uncomfortable as she had feared. Concentrating on Roderick's smile, his face, his lips, holding his head, stroking his hair – and adoring him as she did – she let him take care of what happened down below, and felt glad and womanly at the release of pleasure that convulsed him. That wasn't too bad, was it? And lying in his arms afterwards was the best of all. Each morning she stepped out with special confidence. She was at one with them, the married women of the world.

With the distant sounds of greetings and arrival, Cynthia straightened her papers, fidgeted with her three fountain pens and rose from her desk. Josh had arrived. She could hear his warm Scottish voice. And there was another voice she didn't know. She paused, looking round the room. Suddenly she reached for Brian's photograph in its silver frame and folded it away in her desk drawer. Grace ushered the guests into Cynthia's study and noticed at once that it had gone.

It was certainly a surprise to see Jessica striding into the room, like a galleon in full sail. Josh, beside her, stepped forward to make the introduction, and Cynthia moved towards them with ease and charm, as she had learned to do with parents when she was first a head-mistress. It had become natural to behave like that, but her instinct was to be retiring and watchful. Today, though, her professional skills were on full alert.

Jessica responded warmly. So much in the company of women these days, she recognized Cynthia as a match for any of them, strong yet gracious, confident without display. She noted the neat ankle and fine shoes, the pale fluffy hair and the upright way she held her body. She admired the mauve silk dress with its pattern of tiny red flowers and floppy collar. She noticed, as only a woman would, that the skirt was cut on the cross so the fabric shaped itself round her hips and clung at her knees.

Jessica realized she had imagined some sad, grey

person, left behind by life and satisfied with dull routines. Yet here was this bright, stylish woman, not much more than her own age, surely, and with such penetrating blue eyes. She wondered how Josh felt about such scrutiny. Perhaps he hadn't noticed.

Cynthia saw a buxom woman in an immaculate Wren's uniform, with dashing tricorn hat, shapely calves, black stockings and laced shoes. One was precise, where the other was hearty. One was discreet, where the other was lively. They were resolved to like each other, but there was a sense of tigers prowling in the room, a crackling in the air as they made the thousand fleeting calculations that are the stuff of female encounters. So, Cynthia thought, a wife, the woman who went to the altar with the man who is writing me such familiar letters, a woman who has lain with him, borne his child, is touched by him still. As wives are. Cynthia was in the desert of loneliness compared with Jessica. So why did she not feel lonely? Why did she feel she had access to something in Josh of which Jessica knew nothing? Cynthia gave him a brief but wary smile.

Maggie Clayton came rattling in with the tea trolley, proud of her freshly baked Victoria sponge. She had dispensed with her apron and, having promised to report back to the cook, stared greedily at the exotic guests. They all took seats, smiling, and were given small plates with floral designs and tiny paper serviettes. Maggie was playing waitress with *faux*-gentility. It passed unnoticed. Jessica was preoccupied with Cynthia.

'You should know that the boys call me "the Admiral". It's my nickname among all Josh's crews. So I think the school should adopt it too.' It was an instruction, not a suggestion.

'I'm sure they will. You must come and look round. The girls will be eager to meet you.'

'No, no, thank you, this is just a brief visit . . .'

The women talked together, an aimless conversation that left Josh to pick at his slice of cake. Each was speculating on how the war was changing the other. Was the stalwart wife all that secure? Was the brittle headmistress softening?

Eventually Maggie returned to collect the tea trolley. 'What's them tortoises doing on the floor in the vestibule? Am I to take them off with me?'

'I hope you think they're a good idea.' Josh had yet to explain the gift to Cynthia, but even as he spoke there was an almighty crash from outside the study.

'What on earth— What in heaven—' The exclamations got louder as distress turned to outrage.

Maggie was first through the door, Cynthia following, then scrambling to help to her feet the large tweed-clad figure that lay sprawled on the floor. The tank had spilled its water across the tiles. The terrapins, beleaguered, were moving away in different directions.

'Oh, Mrs Murgatroyd! I'm so sorry. Let me help you up.' Cynthia was solicitous, but puzzled. Had she overlooked an appointment in the school diary, and if not why was Mrs Murgatroyd making an unexpected call? And why were these animals in her front hall?

She was struggling to her feet. 'Don't fuss, woman! Worse things happen at sea!'

Maggie returned to the trolley to fetch a cup of stewed

tea from the cooling urn, grimaced stoically at them but offered no explanation. Jessica, who enjoyed her own kind of mayhem, grinned at Josh, who raised an eyebrow. He moved across the room to where he could see what was going on. He recognized the overbearing woman from the Midland Hotel. She was sitting now in the vestibule's lone armchair, recovering her dignity.

'What exactly is happening in this school, Miss Maitland? Is this one of your Tea Club extravagances? I was coming to enquire about them, but I find utter chaos all around me. What are these creatures doing here? And where have I seen that officer before? I have a feeling he is an undesirable.'

With clarity and patience, Cynthia explained.

There was no mollifying Mrs Murgatroyd, who salvaged what dignity she could, and lost it as she hoisted her ungainly bulk on to her bicycle and wobbled away. Josh and Jessica, watching through the study window, saw her go.

Cynthia returned to her room and leaned on the closed door with a sigh of relief. Her guests had struggled to keep their laughter subdued, but with Mrs Murgatroyd's departure it burst out with complicit pleasure.

'Is she really called Mrs Murgatroyd? What can Mr Murgatroyd be like?' This from Jessica. 'Poor man! Probably some hen-pecked little figure, who couldn't say boo to a goose.'

'Perhaps, but he died years ago.' Cynthia wondered, as she said it, what the Murgatroyd marriage had been like. She wondered often about marriage. And here before her was another: Josh and Jessica, long and loyally together.

173

Their shared laughter betrayed an intimacy she couldn't share. Marriages, Cynthia realized, were secret, private, not to be known to others. Josh and Jessica stood before her, within the world's approval, sanctioned by Church and community, inviolate. A shiver of sadness ran through her.

When the guests had departed it was Grace who dealt with the terrapins. She scooped them up and took them, with the sturdy fish tank, which had survived the accident, to the lab. It was she who had the idea to paint each of the six with the colour of one of the school's competing houses. And so it was done. Red, green, yellow, orange, dark blue and pale blue poster paints were fetched from the art room, and Miss Hayter went to work. From then on girls would call at the lab to see how their own house terrapin was thriving. The creatures didn't seem to mind or notice. The label on the paint said it was waterproof and long-lasting.

Loving

Tim called for Jen at home. She didn't like him to see her in her school uniform, even if she was past the gymslip stage. Was there ever a more humiliating discrepancy between a schoolgirl in the lower sixth and a man who'd been at sea for five years and gone round the world to places she'd only seen in films? 'I'll be in the upper sixth from next October. I'll be almost eighteen then, and a senior prefect.'

But Tim wasn't impressed by any of that. It was Jen he wanted: there was something about her that was just his type – her compact little body, her bright dark eyes and bobbing black hair. He had kept her image in his mind's eye ever since they'd met months before. She had so much spirit, dancing as though there was a spring inside her, and she had laughed easily and often. He even liked her bolshiness, her fearlessness in argument. His father had reported as much when she'd done as Tim suggested and called round to see them.

'They shouldn't be striking while there's a war on.

That's a wicked thing to do, surely, Mr Beesley. I can't see what reason would be good enough.'

A sprightly lass, his father had said approvingly, perhaps because she had made him think about the rumbling threats of a pit strike.

With the arrival of Tim's regular letters from the ship and Jen's immediate replies, it was tacitly assumed by both families that she was becoming his girlfriend. It was a status that slowly assumed exclusivity as, through the spring and into summer, Jen refused invitations to the cinema, to the dancing classes, even to an enticing Saturday-night hop. And without his physical presence she was free to romanticize their bond, to picture him as her hero, to write his name aimlessly on school exercise books, to sign off her letters with the schoolgirl code 'Holland': 'Hope Our Love Lasts And Never Dies'. When he had telephoned to say he was back and to invite her to a dance, it was to the Tim of her imagination that she responded.

Tim's hopes were much more straightforward. From his mid-teens he had been taking women to bed whenever he was on shore leave. After weeks at sea he was happy if a girl was pleasant enough and kindly. Other sailors who spilled from their ships eager for drink and sex would pick up obvious and available women in the dockside pubs, but Tim held back: with the disruptions of war, different kinds of women were ready for sex. It didn't have to be whores – secretaries, clerks and factory girls were away from home and living for the moment. And that suited him. He made his choice from among the quieter, less strident ones. And he was growing fluent at sex, no longer awkward or abrupt, neither shy nor bully-ing. He stayed around for a chat and a cigarette. Girls sometimes beseeched him to stay in touch, but he rarely did. He wasn't looking for love. But Jen didn't fit the pat-tern.

'Good evening, Mr Wainwright. Is Jen ready?'

'No, tha'd best come in and wait. She's been prettify-ing herself the past half-hour. You know these women!'

'Oh, I do, yes.' They were strangers exchanging ritual male phrases to ease the social awkwardness of one knowing that the other was after his daughter.

'You'll be dancing at the town hall, then?'

'I reckon so.'

Tim and, more vaguely, Jen knew they had a problem if they wanted to be alone. They could visit each other's small terraced houses, but the war kept their parents in at nights and retreat to a bedroom was unthinkable. So, there would be no privacy at home. They could get together in pubs, but they were noisy and full of drunken ribaldry. Cinemas had the accommodation: double seats on the back row were meant for sex, and were booked well ahead by eager young people. And, anyway, the sex was strictly limited to fully dressed fumblings. Jen was aware of all this when she heard Tim assuring her father that he would walk her home from the dance. It was a summer night and not raining so they could take their time strolling along the streets, perhaps take a short-cut through the park.

Jen was fascinated by the flesh-and-blood Tim. He wasn't the flawless hero any more: he had bitten fingernails, slurped his beer and wiped away the dribble with the back of his hand. Tattoos laced the muscles of his arms. But he was a rough approximation of the man she'd been thinking of. His hand on her back as they took to the floor now had a proprietorial feel that pleased her. The strength of his wrist as he caught and threw her in the dance marked him out as reliable; his surefootedness as the music swung them away and together was all she'd dreamed of.

Again, they drew attention as they danced. People watched, even applauded. Jen caught sight of Brenda Alsop in the crowd. And later, during a more sedate excuse-me quickstep, it was Brenda who came between them to claim Tim for herself. He limped off reluctantly but was back with Jen at the first opportunity. 'She's a handful. I thought I'd never get away!'

Later as they wandered outside to cool off, he held her gaze, his large dark eyes widening. He watched her mouth: the generous lower lip, moist and delicate, the curve of the upper lip, smiling always for him. When he kissed her she tasted delicious. They laughed at nothing and often, but for each other. The moment was theirs. They knew what it was to be happy. Tim never mentioned the sea.

Eventually they left the revellers at the town hall, dust from the day hanging in the air. There had been no air raids for months in the north of England – the war had moved into other arenas, with the German push into Russia, the endless tussle in North Africa. Briefly Tim had mentioned that his brother, Colin, had been taken prisoner at Tobruk, but refused to say more when Jen pressed him with questions.

'Lay off, will you? I'm trying to forget about it!' Those

were the sternest words he had spoken to her, and she respected his insistence.

As he walked her home they stopped occasionally in shop doorways and he felt her sturdy body through the folds of her flowered silk dress. She felt him stir against her thigh. Then they walked on, past other couples in other doorways. The girls had talked about sex at school, pooling what little they knew. They speculated about which of the upper sixth had gone the whole way. One or two were censorious when it was agreed, on no more than a guess, that Mandy with the flame-red hair and defiant swing of the hips had probably done it. Did that make her loose and common, as Patsy declared, or racy and glamorous, as Evelyn hinted? Jen felt it was sometimes one, sometimes the other. The borderline was fine.

It's what young people do, she thought, and I'm one of them doing it. By the time they reached the park the peachy sunset had mellowed into a soft darkness. The trees, heavy with summer leaf, stood sentinel round the lawns. The dusty flowers had lost their colour. Ranks of ghostly white stocks filled the air with their intense, sweet scent. Tim leaned Jen against the bark of a large beech tree, its lower branches stooping low to enclose them in a haunted shimmering cave. And it was here she suddenly became less vague about these things and wanted him as much as he wanted her.

Later, much later, she was careful to brush away the debris of grass and leaves that clung to her clothes and hair before she turned her key in the front door. She was thankful her father had gone to bed.

*

Mrs Murgatroyd seethed at the memory of her tumble by the fish tank. She would move against this wayward headmistress and call her to account. She summoned Miss Maitland to see her. She arranged her numerous duties, as magistrate, school governor, WVS co-ordinator, from the plush comfort of her over-furnished home. It was as well upholstered as she was, with cushions and carpets as varied in colour as her elaborate tweed suits. Plainness was reserved for her features: a square jaw, stern mouth and blanched cheeks criss-crossed with a network of tiny blue-red veins. She had milky grey eyes, which stared with unforgiving scrutiny at whoever she was addressing. It was hard to believe she had ever loved or been loved. She was certainly out of practice: Mr Murgatroyd, supremo of the local sausage factory, had long given up the struggle, bequeathing to her by his death the financial means by which she now dominated those around her. She rattled orders to her cleaner, nagged the gardener and fell asleep at night out of sorts even with herself.

'Ah, Miss Maitland. Thank you for making the time.' The fulsomeness was back. 'I hope it hasn't taken you too inconveniently from your girls.' Behind the bluster Mrs Murgatroyd had an uneasy fear of the headmistress. She was a professional woman, after all, qualified at a university, whereas she herself had been a wages clerk until the insistent Arthur Murgatroyd had bestowed on her something of his own social standing with his name. 'Please make yourself comfortable.' It was not an invitation that could be taken literally.

Cynthia waited apprehensively for what was to come.

'I want to share with you some concerns that have been expressed to me about the club that meets in your school. It is felt to be subversive of the war effort, and I can't have that in any school of which I am a governor. I even hear it has a secret encoded name – the T Club, I understand. Quite mysterious. Am I right, Miss Maitland?'

It would not do to laugh at the absurdity of the allegations. Cynthia did her best to look grave and thoughtful. 'I can't tell you how seriously I take what you say. And it is most alarming that such confusions have arisen about what we do.' She explained the purpose of the group, and as for the name of the club: 'It meets at four o'clock each Friday when we have a cup of tea together. It couldn't be more harmless.'

'Harmless? I'm not so sure.' Mrs Murgatroyd was off again.

Cynthia left the dingy portico of the Murgatroyd villa and strode briskly away down the gloomy laurel-fringed drive. She was both relieved and anxious. She had recently arranged for the Tea Club's next guest to tell the members about what was happening to the Jews. Mrs Murgatroyd might not take a favourable view.

It had been Polly who had asked. There had been another incident involving Hans. Home late from school, he had tried but failed to conceal the purple bruise that blossomed on his hairline like some rotten fruit. He had refused to give any explanation, embarrassed to be found wanting as an able young man, but also confused as to why he was so consistently singled out by the bullies.

Polly's mother Daphne had taken him aside and, holding

his hand in both of hers, told him he must always feel proud to be a Jew, that they were a remarkable people, full of impressive talents, resolute and patient in the face of the world's troubles.

Her husband was more strident: there were people in Britain who hated the Jews and spread untrue rumours about them, he said. We must always defy such people, and tell the truth about the terrible suffering the Jews are undergoing. He didn't say this in front of Hans. There was a family understanding that what they knew should be kept from him. But what exactly did they know? Polly had asked Miss Maitland for more information.

Mr Samuels was a dapper man of medium height with pince-nez glasses over dark, glancing eyes. He ran a shop that sold pianos and sheet music, and was known to be a fine pianist. Sometimes people pretended to be buying a piano simply to hear him play. He would crack his knuckles and dash off a flamboyant piece of Chopin for their delight. He knew they wouldn't buy. Sometimes he gave concerts in Manchester halls for groups campaigning to rescue Jews from Germany, but they were mostly attended by other Jews and not reported in the papers.

He sat with his knees together surveying the row of uniformed sixth-formers with calm self-containment. They scrutinized his neat dark clothes, his large soulful eyes, and found him foreign and different. They weren't conscious of having met a Jew before, not someone who owned up to it, and would even talk about it. It seemed odd to devote a Tea Club to him.

'The German government began the persecution when you were all still little girls, and it has been getting worse.' Slowly he took them through the litany of increased proscriptions, his voice growing in firmness, his shoulders bearing a quiet dignity as he told of Kristallnacht and, finally, the deportations. The girls listened in shocked, saddened silence, their eyes fixed on his face. They almost forgot to offer him a second cup of tea.

'But it's against the law. Hitler must be breaking the law.'

'No. He changed the law to make it possible.'

'But you can't just do that, can you?'

'Unless people are vigilant, that is what happens.'

'But they must have done something to bring it on themselves. I've heard people say they're difficult.'

'She's right. I've heard that, too. They say you never see Jews doing manual labour or something like that. Why don't they, Mr Samuels?'

'Dear girls, you'll hear lots of unfounded rumours, and you must always seek to verify what is said. Evidence is the enemy of prejudice. The Jews are devout family people who work hard, I assure you . . .'

When Polly met Robert the following evening she was brimming over with the distress of it all.

'That's why we're fighting the war, Polly, to stop Hitler – he's doing so many terrible things. This about the Jews is just part of it.'

'Well, Mr Samuels said they want the Pope to denounce it. You're a Catholic: why hasn't he?'

'You're being childish, Polly. It's far more complicated

than that. Anyway, I'm not answerable for the Church.'

Polly felt rebuked.

Robert was piqued. He had brought her nylon stockings from America as a treat and had hoped for a softer welcome. Somehow the sweetness of their coming together had been blighted and they parted in disappointment.

Once her mother had been despatched to church on Sunday morning, Cynthia made her move. She left an inadequate note on the sideboard and caught a train from Staveley station. On the platforms young women clung to departing servicemen with fierce, false cheeriness. She felt buoyant to be among them. Someone she cared for would be leaving soon.

She arrived at Liverpool's Lime Street station and didn't know what to do next. Among hurrying crowds in every kind of uniform, the heat and swirling steam from the throbbing engines, the incessant noise of muffled platform announcements and whistles blowing, she stood there, oddly out of place, an attractive woman conspicuously in her best Sunday suit, with light summer gloves and neat leather shoes. She was carrying a fawn gabardine coat, and although it was not yet raining she put it on as a sort of civilian disguise. A speck of coal dust lodged in her eye but there was no one to help as she took the corner of her handkerchief and flicked it out. With streaming eyes, she decided to walk. There was nothing else she could do.

Cynthia had not been to Liverpool since the Blitz back in 1941, and hadn't imagined the scale of the destruction it had brought. After the explosions and fires had ended, there had been time only to clear the streets so that the traffic could run, to tidy into bombsites the strewn debris of homes and commerce. Since then the damage had settled into heaps of inert but permanent rubble. A drift of rosebay willowherb muted the broken concrete and jutting timbers. Repairs would have to wait until after the war was won. Sometimes a rabble of children clambered over the ruins, shooting wooden guns and demanding surrender.

Light rain had begun to drift from the Mersey. She could taste the tang of the sea air and walked towards it. She had found her way down to the Pierhead and saw that the entire extent of the quayside was contained within a high, impenetrable wall. At the entry to each dock, a policeman in a cubicle presided over large metal gates through which she could make out the stuff of mercantile traffic: tall cranes loading and unloading, masts and derricks, sometimes a ship's funnel, freight lorries moving in and out. And alongside the wall the long curve of Liverpool's elevated railway, with beetle-like figures scurrying to and fro. She found a staircase running up to one of the stations, sheltered from the rain under its timber canopy, and clambered aboard the first train that came along. It was a drab and dingy world she saw spread out below her, a serious and purposeful place, in which everyone seemed to move with concentrated intent and little joy.

She hadn't stopped to consider what she expected from this visit. Acting on impulse was new to her. She wanted to release herself into it, to feel her visit unstructured and her motives unexplored. She moved through the city, travelling up and down on the overhead train, then walking aimlessly among the tall buildings and dirty streets, past ramshackle boarding-houses and seamen's hostels, intrigued by a Chinese restaurant, then a Chinese laundry.

She had known all along she had little chance of seeing Josh. Now she realized that he was caught up in something entirely alien to her: the world of men, of seafarers, of physical endurance and implacable enterprise. She felt with a thrill how he belonged there and she didn't. She fancied adventures: she would stow away, she would be the cabin-boy, watch in the dark hours of the stormy night, grab food in haste and gulp liquor to keep up her courage. Did women ever do such things? she wondered.

The Kardomah café where she sought refuge was stuffy with summer heat and many bodies, each table crowded with little space for legs or privacy. She found a seat in a corner alongside young lovers too engrossed in each other to notice her. She hung her coat on a peg, ordered a pot of tea and a teacake, and looked around. The ceiling was low and cigarette smoke curled up towards it. The waitresses emptied ashtrays as routinely as they gathered up dirty cups. Mostly people were young and in pairs, many in uniform.

Then Cynthia saw something that made her bow her head and turn to the wall. In the far corner, their hands clasped fervently together, eyes locked on to each other, sat Robert and Polly.

*

'Don't look now, but Miss Maitland's at a table in the far corner. I don't think she's seen us.'

Polly and Robert had been chastened by their brusque parting. Instantly forgiving, they were snatching a last meeting.

'What if she did see us? We're allowed to meet.'

'You're right. There's nothing wrong in my coming here. I can't be in any kind of trouble.'

'Poll, of course you're not. But is she? What's she doing here?'

'Perhaps she has relations in Liverpool. She must know someone here.'

'Then why's she alone and not with them? At their home or somewhere less scruffy? She is a headmistress, after all.'

'Do you think she's here to visit the ship?'

'Maybe. But I bet she's here to see the Old Man. I think she's taken a shine to him and he to her. I think he'd be pleased.'

'Oh, that's an awful thing to say, Rob! She's too old for that sort of thing – and, anyway, as you said, she's a headmistress.'

'What's awful about it, eh? And I'll tell you something else. When I was buying nylons for you, the Old Man was there, too. He grinned at me in a particular way.'

'But he's married to a Wren. They wear black stockings.'

'I think they were for Miss Maitland.'

'Well, she does like nice things. And why shouldn't she?'

'Exactly. And nylons are enough to make any woman sweet on you, these days.'

'Like me, I suppose you mean!' She dealt him a fond blow. They were back to their silly banter and soon forgot Miss Maitland, who paid and left discreetly with her back towards them.

Delaying

2003

'D'you think in those days war made things more romantic, heightened the excitement, all that wartime separation?' Another wearying dialysis session has just finished and Kate is spending time with her mother. It doesn't seem that the recent march has swayed Tony Blair's intentions at all, and the country is facing the prospect of war. Millie considers her question. They've grown closer recently; Millie is finding it easier to talk – there seems more to talk about.

'I suppose there was a certain frantic passion . . . fear of death, that sort of thing. But lots of unhappiness too.'

Kate thinks she hears a cry and tiptoes to the door. Freya is having an afternoon nap, cushioned in her granny's four-poster bed. It's a false alarm.

It gives Millie a moment for reflection. 'This war's not a real war in the old-fashioned sense, "the nation united", that sort of thing. It clearly isn't. It's sad, that we've no sense of common purpose. I mean, it must have felt good once.'

'I can't believe war ever feels good.'

'Well, what I've been reading suggests in the last war they were all fired up to win at almost any cost. Look at the Blitz and that plucky London spirit.' Since the box has arrived, Millie has been reading books about the Second World War. Somewhere her mother fits into the story, which must mean she does, too. The idea pleases her.

'Oh, it was a bit of a con, Ma. Government films and newsreels tell it like that. I bet the truth was much more complicated.'

'Your grandfather was wounded in the war, you know, the North Africa campaign. I tried asking him about it before he died, but he'd just offer the obvious stuff: hating the Hun and such.'

'Why were we fighting in North Africa? It wasn't German, was it?'

'No, Italian. They had Libya, we had Egypt.'

They are silent for a while, but it is a comfortable silence.

'Oh, Ma, those look great!'

'Yes, they do, don't they? I like them next to your father's Lucie Rie.' It's true that the brightly painted terrapin shells add vivid colour to the ebony shelf. 'They have a feel of aboriginal painting, I think.'

'Perhaps they came from North Africa – a possible link, d'you think?'

But Millie is keen to show Kate things are changing. 'Look! I'm bringing all that stuff from Mother's hamper out into the light. Since your pa died I've begun making the place more my own.' She indicates the replica of an African dhow placed to catch the shaft of winter sunlight in the big bay window.

'What else have you found? Any further clues?'

'Oh, I'm past the clues stage. I don't think Mother was leaving me a trail of mysteries to decipher. It's more about the sort of woman she was.'

'And how are six coloured turtles going to tell you that?' Kate has a brusque, impatient air now. Is her illness affecting her mood? How could it not?

'No idea. It's a little enigma in the corner of my life.'

As Kate gets up to go, Millie rises, too, and impulsively gives her a warm hug, holding her daughter close enough to sense her frailty, and to pick up the faint vibrating mechanical throb of her arm. It's where the dialysis tube fits. She recoils from it, leaving Kate bemused, then she goes to the corner of the room where a silk throw with a tinsel thread covers the box. She stoops and brings out a scruffy package and holds it out towards her daughter. 'Take these with you. See if you can find anything out from them.' And Millie hands over what appears to be a stack of birthday cards tied with a fat and faded red velvet ribbon.

Kate unties the stained red velvet ribbon, like an umbilical cord leading her into her mother's inner life. She has brought the cards home, surprised to be included in her mother's quest, but she has a vague curiosity about her own past. The hospital asked about kidney failure in the family, but no one knew of any. There's so much talk these days about genetics, inherited characteristics, television programmes about finding your ancestors – not apes and things but Victorian parlourmaids and cruel factory owners. Why not go exploring into her own family? The arrival of Gran's box, which had seemed so incidental and irrelevant, matters to her mother in a way Kate can't understand. It seems to be taking centre stage in her life, while Kate's illness just goes on and on. Kate fidgets with the throbbing place on her arm. If she helps sort it out, this search of hers, perhaps that will help.

There are ten birthday cards, the first a shiny sepia photograph showing a chubby little girl holding a basket of flowers. The child's dress and the flowers appeared to have been tinted pale pink. She is winsome in a sickly way.

Kate turns it over in search of messages, names, greetings: there are none. The birthday numbers persist up to ten, each charting changing styles and tastes: there are Mabel Lucie Attwell cards, Cecily Mary Barker Flower Fairies. Gradually the tone becomes older, more adult, until finally there's an eccentric one that looks home-made, a photograph of a naval ship sailing rough seas, stuck on a large postcard. This one alone bears evidence of having been posted: on the reverse side, a stamp for twopence-ha'penny, a Cotswold postmark, the franked date 1 Dec 196–. The final number is smudged. The message, handwritten, reads: 'Happy Birthday to my daughter'.

But that isn't all: among the stack there is another, larger card, its corners curled over, not a traditional birthday greeting at all. It is a formal document headed 'Christian Baptism'. Within a border of cherubic heads entwined with leaves there are four pieces of information. The first is 'Church' and someone has filled in 'St Martin's Church,

Llangollen'. There follows space for further names to be listed, the name of the baptized, and three witnesses. The child to be baptized, whose name is written in a firm hand on the first line, is 'Millicent Rebecca'.

The Third Visit

1942

Things were bad that autumn when they got back to Liverpool. A flight of German bombers out of Brest had harassed the convoy on the way home, but Fighter Command had been quickly on the spot to drive them away. It seemed that someone was at last winning the case for more air cover in the battle of the Atlantic. But there was bad news waiting.

The moment the *Treverran* docked, Josh went with his ship's papers to the company agent. On his way he ran into Jamie MacGregor, a crusty master with a skin like pleated leather, a voice always on the verge of coughing, and a flask of drink in his pocket.

'Aw, Gawd, Josh, them's well and truly buggered us up this time. Them fuckers in the Royal Navy did the dirty on our lads well and truly.'

'What's that?'

'The bastards! They drowned many a mother's son as sure as if it were with their own wicked hands. They'll never be forgiven, never.' Josh was eager for details but

Jamie was too bitter and too drunk to be coherent. 'Christ almighty, they should be hanged from the yardarm, damned old men full of bloody medals.' He shuffled off, still muttering, into the brightening day.

Josh hung around picking up scraps of gossip from other seamen. It had happened around the time the *Treverran* was leaving early in July. Convoy PQ17 – thirty-five merchant ships – taking armaments to the Russian ports of Murmansk and Archangel, was only four days out from Hvalfjord in Iceland when it was spotted by U-boats. Right away they were in trouble. Disagreement at home between different commanders meant the wrong order was sent – for the convoy to scatter. Not to disperse, to scatter.

'Every man for himself, it seems it was. Literally. Each ship left to her own resources.'

'God . . . and in enemy waters?' Tim and Robert were appalled when he told them.

'They say it was terrible.' Josh had the details at last. Bad feeling between the merchantmen and the Royal Navy was running high. 'General massacre. Horrendous. Only eleven of the merchantmen that sailed made it to their destination.'

'You wonder who sent the signal, sir, but we know who gave those orders well enough. That old duffer Sir Dudley Pound.'

'He's old, all right. Too old for the job.' Tim indulged his regular quarrel with those in authority. 'He's past it, we all know that, but he's Churchill's chum, that's the problem. This country's run by dimwits and cretins. Degenerate stock, I call it.'

'Can't he be called to account, whoever sent the order? Was it Tovey or Pound?' This from Robert, who still somewhere at the back of his mind cherished a belief in divine retribution.

'The First Sea Lord? Give me strength!'

'I bet things are buzzing at Derby House.'

'Yes, sir. You'd best see if your missus'll give anything away.' Robert meant it as a joke, but Josh bore the burden of his service's loss hard, and wasn't looking forward to sharing it with Jessica.

It sounded, on his arrival, as if he wasn't going to share anything very much. He found Nellie Scragg outside the tall terraced house.

'I must get round to doing my step. It's taken a good deal of scuffing, these last few days.'

Josh knew of the Lancashire way with doorsteps, the daily use of the donkey stone to render them a spotless creamy yellow. It was a way of scoring over the neighbours, and of no interest to him. 'Oh, really? Jessica's in, then?'

'No. On duty, she is, but the others are in.'

'Others?'

'Yes, the girls. Quite a gang of them now, swapping clothes and coupons – swapping blokes, too, if there's any around.' Then, realizing her mistake, 'Other than you, Captain Percival.'

But Josh was already halfway up the rickety stairs.

Babs was there, and two others he didn't know, a thin, angular girl with an air of classy languor, and a neat, pretty one with a heavy plait down her back. All three were in bright kimonos, painting each other's toenails.

Josh gulped but refused to be surprised. 'I supposed Jessica would be on duty. I hadn't time to phone her, thought I'd just arrive.'

Babs was phlegmatic. 'You've just missed her. She won't be back till six. Fancy a drink?'

This was his wife's flat, he thought, and he was entitled to stay. Despite its passing resemblance to a provincial French brothel, he decided to make himself comfortable. He accepted the drink.

'This is Frankie,' the aristocrat raised a laconic hand, 'and this is Kay.' The other gave a curt nod. Neither made any further move nor seemed remotely interested to learn that he was Josh, husband of Jessica. Jessica was so much one of them now, a girl among girls, Wrens and other women's services, partying together and sharing their favourite drinks. They appeared to treat the flat as home, and went on painting their nails.

'How have things been here since I've been away?' Josh sipped his gaudy drink with distaste.

'Oh, you know, the usual. Wartime stuff.'

'But we don't let it get us down.'

'You still think we'll win, do you?' For some reason Josh wanted to irritate them.

'Any minute now.' Kay planted her orange toenails on the floor, and looked Josh aggressively in the eye for the first time. 'Why? Don't you? Are you saying we could lose?'

'I'm not saying any such thing, but it does get you down – at least, it gets me down, what's going on.'

'Exactly which part of what's going on?'

'The losses. Lost mates. Ships going down.'

'Ah,' Frankie shrugged sleepily, 'that.'

Josh felt as if he was talking to them through a sheet of plate glass. This community of women holding themselves separate, apart, untouched by loss. They had created their own world, these women, perhaps from fear and for comfort. Was Jessica part of it?

Jessica came off duty in Derby House and walked back through the autumn evening. Nellie Scragg had been watching the comings and goings and pre-empted any surprise.

'Babs's gone fire-watching, Frankie's on nights at the hospital and Kay's doing a cabaret somewhere over Formby way. But your man's here. Been here most of the day, he has.'

She rushed up to the top landing and stood on the threshold. 'Josh! Hello, stranger!' Last time they'd been together, months before, Peter was on leave and they'd stayed at a small boarding-house, celebrating his safety. Their conversation had been shot through with 'Do you remember when . . . That time when Peter . . . and how you once . . .' Their close bonds were of their shared past, the family years now drifting away with the smoke and noise of the war.

'Jessica. How are you?'

'Fine. So much has happened.'

'It certainly has. I only heard this morning—'

'Oh – what? What particularly? There's so much going—'

'Well, I don't mean Babs and Kay and Frankie, that sort of thing.'

'What sort of thing is that, then?' Jessica bridled.

'Oh, I don't mean any of this rubbish going on here. I'm not interested in that. I mean that PQ17 mess-up. I only heard this morning. Jamie MacGregor had been there – he was well oiled at eight o'clock in the morning. Gave me his version of events and it's pretty terrible.'

Jessica was instantly downcast. 'Yes, it was. It happened just as you were sailing. We only got to know as the news leaked out. It was awful being here, at the heart of it.'

'You weren't at the heart of it! Those men out there on the icy seas were at the heart of it, Jessica. Don't give me any of that pious Derby House chat!' He'd clearly had more of Babs' cocktail than was wise.

'Josh, I know it's a shock, just hearing about it like that. I don't even know what Jamie told you. There are so many rumours.'

'Well, what do you know? What's the view at Derby House? They're in charge, after all. All our lives depend on them.'

'Well, if you'll calm down, I'll tell you. It's been in all the papers that, well, there was a signal the convoy should scatter. But quite why isn't clear. A friend of mine heard a senior naval officer saying they thought the *Tirpitz* was a threat and needed to be dealt with. That would explain why the destroyers and cruisers were withdrawn – that's what he said. Everyone knows now that the convoy should have stayed together.'

'And were they right about the *Tirpitz*? Did they get it?'

'I don't know – no, it's still out there somewhere, I think.'

'God, the Royal Navy, blunder after blunder.'

'Oh, that's hard, Josh. They're doing all they can.'

'While we get clobbered, eh? That fucker Pound's too old for the job, for Christ's sake.'

'Don't shout at me, Josh, and don't swear like that.' Despite the dusty air of Bohemia about the place, Jessica's schoolgirl manners quickly snapped back into place. Without intending to, she found herself on the defensive. 'And you shouldn't blame Pound. He's a fine man. We're all overworked and it's not easy.'

'Well, all this about *Tirpitz*, who got that wrong, eh? Where's our information coming from? Clearly not the right people.'

'Oh, I'm sure we've got spies out there. We're bound to have.'

'Well, not enough. It's obvious.' He paused and they faced each other, locked in argument before he'd even embraced her. Suddenly it wasn't something he found easy to do. 'And what's happening to this flat? It's like a Marseilles bordello!'

Jessica's laughter broke the tension. 'We often say that. They're my friends, if a little dotty.'

Josh relented and drew her to him for what turned out to be no more than a routine kiss. 'You've always had dotty friends, Jess, but these are dottier.' He smacked her ample rump. She squirmed at the familiarity. 'For good- ness' sake, hold on to your old self, lass. I don't want to lose you.' For a moment it was as though an angel's wing flickered over them. It cast a shadow. They both felt it. But whether it was benign or not they didn't know.

*

Maud Sheridan was to be the next guest at the Tea Club. It was an odd idea because Maud was far from a pillar of society. She lived alone in a ramshackle cottage and was baited by local children as a witch. Their parents did nothing to discourage such unkindness. After all, Maud carried threefold guilt: she was Irish, an artist and a con-scientious objector – a conchie. The children didn't inflict serious harm – the occasional smear of cow dung on her front door, bottle tops removed from her milk and a gulp taken before she could bring it indoors. Maud refused to be goaded – she was even sympathetic to the muddy urchins who screamed and ran away lest the witch cast a spell. She didn't believe in frightening children.

When the time came for single women to be con-scripted she had gone before the tribunal, pleaded her case and been heard with gentle disapproval by a judge who admired the conscientious objections made by Benjamin Britten. Maud had been agreeable to doing something short of fighting to show her patriotic spirit so had signed up for the War Artist Scheme and had been commissioned to paint a sequence of old city buildings as a record of England before it was lost. She looked the part, setting up her easel in city streets, dressed in work-man's trousers and heavy shoes. Passers-by ignored her, part indifferent, part suspicious. Everyone had their role in the war and it didn't do to interfere. Cynthia gave a fleeting thought to Mrs Murgatroyd, but set aside her fears of any more wild accusations.

Maud Sheridan had agreed to come, but she came on her own terms. Her paint-splashed skirt and shapeless tunic were dressed up with a row of large amber beads and a long floating scarf, but the heavy shoes were ungainly and Maud's hair unkempt. Grace Bunting was visibly appalled, and the girls giggled as Maud spread herself on the sofa.

She spoke in a low voice, her eyes steady and unblinking, her large, capable hands folded in her lap. The girls who had arrived to mock were won over by her easy informality. They heard in respectful silence her explanation of why wars never solved anything. Then they were quick to challenge her.

'My brother's with the Atlantic convoys. He's risking his life.' Polly had dared to go first. 'I think we should all be supporting him. Why can't you?'

'But I do. I support and admire his courage. But I regret his having to use guns to kill.'

'But they started it. It's Hitler's fault. Anyone can see that!' Brenda Alsop's perpetual state of simmering rage was already boiling over.

'Well, I think nations should come together to solve their problems, talk about them together.' More scepticism, but some interest.

'How can that happen, d'you think?' Jen was on the edge of her chair.

'You'd talk to killers, would you? You'd have truck with arch-villains? I say unconditional surrender or take what's coming.' Brenda's thrust of her auburn head rounded up a ripple of agreement.

Maud ignored her and addressed Jen. 'Well, there's something new going on. It's supposed to lead to a uniting of nations. In January this year lots of countries – all our allies, France, Russia, America, of course, signed a document, a charter. The idea is that when the fighting stops this organization will plan to avoid it ever happening again.'

'Britain will take the lead, I suppose.' This was Polly, ever the patriot.

'Most certainly, and other European countries. There's even talk that Europe might one day come together, different countries uniting for our common good.'

'Oh, now, that's ridiculous! That really is stupid.' Brenda Alsop's was the loudest voice. 'And you know why? Because *we*'ll be grown up by then and we'll stop it happening. Us and the Empire together. Germany will be punished. It will never again be allowed to be powerful.' And then, with a malicious smile, 'Are you Irish? They're hand in glove with the Jerries, aren't they?'

'I'm pleased to be of Irish extraction, but nationalism has brought nothing but trouble.'

A whimper of objections soon subsided: they were exhausted by the ideas Maud Sheridan had stirred in them and gave way with sullen grace. The point about her being Irish lingered, and several asked Brenda Alsop what she'd meant.

'The Irish are all spies. Didn't you know that?'

Miss Maitland was ushering their guest to her bicycle and didn't hear.

'Have you heard of something called the uniting of nations? It's a new idea.' Jen and Tim were dancing close, to happy music playing on records at a public dance in the Staveley scout hut: 'You Are My Sunshine,' and 'Jingle Jangle Jingle' by the Merry Macs.

'Is it something to do with football?'

'No, idiot. World politics.'

'Have you been talking to my dad again? He keeps going on about our heroic Russian ally.'

'No, it came up at school.'

'Well, you're not at school now.' Tim whirled her close as the music grew louder and pressed his lips against her neck. Fleetingly he saw Brenda Alsop standing alone at the edge of the crowd, watching them. 'Whoa! There's that Gorgon again. What's she doing here, d'you think?' He steered Jen away across the floor.

'Her father's on the local watch committee.' Brenda gave them a bogus little wave. 'She's showing off, that's all.'

'Why us, though? What's she want?'

'What she can't have. What belongs to me.' Jen wriggled in his arms.

'Just as I belong to you.' It was a phrase he would recall over and over.

Polly and Robert went walking. At a point where the Cheshire plain gave way to the rising crags of Derbyshire they humped small brown knapsacks on to their backs and set out into the hills. It was cold and bright, with frosted grass crunching beneath their boots. They slapped thick gloves together and hugged their bodies in the light air. Once they were striding out, their breath rose in white feathers and their skin itched with the heat brought on by the effort.

If this was a world that mattered to Robert, Polly would share it. He stopped by a hedge and found two stout sticks, took a knife from his pocket and slashed off the twigs. They took a winding path up through a small cluster of stone houses round a plain church, their eaves low over their windows as though in a frown against the winter's keen winds. Sunday voices, raised in song, reached them, plaintive and pleasing, as they climbed a stile over a dry-stone wall and strode out across the brown couch grass, the views opening towards the peaks.

The sun, the colour of bleached linen, offered little warmth. As they reached each hilltop they stopped and pointed. Clusters of other walkers bunched together on the slopes, and on the distant road an occasional flock of cyclists moved as one, heads down over handlebars.

They found a place of flat stones and sat to share their Spam sandwiches. Suddenly there was an eerie, unfamiliar echo in the air. It seemed to come from one valley, then another. At first it was alarming: all unexpected sounds were. They scanned the sky for clues. Robert took off his cap and Polly her knitted hood to hear better. They stood up and tried to determine where it came from. Gradually they knew it for what it was: bells. Yes, church bells. For years now they had been silent.

'Of course! It was in the papers. Churchill announced it to celebrate the victory at El Alamein. All the church bells to ring. That's what it is. Our first victory.'

High on a hill in Derbyshire they threw their arms round each other. After all these tiring, draining and depressing years the tide was turning. Had turned. Had been turned by a victory in North Africa.

'Ha, Polly! ' Robert swung her round and kissed her hard. 'You know what Churchill said, don't you? Something about it being "not the end, but the beginning of the end"? Well, for us it's more than that. It's the beginning of the beginning. This is where we start.' And she knew he was serious.

Back in Staveley, Tim was thankful that Churchill was doing something right for a change, then wondered about his brother, Colin, taken prisoner in North Africa some eighteen months before.

Jen wondered what it would be like to live without a war.

They knew they would have to contrive to be alone together. A new intent had taken shape. They were stepping over some mark in the road that had said, 'Thus far, and no further.' They were beyond that now. And they knew it.

Cynthia had stayed up late one night, adding slack to the embers of the dying fire in time to catch the flame and keep it burning. Mother had gone to bed with her usual expectation that the comforting sounds of Cynthia following would lull her to sleep. There were no such sounds. Restlessly, she propelled her stiffening body to the top of the stairs and called down abruptly.

'No, Mother. I'm not coming up just yet. I have things to decide. I'll be staying up a good while. Please go to sleep.'

Something peremptory had entered her voice. It was strange and hostile. Painlessly and in an instant, it drained authority from the older woman, who shuffled without protest back to her cooling hot-water bottle and lay there wondering what had happened, and whether things would ever be the same again. With prayers that they might be, she drifted into a calm and yielding sleep. She would have to let herself be old.

Cynthia had already decided. She was over forty – a virgin – and she was being offered love. It had been offered once before, years ago, and she had turned it down. The embers sagged in the grate with a sigh, releasing sparks and collapsing the red coals. She stretched out her hands to the warmth, and looked at the smooth skin, the veins of age beginning to show, the nails pale and shapely. No ring on any finger. The effrontery of it. Oh, and headmistress of a prestigious girls' grammar school. She seized the poker and riddled the ashes, then renewed the fire, adding chunks of gleaming coal from the brass scuttle. On an impulse she turned off the light and sat serenely in the room's glow.

The risk must be taken. Refusal would be a kind of death, and there was too much of that already. What would victory be worth if it couldn't liberate people from the past and let them make new choices, take new paths? She lit a cigarette and enjoyed the curl of the smoke into the darkened room.

Josh had booked a room not far from the busy life around Manchester's Piccadilly bus terminal. He had chosen it with care: the Melville Hotel was anonymous in a kindly way, handy for the flotsam of overnight travellers on the move in wartime. It was double-fronted with a pillared porch, its windows criss-crossed with brown tape against bomb blasts. In the ground-floor window the dark green leaves of an aspidistra blocked further what light there was from the drab street. The paint was peeling; a chunk of plaster was missing from a balcony on the first floor. The whole merged gloomily into the wartime dinginess of the area.

He met her off the bus from Staveley. She looked different – she was trying to look different. The pert little hat was gone, and in its place a soft wool headscarf, taken smelling of mothballs from her mother's drawer, was tied round her chin, the point of its corner hanging over the collar of her neat navy coat. She had set aside the leather gloves and matching handbag. She was trying not to look like a headmistress. She hadn't known how conspicuous her role had become, nor how proud she was to display it. But not at the Melville Hotel.

Josh was heady with excitement. 'Act on impulse and something good will come of it', had been one of his more reckless axioms. It had to answer small pangs of conscience when things went wrong, but it gave him a sense of the rightness of his own instincts. Now, as this serenely smiling woman came towards him uncluttered by memories and expectations, he experienced an extraordinary sense of security, an inner peace that made him feel he could live for ever in her radiance.

He took her elbow and steered her through the worried crowds. He directed her across the streets between the rattling trams, he opened the swing door into the ill-lit foyer and signed the hotel register.

Cynthia accepted his guidance. It was a new pleasure not to be responsible, not to be in charge. She submitted to his knowledge of the world, as she would in their room together.

She sat on the bedside and took his head in her hands, her eyes searching his. He knelt before her, pulling the scarf from her head and reaching into the fine blonde hair. He lifted her skirt slowly upwards, undid the peach pink suspenders and rolled down her stockings. He stooped to kiss her ankles, then lifted her gently on to the bed. Her eyes never left his.

She had expected it to hurt and was pleased when it did. She had never touched or fondled a man's naked body before, but she wasn't ignorant. She knew what to expect and what would happen. In practical terms she drew on shreds of vague information. Her feelings were better informed: she had read works of literature that expressed the emotional upheaval of physical love. While she remained sceptical of D. H. Lawrence and was inclined to think the Brontës neurotic, she had an awesome sense of impending joy. She was not disappointed. She lay on tossed sheets, glowing and happy, Josh beside her, holding her hand. 'I never expected to feel like this ever again,' he said. It was as though they had inherited their kingdom.

Surviving

1942–3

The first week of the spring term was bitterly cold. The life of the school had resumed its steady pace. Thoughts for the ship's safety became remote and unalarming. News from the Atlantic had not reached them.

The girls had their own comfort to worry about. The heating had been lowered during the Christmas holiday and classrooms were icy. They were allowed to keep on fingerless mittens over chilblained hands. Feet stamped to keep warm, setting up a rhythm that made their owners giggle and irritated their teachers, themselves bundled in shapeless cardigans and thick wool stockings.

The Tea Club guest was Jocelyn Frobisher, editor of the weekly *Staveley Gazette*, scion of its owning family. He was, he said, 'learning the ropes' on the way to what he hoped would be a glittering career in Fleet Street. Parental influence and an exaggerated limp had kept him out of the forces and he was now doing his bit, he believed, to keep Staveley informed. He had his eye on Beaverbrook's *Daily Express* and was well clued-up on Beaverbrook's current role as Churchill's Minister of Aircraft Production. Such status for a newspaper proprietor gave legitimacy to what his mother spoke of sneeringly as the grubby end of Grub Street. The *Staveley Gazette* wasn't grubby at all though Jocelyn wished it was – it would have been a lot more fun. He would have relished a gruesome murder or juicy scandal. Instead, the *Gazette*'s healthy circulation was built on weddings, flower shows, cinema advertising and repetitive reports of local contributions to the war effort. Nonetheless, he thought it might be amusing to take up Miss Maitland's invitation and hold forth to her sixth-formers. There might even be a story in it.

'What do you think of Lord Haw-Haw?' Brenda Alsop didn't wait for the usual niceties. 'My dad says it's a disgrace his broadcasts aren't blocked.'

Heavens, these girls were keen as mustard. He ran his fingers nervously through his ginger hair and swallowed. His Adam's apple bobbed up and down. 'Well, he's a traitor, isn't he?'

'I wonder,' Miss Maitland put in, 'if you all know to whom Brenda is referring.' She had noticed inattention among the chairs grouped round the guest's sofa.

'Some kind of spy, isn't he?'

'I thought he was an actor.'

'Jairmany calling, Jairmany calling.' Jen's tone mocked that of the strangle-voiced William Joyce, the British Fascist who had fled to Berlin at the start of hostilities and now broadcast misinformation regularly on open airwaves.

'I can see you've listened . . .' Jocelyn Frobisher was shocked that such innocents were tuned in to Nazi propaganda. 'I'm surprised your parents allow it.'

'Oh, no, that's not it.' Polly attempted to explain: 'It's just that the papers keep going on about it. Do you think newspapers should be giving him such publicity?'

Miss Maitland was proud of her girls. The Tea Club was waking them to the world beyond gymslips and detentions, to ideas beyond simple patriotism and dull conformity. Jocelyn Frobisher sounded feeble by comparison.

'Well, we're fighting for freedom, aren't we, and that must include freedom of speech, what?'

'But he tells lies, we know that! Should we let him spread lies about us?' There was tension in Jen's voice. There were rumours that Lord Haw-Haw had reported heavy British losses in the Atlantic over Christmas. 'We shouldn't be helping him win the war, surely.'

'The *Daily Mirror* launched a campaign of people pledged not to listen to him.' Brenda Alsop had him in her sights. 'Would your paper do that?'

'Oh, yes, indeed. In fact, we make it our policy. By simply never referring to him, we prevent people becoming aware of his existence. That's a very positive position and ours is a very positive paper. Our business, after all, is the stuff of daily life – local councils, reports from the criminal courts, Church news, and the hatch, match and despatch columns. Those are very popular.'

'But the stuff of our daily life is shortages, bombsites, rationing, all that, too, don't forget!' Brenda Alsop was on the edge of her chair now and wagging a pencil. The rage was surging.

Miss Maitland considered this less than polite. 'Perhaps you could tell us, Mr Frobisher, how one of us might become a journalist, make a career of it. Which Higher

School Certificates would we need?' Relieved at the change of subject, Jocelyn Frobisher sat back, lifting an ankle across his knee, revealing a shocking stretch of bright red sock, worn without suspenders. There were nudges and smirks. He made a mental note that Ashworth Grammar School was encouraging its girls to challenge authority. He might mention it to his mother-in-law, Nancy Murgatroyd.

Josh was on the bridge of the *Treverran*, straining to survey the vast convoy around him: it was Christmas night and officers and crew had all enjoyed a good dinner. For the moment morale was high. In a good humour, he had called to exchange a word with Robert, who was officer of the watch, then retired to his cabin. The moderate swell was steady enough for him to take a pen and start a letter home. 'My Dearest Cynthia . . .'

The convoy of forty-five merchantmen had hit heavy weather two days out from Liverpool and the ships had had trouble keeping their immediate neighbours in sight: some had been driven from their allotted stations. Now they were worrying more about the weather than the enemy. But by Christmas Eve visibility was good again, the convoy was gathering speed and back in formation. They were heading south with a cargo for South Africa, in convoy as far as Sierra Leone, and approaching the dangerous air gap. The watch change at midnight had bid each other happy Christmas and meant it. It was not to last long.

On Boxing Day a gathering German patrol of eighteen U-boats received the order to 'await darkness and attack without further orders'. In London the Submarine Tracking Room, realizing an ambush was in preparation, sent a warning to the convoy's escort commander and commodore, copying the signal to Derby House. Did that message pass through Jessica's hands? Did she wince at what it told her? Was she even on duty on Boxing Day? In the fading daylight the convoy commodore hoisted the signal 'Convoy close up'. Everyone understood. They did not have long to wait.

It was no surprise to Josh that an attack was imminent. At the convoy conference in the Liver Building before they left, the briefing officer had apologized to the assembled masters for the lack of escorting warships. As the meeting broke up there had been an air of foreboding among those leaving the building. Josh had said an abrupt goodbye to Jessica, and the seamen's spirits were low. There were grumbles in the pubs. Sometimes bitter, despairing fights broke out. Rumour was rife that their interests and safety were being sacrificed to support the operation supplying the North African campaign. The old quip – if you turned the MN badge upside down it read NW, Not Wanted – was doing the rounds.

There had been a recent change at the top of the battle of the Atlantic command: in November 1942 Sir Percy Noble had been relieved by Max Horton as Commander-in-Chief, Western Approaches, an intense and persistent leader, intolerant of fools, a demon for detail. It was being said that he meant business. His harsh, abrasive manner was forgiven in the hope that he could deliver. Jessica had picked up the buzz and enthusiasm around his arrival. When she hinted at what she saw as good news, Josh had shrugged it off contemptuously. It wasn't making any difference out there on the high seas.

They had rendezvoused off Malin Head, with merchantmen from the Clyde joining them, and set out below overcast skies, into the predicted bad weather. Robert and Tim were with him, as first and second mates, so too was Charlie Rawlings, and the ever-grumbling Able Seaman Ross. The chief engineer, Lofty Clarke, had sailed with him before, of course, and so had one of the radio officers. Otherwise he had signed up a crew of unknowns, in the traditional way, from the pool at Liverpool after their leave from previous voyages.

The first the *Treverran* knew of the attack was a radio distress message at 1952 hours from a ship far out on the other side of the convoy. Tim was officer of the watch, wrapped in his duffel coat, binoculars trained on the horizon, Able Seaman Gibbs at the wheel, and Rawlings standing by the Aldis lamp, ready to send Morse signals. Seamen and greasers, the carpenter and deckhands, off duty in the mess-decks, had been sitting about eating, smoking, some playing cards. But readiness was in the air, each man alert.

Those on the bridge saw a faint glow in the night sky on the far side of the convoy. Snowflake flares went up from a flanking escort, filling the air with sudden but short-lived dazzle. There were two further hits nearer home, the boom of explosions intensifying. Where the hell were the buggers? The enemy was as dark and deadly as the sharks that swam the waters alongside. Then, from the lookout forward on the forecastle, a deadly shout: 'Here comes ours, sir!' Seconds later, in the dark night and heaving seas, the torpedo struck the *Treverran* on the starboard bow. They were the last words the lookout spoke.

The impact blew a gaping hole in the side, sent a traumatic shudder the ship's full length and a huge column of foam and debris into the air. The noise was volcanic, reverberating like the end of the world, an amalgam, in one mighty roar, of tearing metal, crashing objects, and the inrush of water. Josh, half asleep but fully dressed in his cabin, felt the jolt through his entire body. The knowledge of what was happening, the realization of all that each man dreamed of and dreaded, feared and awaited. His brain was on adrenalin-fuelled alert. And somewhere deep within, he felt an awful exhilaration. This was it, his proving moment. It had arrived. He pulled on his sea boots, seized the rough canvas bag that held the confidential code books, a smaller bag of personal items made ready for just such an event, then dashed for the bridge. In the radio room the first radio officer was already transmitting a distress signal, giving their exact position: no point keeping it secret now that they might be about to sink.

Tim, on the engine-room telegraph, ordered 'stop engines.' Josh was with him on the instant. 'Right, Tim. Alarm bells and muster the crew.' As master, he took control of his damaged ship.

Down below the chief engineer had already vented the boiler's steam, which added to the bedlam as it surged out round the funnel.

The *Treverran* veered wildly from her course, then listed to starboard and began to sink by the head. There was little light to see what was happening. Carpenter Pilbrook rushed forward and crouched, his ear to the deck, listening for a betraying creak: he could hear and sense that a massive bulk of water was slamming into Hold One, engulfing the cargo. So far, the bulkhead to Hold Two had not given way, but it could be only a matter of time. He yelled to the bridge, not knowing whether he'd be heard, 'She's holding, sir, but not for long.'

Engineers and greasers were still at their posts. There was time before she sank. Time to live or die.

Robert, like the rest, had been flung off his feet but made the bridge, where Josh ordered him to bag the sextant, chronometer and charts they'd need to survive in the lifeboats, then dump the code books overboard. Unconsciously Robert fingered the gold crucifix his mother had tucked into the top pocket of his uniform and muttered, below his breath, *'Credo in unum Deum Patrem omnipotentem . . .'* He felt in a strange way he was in safe hands, eternal hands, the hands of the God his family believed in and he had doubted.

Josh took the engine-room telegraph: 'Finished with engines. Finished with engines.' They were now officially sinking: the engineers, firemen and greasers left their posts. After the briefest final glance Josh abandoned the bridge.

In the moments before Tim could reach them on the boat deck there had been mounting panic among the crew. She was going down bow first and seamen were rushing and hustling, fear clouding judgement, impatient for their own safety. Some had begun, without orders, to lower the starboard lifeboat. But the rope falls were hanging away from the ship, which was now heeling over at an ever-increasing angle, the roll taking the lifeboat beyond their reach. All they could see in the space between was dark chaos. Men were shouting, cursing, slipping on the wet surface, losing their grip on the tilting slope. Tim was soon with them, tense and concentrated, his directions clear and swift. The lifeboat swung back within reach. He brought order among them, mustering and checking numbers as they gathered in their life-jackets. A steward was missing.

In fact, the steward was below, making a dash for the storeroom where he hoped to lift a few bottles of whisky to fortify himself and others if they made it to the boats. From there he heard a deep rumble from the bows. Turning, he saw the bulkhead heave and buckle, and finally a torrent of water cascade towards him. He reached for the rail of the companionway, dragging against the pull of the water to get one foot after another up the ladder to the deck. The water swirled round his waist, surging ahead until, his hands still grasping the rail, his shoulders collapsed and his fingers released their grip.

Josh was now on deck among his crew. 'The Old Man's here,' rippled among them, giving them confidence, his tall figure seen and trusted by those around him.

Suddenly within the surrounding chaos he had an eerie sensation of enveloping and serene contentment, as though he were in a protective bubble and all the cacophony belonged to a distant, different dimension. In that moment, he knew himself for what he was, and where his life was going. Even in the crucible of disaster it felt good. Then the moment fled.

Where were the escorts, the ships supposed to be defending them? The U-boat must still be prowling, waiting to do more damage. Robert had been quick to switch on the *Treverran*'s red light above the bridge, signalling distress, and in the radio room the sparks was sending out repeated calls, giving their position as they drifted out of formation, knowing the convoy was passing them, moving steadily on without them. His sense of urgency could not speed transmission: frantically, he sent it over and over again, refusing to give up hope of help.

Men had scrambled into one boat and were lowering it to the water. Some had wedged on their davits, and would be no use. Crewmen were now detaching rafts and throwing them overboard: as the ship plunged downward, bringing the water ever closer, they reckoned to swim out to them and, steeling themselves against the shock, flung themselves into the sea.

The radio engineer was still sending out messages. Tim noticed he was missing, and rushed to fetch him.

Suddenly the pace accelerated. The *Treverran* made her final move, heaving towards the depths with a great sigh. Those in the boat, on the rafts, the bobbing heads of swimmers, the red lights of their life-jackets winking feebly in the black night, paused, turned to watch her go down, plunging from sight with a slow, solemn thrust of her great metal bulk. A single figure silhouetted against the sky leaped from the stern rail. And then there was no trace. A black slick spread across the water and with it the pungent stink of oil. The lap of the wide ocean was all around them. None of the convoy was in sight.

Josh struck out to swim strongly towards the lifeboat fifty yards away, oil on his clothes, his face, his hands. He gulped seawater and with it a gob of oil. Finally hands reached out and Robert hauled him on board. Within minutes he had vomited the black stuff. But where was Tim? No one knew.

When daylight came they were alone. The rafts had vanished. They were far enough south for there to be no immediate threat from the cold. There was a silver sheen around them, a pale translucent light above the steadily rocking waves with a haunting beauty that dissolved time and smoothed away any sense of place. After the noise and rigours of their escape it felt almost as though they had drifted into a different destiny. Robert counted: sixteen men, now bound together in need. Charlie Rawlings was with them, which cheered him up, and so was misery guts Ross. That might mean trouble. Three Chinese greasers from the engine room sat stoically silent and shivering in vests and cotton trousers. Robert gave them one of the three blankets someone had thrown into the boat. His thoughts went to Tim: might he have survived?

The first matter was injuries: an engineer had a severe steam burn. There was stuff in the medical box for that, but it couldn't do much for shock, and his shivering was beyond control. One man wrapped his arms round him, for warmth, strength, comfort. For humanity.

Others, traumatized, were shivering too. The blankets were welcome.

Josh explained his plan. There were oars on board so he set four to row: they would all take turns. They raised the sail, but there was only a sluggish wind. With the help of the compass they set course nor'-nor'-east, which offered their best chance of land or of encountering other ships. Josh didn't let himself focus on that: the immediacy of the present was what mattered. The lifeboat had been stowed with emergency stores: chocolate, Horlicks, malted-milk tablets, barley sugar, ship's biscuit, condensed milk – and water.

They all wanted water. The excitement, the rush of adrenalin, the Christmas alcohol souring in their guts made their craving great. Josh issued a half dipper each, warning that they should sip it slowly, slosh it round their mouths. They moistened their lips, did as they were told, then let it trickle slowly down their throats, registering how it felt, nursing their greatest fear that it might run out.

No one spoke much, but it was dangerous to let minds wander, so Josh suggested that each recount his own experience of the sinking. He was hopeful someone would know what had happened to Tim, but no one did. Their drifting accounts grew into a swell of affection for the ship; they spoke of her as their home, joked about her cramped shit-house, and the fetid smells from bunks stacked and packed tight in little space.

'Plenty of space out here, sir.' Charlie Rawlings was never down-hearted. He was still only seventeen; Josh thought of his mother, and his fisherman father back in Norfolk. Fishing communities knew about the sea, but did that make it any easier for them? He slapped Charlie's knee affectionately. He needed his good spirits.

'How about giving us a song, Charlie? One of those Norfolk tunes of yours.'

'Well-nigh unintelligible, sir.' This was from Charlie's bunk mate, but Charlie sang nonetheless. It even raised a smile from the stoic Chinese.

The sun rose and the day grew hot. From the chill of the night they sailed into bare open skies and a sun that cut through the early sheen. The paler-skinned among them felt its cruelty. There was no cover, only raw naked exposure. They sat in the well of the boat, even if it meant getting wet. Able Seaman Ross – bald and freckled – spread a blanket as an awning and crawled beneath it with several others. Only the sun's dipping in the western sky gave relief. But it brought other problems.

With night the temperature plummeted and with it their frail hopes. The rowers took turns, with long, splashing strokes. It served to keep their bodies warm, but their energy was low and there were grumbles that they were getting nowhere. If a current was running they had little sense of it. As they tired, they had less and less sense of anything. Some fell asleep where they sat, leaning together, sometimes crying out in their dreams.

Josh forced himself to keep awake. Again that strange sense came to him that he was in a bubble of his own consciousness, and from within this detachment he looked up at the sky, choked with a multitude of stars and a gibbous moon casting a wavering silver path across the swell. Idly he watched Robert in the stern, and saw him unobtrusively pull from his pocket a folder and a photograph, and sit looking at it, his face clear, blank and young. Josh had no photograph of the woman he loved.

With morning there was a need to extend the rations. Having swallowed their meagre allowance and washed it down with a precious dipper of water, they fell to discussing how to catch fish. Lines were improvised from bits of rope and left trailing behind the boat, but without bait they caught nothing. They were reluctant to sacrifice even a morsel of what they had in the hope of catching fish. 'Not mine, I tell you, not mine' – the squabbles were made fierce by fear.

Finally a meagre scrap of biscuit was fixed and the long lines trailed hopefully. It took most of the day, but they caught four good-sized fish, which they seized ravenously and tore into shares. Afterwards, the raw fish sat in their yawning bellies like lead, and more lines were cast with the bones and fins as bait. A mistake. Sharks – not big ones – began to swim at the stern, not taking the bait, not going away. The sun blazed down, the horizon stark and white. No ships passed.

'Did you ever read *The Ancient Mariner*, sir?' Robert asked.

'Don't tell me he was eaten by sharks.'

'No, he lived to tell his tale – at a wedding of all places. We read it at school. He saw terrible things—'

'Stop! It's not the time for that. We need to think of palm trees on white beaches and will ourselves to get there.'

'I'm not sure will-power's enough, sir. Perhaps a prayer. People pray a lot in wartime.'

'And a fat lot of—' Josh checked himself. Generosity of

223

spirit would get them through this, not confrontation. Besides, Robert had helped with the ship's Easter services earlier in the year. He took God seriously, far more so than Josh. Then Josh remembered the photograph and thought Robert's mind must be running on weddings. He let his own do the same: in some idealized future he saw himself free to marry Cynthia. That was how it would be.

He rolled the idea in his imagination; he played with it, let it dance behind his eyes, ran it away into the distance, then hauled it back and hugged it close. The minutes were full of it – the hours consumed it. It was what he would do. He imagined Cynthia in a hundred different places: on heather-strewn hillsides, beside churning rivers, shoeless on golden beaches, always smiling and laughing. She didn't laugh often enough, he thought. He would make her happy – he would make her laugh. He would make them both happy. He was almost delirious with the idea. There was no time to lose. He laughed out loud.

'What, sir?'

'Just thinking . . . It's too late to do all the things I wanted to do . . .'

By the next night, the engineer's injuries had turned black: the raw skin was blotched and ragged. He was lying semi-conscious, gasping at the pain, his mouth dry, lips cracked, tongue like a stick. Josh took a little water and tried to moisten it, but the drops dribbled away down his chin. He died moaning, around midnight, lolling in Robert's arms.

Robert had learned about death, had accepted it as the

crux of his family's faith: the resurrection and the life. He had grown up in the knowledge of God's love and familiarity with grace and salvation. As a young man given to questioning and independence, he'd rebelled against the dogma, and its cloying hold on his family. He'd run away to sea, rejecting it, and feeling freer for it, free to be himself. But the prayers never went away and the love his family vested in their God came back and cradled him even as he held a dying man.

Those who were awake helped to lift the dead man to the boat's gunwale where they held the deadweight of him, poised, while Robert ceased to be a mere crewmate and assumed a proper solemnity. He improvised a service: 'His was a good life. He tried always to live it well, and to us his friends and fellow seamen he always did. We are here far away from all those he knew and loved, but we think of them now and speak in their name. O, God, take him from this cruel world and into thy love and care. Amen.'

'Amen' echoed from other choked and drying throats. A few managed the first verse of 'Abide With Me'. They paused a moment over their silent goodbyes, thinking too of how their own deaths might be. Then they slid the body into the silent sea. Robert crossed himself and, copying him, several others did the same. They were too moved to think of the sharks.

By the time the fourth night came, the eager survival activity of the first hours seemed years away. The discomfort had increased: the thwarts were hard, wet, and chafed against the skin. They still observed the daily routines. Josh insisted they did a little exercise, stretching and bending limbs. And there was the daily excitement of food distribution. At first Able Seaman Ross kept an eagle eye, making sure no one had a drop more than his due. But even his keenness flagged as the heat and despair grew. Men took turns at the oars, but the less willing were allowed to miss their turn. There was no energy for disagreement, no strength to insist. Someone always had an eye on the horizon. Nothing. Always nothing. They were slowing, now, losing strength, and some were losing the will to carry on.

Several had developed salt-water boils on their hands, forearms and buttocks. Wet clothing irritated them however they sat. The sores became infected, red, stinging and swelling with pus. As a distraction Josh forced childish games on them – counting, spelling – but their wits were slow, and the jokes came rarely. They began to expect to die.

It was while they were sleeping, strewn against and across each other, that something deep in their unconscious noticed the change. The sea was moving differently. It was lifting and falling with increasing violence. Some dynamic other than the ocean's drift lay behind it. In the sleep of sailors the sea sends messages. One or two woke; others' limbs stirred as they responded to the ocean's subtleties. Within the hour everyone was awake and alert, not daring to say what they were all thinking. Each strained his ears and imagined he heard a dull roar.

'Stay still . . . and wait.'

Josh's words were wise, they knew. Elation, wide-eyed, glittering. Glances from one to another. Sleepers shaken awake. Listen. They knew it for what it was. They were drifting inshore and the changed motion of the boat was the swell forming into distant breakers. Their hoped-for chance. But another kind of danger. Bringing the boat through heavy breakers would be difficult. Josh was tense. They waited.

'OK, steady now. We're going to lose her if we're not careful.' In the dark Josh struggled to interpret the sounds, and what the size and power of the breakers might tell him. They could try to coast in on them, running up to the land, but the shoreline, now faintly visible, gave no indication of whether it was sand or rocks. Better to wait out the night, resisting the pull of the tide. Josh ordered them to ship the oars and bring the boat head to sea while he reconnoitred their prospects and tried to find a sheltered cove where they might land safely. He then set four men rowing furiously to stay where they were. New hope gave them new energy.

At first light they peered forward. All was grey in the colourless dawn. Gradually they made out a stretch of shallow beach ahead, pounded by enormous breakers.

Now began the steady handling of the boat inshore: for an hour they worked at it, riding the swelling water, turning and catching its thrust. Josh and Robert were as one, directing their crew, steadying their excitement. The task got harder as they came nearer to land. They were a hundred yards from the beach when a large wave curled above them; its crest broke into the boat and capsized her, scattering everything that had kept them alive and hurling the men into the sea. Josh just had time to cry, 'Swim for it, lads!' before the water crashed over his head.

He managed to get rid of his boots and jacket and was free to swim, but with no sense of distance or movement. The undertow was powerful, pulling him back from the small progress he made. Time passed, the sun shone, he thought only of keeping going, forcing himself not to give up. The increasing noise was his only clue. Finally the water thinned and a spread of grey sand came up to meet him. He felt his toes grasp at it, then digging in, holding on, pulling him up the narrow strip of beach. As he cleared the shoreline he was spent. Sprawled among the shells and seaweed, he lifted his head and gave a raw animal cry. It sounded in his ears like the moment of birth. It was the sound of survival.

Grieving

The ensign flew at half-mast at the school's front gate. It was a crisp January day and a sharp breeze lifted its red folds into the blue air. The call had come to Cynthia from the Ship Adoption Society offices in London: a strained formal voice dulled by the pain of having regularly to make such calls. The British Ship Adoption Society wished to inform Miss Maitland and the Ashworth Grammar School for Girls that the SS *Treverran* had been posted sunk off the Azores, some time on the night of 26 December. There was no news yet of any survivors. In due course they would be pleased if the school was willing to adopt another ship. Perhaps they would like to stay with the same shipping company that had owned the SS *Treverran*. And, yes, yes, the voice sounded impatient, of course they would forward any news of what had happened to the crew.

The flag had been a gift from Captain Percival and the crew on their last visit to the school. On that occasion Cynthia, with Miss Hayter and Miss Fletcher, had gathered round the flagpole and raised it then and there. In classrooms running the length of the building girls had crammed at windows, mouthing cheers and neglecting their lessons. It had taken them several minutes to settle back to the Latin pluperfect and the parsing of sub-clauses. Now there were no faces at any window. Girls bent over their exercise books in silence and regret. They knew of people getting killed, of course. That was what war was. But an entire ship's crew?

Cynthia was frightened that all the crew had perished. But something in her refused to let it be so. She would hold on and wait for news. She made an announcement at morning assembly to that effect: 'No news yet of any survivors. Now, those of you who had a chance to talk to Captain Percival know that our ship, like all seaworthy ships, was well provided with lifeboats. A sinking is an awful thing to happen but it need not be the end. We must hope and pray for their survival, and await information from the appropriate authorities.' Then they stood and sang 'Eternal Father Strong To Save' and filed from the hall, suppressing sniffles and being brave.

In the staffroom the talk was subdued.

'It's Polly and Jen I feel sorry for – they were really stuck on those lads, you know. First love.'

'Oh, as serious as that, was it?'

'Well, puppy love, perhaps. What's serious at that age?'

'Oh, everything, surely. Everything.' This from Lorna, who had never recovered from the loss of her young man at the battle of Jutland.

Polly and Jen were frozen by the news. Someone looked up the Azores on the map. 'It's not ours. It belongs to Portugal.'

'There's still hope, you know . . .' someone offered, but mostly they left the two girls to their shared silence. After school, they huddled together, scarved and gloved against the cold and the sorrow, then walked their different ways home. They said little, Polly's silence hiding the calm of shock, Jen's a turbulent resentment.

But then hope, the succour of youth, the child of innocence. It came spontaneously and fed their spirit. They had heard of people going missing and turning up. Battlefields were chaotic places. Of course people went missing. Then they were found. You only had to miss the bus for your parents to get anxious. Stay out late with a friend and they went braying to neighbours that you were missing when all the time you were just listening to someone's Hoagy Carmichael collection. 'Missing' wasn't lost: it was just a gap in the continuing order of things.

Cynthia was no longer familiar with hope. It had been anaesthetized in her decades ago and she knew not to awaken it. Hope was treacherous, scattering random grief in its wake. Instead she would go by hard-headed calculation. But even that made her heady with expectation. Her days took on a new sense of anticipation. Each time the phone rang or there was a letter with unfamiliar writing she flinched. And it was in such a mood that she made an unwise decision.

She would persist with the Tea Club. She had received a hectoring letter from Mrs Murgatroyd, but she would

231

continue to do as she thought right within her school. She went to find Grace in her poky little office to make plans and came upon her red-eyed, slumped on her ladder-back chair, blank and idle.

'Grace, don't give up hope. I've every trust there'll be survivors.' Then, on an impulse: 'I'm sure your prayers will help them.' She felt impatient at having her own grief leached from her by others.

'It's not the sinking of the ship – that's terrible, of course. It's something else, something private.' Grace was morti-fied to be discovered weeping. 'I'm so sorry, really I am. It's not like me, is it?' She gave a bleak smile.

'No, it's not. Not like you at all. So it must be serious.' Now she seized gratefully on someone else's problem. She led the young woman briskly into her study and sat her down. She could spare a few moments before her next meeting. 'Now then, Grace, tell me.'

'Well, Roderick and I, we're very happy together, you know. It was meant, our being together, it really was.'

'Yes, of course. I can see that. It was a lovely wedding. I was there.'

'With God's blessing, we thought nothing could go wrong.' Cynthia waited. 'And . . .' If this was a lovers' tiff she wasn't in a mood to deal with sob stories.

'You see . . . It's not anyone's fault . . .'

Cynthia resisted the impulse to look at her watch. How long would this take?

'The doctor explained to me . . . We didn't know. But we do now, of course.'

'What did he explain, Grace?'

'Roderick was injured in North Africa, back in 1940.

232

Invalided out. He was fully recovered ... or so we thought. Everyone did.'

'I remember.' Where was the story going? Cynthia had always admired Grace's crisp sense of a job to be done. And here she was meandering all over the shop. In times of war people's private lives needed to be just that, kept to themselves. There were bigger things at stake. You had to swallow your grief and get on – keep going. 'So?'

'The injury was ... well, it ... We can't have children.' A pitiable wail twisted Grace's face. 'I'll never be a mother, never. I've prayed to God about it. But only a miracle ...'

The tears came again, and Cynthia held Grace's arm. God was all she could offer. 'God comforts many people in this terrible war, Grace. And he will comfort you and Roderick together. I'm sure of it.'

'I am too.' She had the answer she wanted, but the pain needed one final cry. 'It's just so sad. So sad.'

'Yes, my dear, it is. But life – your life – goes on.' Tactfully, Cynthia steered her back to arrangements for the next Tea Club.

And my life goes on, too, she thought, and shook out the sentiment from her day's routine.

Cynthia turned the key in the lock, calling reassuringly, 'It's me. I'm home.' She returned the key to its place in her handbag, unbuttoned her navy serge coat and hung it on the hallstand. Then she saw on the table a small orange envelope: a telegram. Its colour sang out to her like a square patch of sunlight in the drab hallway. It had the earthiness of orange peel. Not that she'd seen an orange for a year or two. She registered a thousand tiny reactions: her stomach turned over; the hairs on her neck flicked; her hands went clammy; she dropped her bag; her mouth went dry.

Then she gave a small explosive cry, snatched up the flimsy paper and ran noisily upstairs with her mother's 'Cynthia, are you ill?' floating behind her.

Was she ill? No, but she was suddenly feverish, her heart pounding. She dumped herself on the bed, her gloves and bag beside her, held the telegram for one breathless moment, then opened it. 'AM SAFE STOP BE WITH YOU STOP J.' No explanation. She scoured the envelope for clues. It wasn't from an official address or military establishment, just a post office in Liverpool. It had been sent that morning. Josh safe. Nothing more.

She sat bolt upright, questions and excitement chasing round her head. What about the others? Was he injured? In hospital, perhaps? He must be with Jessica. How soon could he and Cynthia meet? No phone number, no address . . . What should she do?

Downstairs Beryl put on the kettle then went back to her knitting, popping a mint imperial into her mouth. Half an hour later she went to the foot of the stairs. 'Your tea's ready.'

Following their return to Liverpool Josh had contacted the *Treverran*'s owners. The company was benign, keeping up the wages to its shipwrecked mariners even after their ship had gone down and they were deemed to be technically 'off pay'. It was a private choice and many civilian merchant-shipping companies chose not to make it. Plenty of seamen rescued from torpedoed ships fetched up in a British port with no money due and no prospects of help. Survivors who were on company books, like Josh, Robert and Charlie Rawlings, were allowed four weeks' leave to sort themselves out. The Handley Company had heard nothing of Second Mate Tim Beesley.

Josh had lost everything: identity card, clothes coupons, sextant, nautical tables, binoculars. He had to re-equip himself and negotiate through the company's agent in Liverpool, who shook his hand, holding his arm at the elbow. But there was little time for more. There were too many survivors, shocked in mind and withered in body, prowling the docks of British ports to make each rescue any occasion for celebration. Merchant jacks felt neglected, at best patronized. The Seamen's Welfare was overwhelmed and coped with a brisk efficiency that left little space for smiles. Everyone had tales to tell, and no one had time to listen. The pubs did a roaring trade. Only the debriefing by the sympathetic naval officer gave him the chance to tell the full story.

Josh and eight of his crew – Robert and Charlie among them – had fetched up on one of the Azores, and been found by an old man who was becoming used to this sort of thing. 'You are my third lot. Stay. Please stay. My wife fetches food.' Along the shore came a small busy figure carrying two mighty flagons, too heavy for her strength and splashing water abundantly on to the grey volcanic sand. It was a precious sight.

The British consul at Ponta Delgada was informed and

took charge, arranging clothing and accommodation: three men, including Charlie Rawlings, needed to go to hospital; some were lodged on a Belgian ship in port for repairs. Josh was given a room at a small seafront hotel. He lay on its white sheets and stared at the ceiling, thankful, ever thankful. And changed.

A week later a troopship arrived to fetch them and others who had landed there. The battle of the Atlantic was bringing a flurry of activity to the sleepy islands.

Josh had gone at once to Jessica's flat. He was blank, wasted, scoured by misery, needful. He climbed the stairs with grim, heavy steps. On the landing, the noise hit him like an assault. Female voices, some singing, some shouting, all drunk. Among them he could distinguish his wife's rich contralto – 'I'll see you again, whenever spring breaks through again.' He held the banister with both hands, eyes closed. All this way, all those tracts of ocean, of suffering . . . towards a world of silly women, giddy exploiters of the war's freedoms to be drunk, sluttish, dissolute. He turned and, with as measured a stride as he had come, he left Jessica's home for good.

There was a queue of returned sailors at the post-office counter, but he waited until he could despatch his telegram. Then he moved into a hostel for seamen.

The receptionist at the Melville Hotel registered them as though she had never set eyes on them before. They were grateful for that. Cynthia's flair for making arrangements had come in handy. She had explained to Beryl, in tones that brooked no challenge, that she would be away for several days. She grew inventive, concocting an elaborate and unverifiable tale of a course somewhere in Wales where head teachers were being brought together to consult on educational changes that might come about once the war was won. If Beryl referred to such activities in the wrong company – an unlikely circumstance, though in wartime all sorts turned up at church – there were enough snatches of truth for it to be plausible. The country was rife with undercover activities, covert arrangements, signings of the Official Secrets Act by people from Bletchley Park to Scapa Flow. And she knew there were plans to revolutionize the country's schools. Ashworth Grammar School was told that she was ill.

She packed her nicest clothes – smart Gor-Ray skirts, blouses made from parachute silk, two jumpers recently reworked from unravelled wool, and a silk nightie, a present from an indulgent aunt before the war and still unworn. She stowed everything in her brown cardboard suitcase as though it were her trousseau.

Her vanity made her ashamed when she saw Josh. Liverpool's Mission to Seamen had kitted him out as best they could: the chaplain at the Hanover Street Institute had explained that they tried to hand out clothing appropriate to a man's status. Josh, as master, should have the best, but the two suits they offered hung limp and depressing on their second-hand hangers. As for woollens, he had the pick of socks, gloves, jumpers and vests knitted in a thousand styles by a thousand well-meaning hands. He could hear the clacking of the nation's knitting needles as he rummaged through the multicoloured stack. The monochrome of wartime life had clearly fired up these enthusiasts into a frenzy of rainbow offerings, shreds of different colours finding their way into sleeves and waistcoats rather than go to waste. Sometimes on the quayside you spotted some hapless jack sporting the dazzling stripes of a civilian effort. Smoke, grease and rubble dust would soon tame the excess, no doubt, but Josh said he'd take the only plain one offered: 'Nice jersey, this, in rich nigger brown, sir.' It was ample, warm and shapeless.

They hardly left their room. Apart from draughty sorties to the bathroom and lavatory along the corridor, and brief excursions to fetch food and drink from dingy local shops, they stayed put. They nested in the room's cheap bric-à-brac, and in each other. They tipped the cleaner to stay away and not report them for remaining there throughout the day.

They would each remember it as a blur of time undefined, a long unwinding of themselves into each other, sometimes all talk and smoking, telling of each other's lives, laughing at insubstantial detail. Sometimes episodes of making love, sometimes laughter and sometimes silence – the pleasure, as they become closer, of not having to talk. Cynthia grew from shyness into a woman surprised by pleasure. She was proud of her body, watching Josh caress it, his hands tracing the arch of her spine, the concave spaces of her armpits, the dome of her belly. Sometimes she would stop him there, and hold his gaze as he moved below and into her. It was new and sometimes clumsy: she didn't like staining the sheets, or the reek of it. It was then she felt her gaucheness.

Josh enjoyed her innocence, steering her hand and her mouth, allowing her time to understand his own moods and impulses, teaching her to let go and come to his mouth, to his hand and with him inside her. He had learned how precious and vulnerable the human body is. He had promised himself that if he survived sufficiently unscarred he would savour its every movement, enjoy the sweetness of flexed limbs, healthy, striding walks, the comfort of a warm fire on his skin, the tang of frost in his nostrils . . . and now his renewed sexuality. He, like Cynthia, was experiencing something new.

When the week was over, they agreed the routine for parting. It would be practical, unsentimental: he to be master of a new ship, she to resume the care of her girls. They strode together from the hotel with light hearts, and no looking back. Both assumed too much about their future.

'Oh, Miss Maitland, thank goodness you're well in time for the captain's visit.'

It had been Grace who had taken Josh's call. Cynthia had been at his elbow in the phone box when he had pressed Button A and heard the money clatter down, but Grace wasn't to know that. Indeed, she had fussed about Cynthia's absence, but he hadn't seemed to think it mattered. He explained that the school now had a new ship. Robert and Charlie Rawlings would come with him. He asked that the visit be very low-key. He also asked for Jen's address.

'Yes, Grace, thank you for coping. We shall call a

general assembly so that Captain Percival can speak to them of the *Treverran*'s loss.'

It was eight o'clock in the morning and Bert was tuning in to Alvar Liddell reading the news on the Home Service. 'Our Russian allies are pressing forward with their encirclement of the German forces outside Stalingrad. Yesterday ... Colonel ... drove back the ... regiment under ...' The front door opened directly from the street into their living room, so the knocker made a sharp crack and Ruby bobbed out of the back kitchen. 'Who can it be at this hour, Dad?'

'Only one way to find out.' He went to answer it, wiping a trace of porridge off with his shirtsleeves. He thought it must be a mistake, a seaman in full uniform, brass buttons and all, holding his cap under his arm.

'Good morning, sir.' He treated Josh as he would a passenger at the station. 'Number thirteen you wanted?'

'Yes, it is. I understand Jennifer Wainwright lives here. I hope she hasn't left for school.'

'Our Jen? No, she's on her way down.' Bert switched voices and volume: '*Jen*, there's someone here to see yous.'

Josh stepped across the threshold on to the bright but scuffed lino. 'I should explain. I was master on the SS *Treverran*. I've met Jen before.'

Bert was shocked. Hadn't the ship gone down? Hadn't the school flown the flag at half-mast? Hadn't Jen been convulsed by grief?

'Oh, aye, sorry to hear about that, sir. Very sorry we are. You'll know young Tim. We've grown very fond of him, one of the family, like.'

'That's why I'm here.'

Jen had arrived in the doorway, pale and trim, with a bulging school satchel on her shoulder. 'Captain Percival. Oh, heavens, it's you. What happened? Why are you here? Are you all back? Please come in and make yourself at home. We'd no idea . . .' She swept domestic untidiness under the sofa cushions.

'Cup o' tea?' called Ruby from the kitchen.

'Yes, thanks – but don't go to any trouble. I wanted to talk to Jen privately.' Ruby hurried the cup to his elbow and signalled Bert to be gone. The door slammed. Jen and Josh were left facing each other in the armchairs.

He took a deep breath. 'Some of us survived, Jen, but . . . Tim wasn't among those who got back.'

'Ah.' It was the slightest of reactions, but her eyes were fixed on his. 'Yes . . . Well, I'd like to know what happened.'

His account offered no consolation.

'You think he was trapped below decks, do you?'

'Almost certainly . . .'

'How ghastly.' She shuddered, and he saw that the nature of such a death, so claustrophobic, so trapped, distressed her almost as much as his loss.

'We thought we saw a couple of figures silhouetted against the sky, very high up, as the ship tilted higher and higher out of the water. We think they must have jumped.'

'Tim? Might that have been Tim, d'you think? Did you look? Did you look for him?' She was agitated now, frantic.

Slowly Josh took her hand and spoke gently to her. 'It

241

might have been Tim, and of course we looked, Jen. We searched long and hard. But the ocean is . . . well . . . it's very big. Of course I searched, Jen. He was like a son to me . . .'

'Yes. Thank you. And thank you for telling me.'

'He was very brave, Jen. He was a hero. He always was. Last voyage he rescued a sailor whose ship had gone down. Tim was like that, impulsive, not thinking of himself. One of the best.' His voice cracked. 'I think I loved him almost as much as you did.'

'As I still do, as I still do!' And she burst into tears.

Realizing

Throughout March and April Cynthia walked with a new air. It was as though her sensibilities were newly tuned. The perceptions that connected her to the real world intensified. The life around her became more vivid, more detailed. She saw beauty in unexpected things: the jet black glitter of a piece of coal, the clang of the trams swaying along their tracks, the dense opacity of milk poured from a bottle into a jug. Where had all those pleasures been until now? And how thankful she was that she was aware of them.

The poets tell of lovers wrapped up in each other, too preoccupied to mark the outer world, but she found her love for Josh opened new paths in her consciousness. She became more alert, more responsive to public events. Her private joy translated into optimism about the progress of the war. Her sense of patriotism took a little skip. And, almost in response to her private confidence, the tide of the war seemed to be turning in the Allies' favour: the Germans had surrendered to the Russians in Stalingrad at the end of January; the Americans were mopping up the enemy in North Africa – there had been a conference in Casablanca where Churchill and Roosevelt had made their plans.

The film *Casablanca* came out at the same time: she and Josh had sneaked from the Melville Hotel one night and gone to see it at the Gaumont in Oxford Road. From then on 'As Time Goes By' was 'our tune' – 'Just like a couple of love-sick kids,' Cynthia had teased.

'But that's what we are,' said Josh.

Meanwhile the RAF had begun its massive bombing runs against Berlin – she rejoiced in that. The latest government campaign 'Wings for Victory' was going strong, and the bombing of British cities had virtually ceased. Yet rationing was getting tougher: there was little paper, fewer schoolbooks, nothing came wrapped and old newspapers did for lavatory rolls. But such scarcities had a sense of purpose about them: people moaned but didn't mind. Cynthia didn't moan. She smiled.

In one battleground the war was not being won. The battle of the Atlantic was a never-ending struggle that had none of war's usual parameters – of land gained or lost, as in Stalingrad, or the enemy driven back as in North Africa. This was a war that went on and on across the shifting waters of the treacherous ocean, its weary combatants unsung in the nation's roll-call of honour. Seamen felt ever more unappreciated, taken for granted. They felt they deserved better. With death in prospect at every sailing, many grew restless to seek what joy they could.

Josh was now ready to take up his new ship, the SS *Tremullion*. Once back from the Melville Hotel and his visit to Jen, he had gone to spend some time with Peter, whose ship had docked at Bristol. They would have several days together. They could share the worries that troubled all seamen.

From Bristol Josh had written:

My dear, dear Cynthia,

I think of you every moment. I can smell your skin, feel the tenderness of your dear body. I want to be with you. I will be with you.

I am with Peter now: he is so tall and handsome, not like his wizened old father. But he is the future. His generation will shape this country. I am so proud of him, Cynthia, and, strangely, I know he is proud of me. That's a rare thing between father and son, and I believe I have the war to thank for that. Sometimes good things come about because of the most terrible. His mother is less close to him than I am. But I'll say no more. You and I have agreed not to talk about any of that.

I send all the fondness and love you know I have for you,

Josh

Upbeat and emboldened, Cynthia decided her girls must be prepared for the world after the war. It would be theirs to inherit and improve. She would invite people to talk to them who would challenge the world-view of Mrs Murgatroyd and her kind. They might believe

Britain was fighting to sustain the old ways, but the war itself was making that impossible. The important thing for her girls was to have a sense of the country's new direction.

The Tea Club had been popular in the coldest months for a particular reason: the heating in her study made it the warmest place in the school. Towards the end of March they had shuffled into their rows of seats with surprising good humour. They were beginning to relish their encounters, even if they hadn't quite got the hang of purposeful debate.

Alf Wilbraham came over from Rochdale to talk about the Co-operative Movement. Centenary celebrations were coming up in a year's time and volunteer speakers were taking the message to schools and youth clubs. A machine accident had ended Alf's work as a weaver, but evening classes had qualified him for a new role in life to which he had not yet adjusted. He wore his hairy brown suit with obvious unease, his stiff shirt collar pressing into his neck. The cuffs of his frayed shirt stuck out too far, and he made clumsy play with a red silk handkerchief.

But coming to a grammar school in no way over-awed him: he was well read in H. G. Wells, Robert Tressell, George Bernard Shaw, the publications of Victor Gollancz's Left Book Club. And his loquaciousness owed something to each.

'I take it, young ladies, that you're familiar with the struggle of working people, even in time of war, to earn a decent family wage . . . enough to allow a married man to support his family.' No one answered. Many knew that the fees of several, including Jen, were paid by the local education authority, but it was considered vulgar to draw attention to it.

He took his time in getting to the really big news, lingering over tales of his days as a weaver, offering gruesome details of his accident, speaking lyrically of how the Co-operative Movement benefited all who used it. The girls fidgeted in their seats, Polly contemplating her nails with especial concentration.

Alf took the hint. 'There's a major change coming to all our lives. I can promise you that.'

He must mean peace. That was the promise always held out to them, a sort of Heaven on Earth a long way off. Attention perked up. Brenda Alsop, her arms folded, leaned forward, challenging him to surprise her.

'It's just been announced by the government. I don't suppose you young ladies have heard of the Beveridge Report.' The phrase meant nothing to them and sounded dull, but he ploughed on: 'You're lucky, you young women! One day all visits to the doctor and hospital will be free. Dentists, too. It's what we socialists have been planning. Now Beveridge, although he's a Liberal, is making it possible. The day is well-nigh here!' And with similar Biblical fervour he went on to prophesy the end of poverty, unemployment, disease. Then, exhausted by such benison, he sat back and smiled at his shiny black boots.

There was an outburst of questions and opinions. Brenda Alsop's father was a doctor and she insisted he wouldn't be treating anyone for nothing. But others were eager to know when this miracle would transform their lives. Alf Wilbraham went away with their praises ringing in his ears. All agreed that the war must be won first.

'That was really good, Miss Maitland!'

'Odd old boy, wasn't he? From a factory, but with all that reading . . .'

'Tim's dad's like that.' Jen liked to bring her lost love into every conversation. 'He doesn't have much of a job, but he knows all about what's in the papers, Beveridge and stuff.'

'And he'll be on the socialist side, too, I bet.'

'He is – and what's wrong with that?' They disappeared, arguing, towards the bike sheds.

March 1943

Dear School,

As you know already, you have a new ship. She belongs to the same shipping company as our dear old one and has inherited the same coded number. But she is newer and therefore a little more spick and span. We are sailing from Blighty again quite soon; you will be pleased to know that First Mate Robert Warburton is with us, as is Apprentice Charlie Rawlings. The three of us will miss our friend Tim, but at least our being together will help keep his memory alive. I have enclosed a photograph of him with this letter. It's rather blurred, and I'm sorry about that, but we took it in the West Indies when we were buying your terrapins. It's good to see him laughing and enjoying himself so much.

It was on our last but one journey home that Tim was immensely brave. I want to tell you about what happened. We ran into U-boat trouble, and one of our ships was hit and sinking. Tim spotted a survivor in the water and, against all usual procedures, insisted that he could rescue the man. He did, and the man was dragged on board. Without Tim's intervention that would not have happened, and that man is alive today because of him. That's the sort of person he was, and I trust you will keep his memory alive for his own sake and for the sake of all those he loved.

Your captain,

Josh Percival

Jen was given the letter to show Tim's parents and her own. She felt proud to do so. The small, smudged photograph was pinned to the school noticeboard, with a written tribute set out below. Only after several months when it grew curled and untidy did Grace take it down and stow it among the school's records.

Cynthia's sense of well-being extended beyond her state of mind. She had never felt so fit. Self-conscious without being vain, she took fresh delight in how she looked. The contours of her face rounded, the texture of her pale skin grew finer, more like porcelain than ever. Her mother noticed, with an approving eye, that her daughter was acquiring a sort of innocent glamour, walking with a lilt, her pert little hats bobbing cheekily. Her hips seemed to have more shape, her breasts too.

She hadn't bothered much when she missed her period late in March. It often happened in wartime. All those years ago her grief had had the same effect. Besides she was forty-one: she'd be forty-two at the end of May, an age when women began to feel seriously old. She'd be happy to see the curse die out: the harsh cotton-wool towels were hard to come by and like cardboard to use. If the change was starting already, so much the better, though it did seem rather early.

She couldn't ask her mother: they didn't talk about such things and, besides, her mother was more ignorant than she was. Beryl had once asked her, in a rare moment of intimacy when Cynthia had just graduated, to tell her about birth control. Cynthia had looked it up in a book and tried to remember it now. She had reckoned that by counting the days she'd be safe when she was with Josh. Besides, she felt wonderful. What could be wrong with that?

It was the end of April and the Easter holiday when she missed another period. Odd that now term was over it still hadn't come back. But the body was a mystery. Who knew much about its daily workings? Biology at school told you about the organs and where they were, but little more. Bodies had their own way of getting on with life. She'd done as the book said. She wouldn't worry.

She went with her mother to Communion on Easter Sunday. Grace was there with her husband, but she scarcely knew the other parishioners. They nodded kindly, their eyes weighing up her elegant outfit. Like her, the other women wore hats.

The church had modest beauty – simple lines, stone pillars, pale oak panelling. The embroidered banners of the Mothers' Union and the Church Lads' Brigade were propped below the pulpit, and the white Easter cloth, with its golden cross, had been brought out to dress the altar, while the pew ends were twined with stubbornly unbending daffodils. An unremarkable church had put on its finery to celebrate the most remarkable event in the Christian year. 'Christ the Lord is risen today, alleluia . . .' The sweet voices rose guilelessly from the choir.

Prayers had always been a matter of routine for Cynthia. Cosy mothers and housewives, serious-minded office workers, wholesome shopkeepers bent over clasped hands to confess their sins in dire and solemn tones: '. . . we have done those things that we ought not to have done, and there is no health in us.' But what sins, exactly? A deal or two on the black-market, a squabble with a neighbour over the blackout, a bill unpaid before the month was out. Minor social transgressions had to stand in for the big stuff. Real sins were betrayal of the country, which was unthinkable, lack of patriotism, despicable, and cowardice in battle, contemptible.

Oh, and sex. Well, sex was tainted with sin, certainly, and anything outside marriage could, heaven forfend, bring its own punishment. Those who dared to transgress risked getting caught out, and then what? Shame and disgrace, social ostracism and rejection. Quite right, too. Pray that we and those we love never stray in that way. On bended knees the woollen shoulders and feathered hats, the knitted scarves and balding heads bobbed at the pews. Amen. Amen to that. Beryl's 'Amen' was as heartfelt as the rest.

Cynthia had sinned. And she didn't regret it. Reciting the confession required you to declare of your sins that 'the remembrance of them is grievous unto us. The burden of them is intolerable.' The words were hollow. Cynthia's sins were some of her happiest memories: they had brought her joy she had dreamed of once long ago and now was hers again. She sighed, closed the prayer book and looked about her. She didn't belong among these people. She must find someone else to talk to.

Maud Sheridan opened the door as if she had been expecting her. 'Well, this is a surprise and no mistake. Come in.'

Cynthia stepped into the ramshackle cottage and knew that this was where she wanted to be. It was spare and makeshift, but a place of clumsy beauty. The floor was bare of carpets, with a single rag rug, the walls dense with paintings, pinned and tacked, unframed, across them: sometimes the recognizable shape of a curving nude, with bright splashes of bronze and brown, which hinted at either a landscape or a tangle of messy hair. All was vivid and cheerful, and before it stood, most comforting of all, Maud herself. 'Would you like some tea? I've nothing fancy like I had with those girls of yours. And I've given up with milk – the little scoundrels round about keep stealing it.'

'No milk is fine. Thanks.' Cynthia took off her headscarf and serge coat, and sank on to the only chair. Maud went to put on the kettle, then plonked her large bottom

252

on the round leather pouffe beside the fireplace. They lit cigarettes and the smoke spooled into the open rafters above.

'It's good of you to come, Cynthia, but I can't think it's genteel visiting you have in mind. Am I right?'

'Lovely pictures. Well, I like them,' she said, as though plenty of others might not – as was, in fact, the case. She stared purposefully at the walls, using this as an excuse to turn her back. Not facing Maud directly, she said, 'I think I may be having a baby.'

'My goodness me. My goodness indeed.' Maud dipped her head to catch Cynthia's expression. 'Is it what you want? Because if it is, that's a fine and wonderful thing, isn't it? A child of your own . . . and of someone else, too, of course?'

'Oh, yes, but no one you know, or would know.' She paused. 'He's away. In the war.'

'So he doesn't know.'

'Not yet . . . no. It won't be . . . convenient. It's not what he wants. Well, I don't think so, anyway.'

'Ah. Married, is he?'

'Yes. Er . . . separated.'

'Oh, we're all separated, these days. By the war or his own choice?'

Cynthia managed a little laugh. 'Well, both, I suppose. The one tends to lead to the other.' And they shared a smile at the state of the world. 'It's disastrous, of course. My school, my girls, my mother, my entire life . . .' She stubbed out her cigarette with some venom and took a sip of the bitter milkless tea.

'You didn't think to . . . avoid it?'

'I counted the days. I thought that was what you did. It's not something I know much about.'

Maud took in the full significance of this. 'Do you still want to avoid it? Is that why you've come to me?'

'Oh, no. About coming to you, I mean. I came because I knew you'd be sympathetic. There aren't many I know who would be.' Cynthia had never felt so forlorn.

'When I was younger there was a woman over Oldham way, who'd help out young girls in trouble. I don't know if she's still doing it, or if the law caught up with her. I can find out, if you'd like.'

'Oh, I don't think . . . I don't know what I want. I can't think straight any more. But I don't think that's it. I think I'll go through with it one way or another.'

'Yes! Have a baby! Become a mother! It's a wonderful destiny, you know.'

Cynthia managed another wintry smile. 'Well, I certainly thought so once, long ago. And it was true then. I really believed it, but I can't believe it'll be true now.'

'Are you . . . close to the father?'

'Very. Very close indeed.' She lifted her head and her eyes shone. 'That's the one true thing I know. The one thing I can be sure of.'

'But that's wonderful – for you both.'

Cynthia's face reflected her doubt.

'Well, isn't it?'

'I want it to be. Oh, I so want it to be wonderful, but I can't see how it can be. I can't think of it in that way.'

'He'll need to know. You must tell him – soon.' But Cynthia's moment of hope had fled and she was cast down once more. Maud spread her sturdy arms wide, like some benign enfolding goddess. 'What's stopping you?'

'He's at sea, the captain of a ship. It's not something I can write in a letter.'

'You're being a headmistress, Cynthia, trying to forestall all problems that might arise. You need to think differently, ride with events. Let things happen. They have already, after all.' She laughed loudly, startling Cynthia out of the dumps.

'You're quite right. He'll be back some time in May, I think. I'll be able to tell him then.'

'Meanwhile, you should see your doctor, just to make sure.'

'My doctor? Oh, I couldn't. He's Mother's doctor, too, and he goes to our church. It's simply not possible. You can see that, surely!'

Maud nodded grimly.

'I'll just wait. After all, I'm feeling fit enough.'

'But you don't know for sure yet, do you?'

Cynthia held her gaze, then slowly gave a glowing smile. 'Yes, I do.'

Reaching

There was sunlight on the quay: the *Tremullion* had docked. Most of the crew had taken their wages and were making their way, with grins and chatter, down the gangway. As they had come down the Mersey channel at dawn there had been light rain, and now, with their arrival, the June sun was warming the city. By midday the paving stones, roof tiles, warehouse walls and rows of red-brick houses would be throbbing with the early heat. It was holiday weather. Along the coast the wide beaches of Formby and Southport, and beyond them genteel Lytham St Anne's and raffish Blackpool would be relaxing their corsets and feeling the benefit.

Josh had handed out permits for the crew to go ashore, called on the duty officer at the Naval Control of Shipping, handed in the ship's confidential books, then made for the company agent's office and the telephone. He left a message with the school that he was back and promised them a letter.

*

The summer term was in full swing. The upper sixth were preparing for their Higher School Certificate exams: revision and cramming had engulfed them. Girls took turns with scarce library books, nagging each other for key works. Some skulked in corners with thickets of paper and inky fingers, bent on memorizing notes. Others spoke aloud set texts – Milton, Shakespeare – battles and treaties, chemistry formulae, meaning lost in the military precision of rote learning. University applications had gone in for the handful of girls with daring ambitions. Others had applied to training colleges – it was the fashion to aspire to be a gym mistress. Many wanted to help the war effort, and knew that good exam results would keep them out of munitions factories. Instead they would find jobs as clerks and secretaries. But the prime option was marriage.

Polly was secretly planning hers. On his last visit Robert had bought a small ring with a tiny stone and asked her to marry him. It was still a secret. His survival and Tim's death had decided many things for him. If the God his parents worshipped had anything to say on the matter, it was that life should not be idled away. It must be seized and made good. Robert believed he and Polly could do that. During his most desperate time at sea he had remembered his mother's favourite prayer: 'And all shall be well, and all manner of thing shall be well.' The thought had somehow lodged and grown, and his resentment of his parents' faith had relaxed its grip. He had returned eager to press forward with the rest of his life.

Polly was thrilled at the prospect of being the first in her year to marry. The losses of the school's spinster teachers lingered in their teaching: the yearning of Andromache for Hector, Elizabeth Barrett Browning's poems to her husband, the partnership of Pierre and Marie Curie – all reinforced the view that life's first and most sublime purpose was the discovery of love and its enshrining in the bonds of marriage and family. Careers were all very well, and bright girls were encouraged to take them up with dedication, but it was implied, hopefully, that somewhere along the way the greater destiny would claim them. Now Polly would arrive there before the rest. Meanwhile the secret had to be kept. She lived out her final term as head girl with the easy grace that had always captivated the school.

The night after she'd heard about Tim, Jen called round to see his parents. Sam, still blackened from the coal dust of his daily deliveries, stood with his back to the empty fireplace, tamping coarse tobacco into his pipe. Ida was slumped in her armchair, her knitting neglected. It was nearly seven o'clock and a few dirty pots from their evening meal were still stacked on the wooden draining-board in the kitchen.

'I'm sorry it's so untidy, Jen. Neither of us felt much like eating and I haven't the spirit for the washing-up. It'll have to wait.' Their life's routine was in disarray. 'Would you like a cup of tea? I've got a packet of gingernuts saved.'

'No, no, don't you get up.'

'She'll need something more than tea, Mother, won't you, love?' Sam himself had stopped at the local on the way home and Beth the barmaid had given him a shot from a scarce bottle of whisky. It had steadied his nerves.

'I'm fine. Just sit down, please.' They knew what she wanted and they were avoiding it. But once the talk of Tim began it came in a rush. They compared what Josh had told them, the detail of the silhouettes against the sky. They decided that Tim had died in water rather than fire. Josh's account of his rumoured dash to rescue the radio officer brought both women to tears. Even Sam had to get up and walk round to stop himself giving way. Instead he talked of what might have been. 'He'll miss it all, now, that's what I mind. All that lies ahead for young people like you. The better world that's coming. He won't be there to share it. To share it with you, Jen.'

'And who'll I dance with now, eh?' She managed a whimper of laughter, and the tears flowed harder still.

'You must see it all for him, Jen. He'd want that. He'd want you to be part of the good changes on the way. You must be even more sure to get to that university of yours, get on in the world.'

'Well, I'm trying my best. We've got Highers in a couple of weeks.'

'We mustn't let these sacrifices go to waste, all those that have died. Think of Stalingrad and what the people there have been through. They say the king's sent a telegram.'

Ida was more practical. 'We wondered if you'd like any of his things, Jen. His room's not been touched. You can take your pick.'

'Oh, that's kind. Thank you.' Jen wasn't sure she wanted this but knew it would please Ida. She paused at the door of Tim's bedroom, given access for the first time. Stepping inside, she opened the wardrobe door and buried her face in his clothes, taking in the smell of him. His worn shoes lay in a heap, the shoes that had been so nimble when he danced. She sat on the floor beside his wind-up gramophone and played through the small pile of records, each taken from its purple Capitol sleeve.

When she came downstairs she had chosen just one souvenir: Xavier Cugat's version of 'In The Mood'.

She called on Sam and Ida often, and played the scratched records over and over again, but she hadn't been dancing since Tim had gone missing. They talked of increasing triumphs at sea. The Allies seemed to know where the U-boats were and the air force was turning up more often, so things were going well. Always Jen came away with a book or two borrowed from Sam's shelf: Harold Laski's *Where Do We Go from Here?*, an odd book called *Put Out More Flags*, which seemed to mock evacuees. She didn't like that. Supercilious. And a book by George Orwell: *The Lion and the Unicorn*. She didn't always agree with him either. Ideas and argument filled her life, and helped to stop the tears.

The plan was that the girls would make a visit to the ship in Liverpool. Josh's letter had explained that now there were fewer air raids on the docks they could come in safety. Robert would be there, and Apprentice Rawlings, possibly a steward, and even the radio officer. There had been a giggling flutter of rivalry as to who should go: Polly obviously, as head girl; Jen asked to stay behind with her books and her grief; Brenda Alsop was keen, and so were other Tea Club stalwarts. Miss Maitland would be at their head. Grace booked twenty third-class railway tickets and Miss Maitland gave a brisk talk about wearing full school uniform and making a good impression. She must find a way to speak to Josh alone.

This time the telegram came to the school. The boy parked his bike at the gate and took off his bicycle clips. He stopped whistling as he entered the elegant vestibule and dropped the familiar orange envelope in Grace's office. Cynthia retreated to her study to read it.

PETER MISSING STOP SCHOOL VISIT GOES AHEAD STOP WILL NOT BE WITH YOU STOP JOSH.

'Ah, that's such a pity.' Her tone to Grace was of gentle regret. 'It looks as though Captain Percival won't be there to greet us.' She retreated to her study and sank into her chair. Josh's son missing. The son who was his echo, his other, his better self, in the Senior Service. Father and son: two peas in a pod, Josh had told her. Back at the Melville Hotel he had talked of Peter fondly and often: 'His mother did the caring, of course, but he would always run to me with his toys, "Da, Da, Da," and I would lift him up and throw him in the air. His mother didn't like that. Thought he might fall. But he was a real boy, ready for anything, after my own heart.' It was said so lightly, and sometimes Josh had brought out a small black-and-white photograph of a tall young man, gazed at it for a good while, even stroked it with his thumb, 'That's my lad . . . That's Peter,' then returned it to his battered wallet.

Speaking with Grace she was quite calm. 'It's disappointing for everyone, of course, but at least Robert will be there. He's as much a friend of the school as Captain

261

Percival, after all. Make sure each girl brings her own sandwiches.' She must reach Josh somehow.

Josh had been summoned as he was leaving the agent's office. 'Urgent call!' He hurried back. Perhaps Cynthia had found a quiet moment. But it had been Derby House on the telephone. Peter's ship, HMS *Somerton*, had been lost in the Mediterranean. Few survivors. 'I'm sorry, Josh. Really sorry.'

He hurried out, away from people, and found himself wandering along the quay, thunderstruck. 'Fuck the war, fuck the goddamned fucking war!'

'I agree there, mate!' from a passing seaman. 'Fuck the lot of them!'

Jessica. He must find Jessica.

Nellie Scragg had been standing at the front door, smoking, guarding her clean step. She had nodded to Josh. 'She's upstairs on her own.' Thank goodness for that. He couldn't have faced the cawing sympathy of Jessica's parrot friends. He had found the door of the flat open, no sound from within. Jessica had been sitting at the desk in the crook of the sloping window, smoking, staring out into the sunlight. She was still in uniform: she must just have come off night duty.

'It's usually raining, isn't it?'

'Mostly . . . in Liverpool. Well, it seems like it.' Her voice was crisp, exact.

He had walked towards her and put his hands on her shoulders, had felt her give way to the comfort of his holding her. 'When did you hear?'

'First thing this morning. They called me out of the

office at Derby House. I knew what it meant the moment they did that.'

'Is there any detail?'

'None.'

'That might come through later. We can hope for that.'

'Hope?'

'Well, it would be good to know.'

She had smoked in silence. 'He's gone, Josh, gone for ever . . . *for . . . ever.*' She had dragged out the words in a hideous drawl, quietly at first but then in a wild yelp of pain. It had gone on and on while Josh held her, sobbing, to him. He found comfort in his boy's mother, her body, so familiar. Only she could know what he was feeling. Through the years they had developed all the irritants of marriage – repetitiveness, familiarity and the arcane hostility between men and women – but now that familiarity was their solace. Their ancient bond came to their rescue. He needed to help her. She was the frailer spirit, giddy and wayward in good times, now fragmenting. An only son: the two of them could bear it together.

'Is there any food in the place?'

'No, I haven't had time. Haven't thought about it.'

'I'll fetch something from round the corner. Put the kettle on. I won't be away long.'

'Don't be, Josh. I need you here.'

'Of course.'

He had sent the telegram from the post office down the road and gone back to his wife.

As sixth-formers they were spared the requirement to walk in crocodile. It felt like freedom. They were a conspicuous arrival on the quay as the gates of the dockyard swung open for them and they were marshalled through. They broke into chattering. 'Not too loud, girls. Remember, you're ambassadors for the school.' But Miss Maitland and Miss Hayter relaxed too, caught up in this male world of ships and cargoes, shouting and machinery.

Apprentice Charlie Rawlings rushed forward to greet them and took them first along the jetty to where they could get a seaward view of their ship. He pointed out its Plimsoll line, and there was First Mate Warburton, waving from the bridge. Once they were on board he led them from deck to bridge, from wardroom to radio. The girls craned their necks, and were impressed.

Cynthia saw it with different eyes: this ship was Josh's domain. She thought of his presence here, his leadership, his authority. They were shown the chart room, and the sextants, the pair of brass chronometers gimballed in their mahogany cases. This was the stuff of Josh's everyday world. They were taken along a narrow catwalk to look down on the huge engine, the atmosphere stifling with heat and oil – the girls whispered among themselves, imagining what it meant to be below the water level when a torpedo hit. As at Ashworth Grammar School, there were disciplines and skills here, too. Cynthia felt a jolt of pride in someone else's knowledge, at his difference from her: his physically active life pitched against the elements, and hers, bookish, close, internal. Going round his ship, she caught the flavour of him, enjoying the strangeness. But when the troop of girls went in single file to peep inside his cabin, with its bed, the single armchair and photographs of Jessica and Peter, she felt suddenly excluded.

This was not her place, neither had she any claim on it. And now there was his bereavement.

Up on deck again, they were soon peering into the vast emptiness of the holds, where men were loading the cargo: locomotive parts, packing cases and bales. Grains of wheat left from an earlier voyage were sprouting in the moisture round the edge and now formed a green border. Stevedores lumbered to and fro, pretending to ignore the clutch of schoolgirls, filling the spaces in the echoing hold below. Beyond, the sun shone on the Mersey where a slight breeze was whipping up little crests of foam.

Miss Maitland and Miss Hayter were ushered into the saloon where they were served lunch, made by the steward in the galley. The girls were left to eat their sandwiches in the smoke-room. Ships, like schools, had their hierarchies.

She must find a way to reach Josh.

After their sandwiches the school party lost something of its formality. There was a modest presentation on deck when Robert and a shuffling member of the crew had handed the school party a replica of a wooden dhow – 'something we picked up on the way' was how they phrased it. After exclamations of delight the girls unwound, lolling in the sunshine on deck, loosening their ties, kicking off their stiff school shoes. Some of the crew took time off to come and talk. One had been on the *Treverran* when it was torpedoed, and had known Tim. 'A right good mucker, he was. A real gent. He had guts, too.' They pocketed the remarks to report back to Jen.

Robert found time to spend with Polly.

Cynthia asked for a moment on her own to walk the decks and smoke a cigarette. She stood, braced against the rail, watching other ships coming and going, feeling lonely and curiously self-possessed. Her pupils were a credit to her, Josh's ship a credit to him.

As they were preparing to leave for the train, a messenger from the agent's office called with a note for Cynthia. Would she be pleased to take tea with Josh at the Kardomah café before she returned? Of course she would. Suddenly brisk and efficient, she marshalled the girls under Miss Hayter's ready control, handed over their return rail tickets and packed them back to Staveley. Robert directed her, with a certain knowingness, towards the café.

She remembered it was below street level with steps that led from the sunlight into the cool, dim interior. Neat but shabby wooden chairs circled plain tables with washed-out checked tablecloths. It was the middle of the afternoon and a desultory few customers were enjoying the rare treat of a Kunzle cake. Her shadow went before her down the steps, and Josh saw her coming. He stood and seized her elbows, crushing them into her body, almost squeezing the breath out of her. His body seemed to have caved in, his stoop become a hunch, his manliness driven out.

'Thank God you're here. Thank God.'

'Yes, Josh, I'm here.' They sat quietly, each searching the other's eyes for contact, reassurance. It wasn't quite there. Instead their memories, their love, glanced between them, caught and evaded, confused, unsure. Needful, always needful.

'Oh, Josh, I'm so, so sorry. I am truly.'

'I knew you would be. I trusted you to understand.' He had no smile for her, just gaunt deep eyes searching hers.

'Is there any information . . . any detail?' She had hesitated before each word, seeking what would give him most comfort, almost enraptured by the depth of his grief. He shook his head hard and suddenly, she suspected to hold off tears.

'No, nothing. Yet. His mother, Jessica, is . . . well, ill with it. She's collapsed . . . gone to pieces.'

'How terrible . . .' It was, of course, in many ways.

'Yes, she's been hysterical since she heard. Her flatmate, Babs, is with her now. I can't stay long. We think she may need the doctor.'

'He might give her something to calm her down.' And then, as the reality dawned, 'But perhaps such loss is inconsolable.'

He hadn't heard her. He was clinging to her hands but listening only to himself. 'He was a great man, you know, my boy. One of the best.'

'I'm sure he was. I would have liked to meet him.'

'Oh, you'd have got on so well. He'd have liked you. Adored his mother, you know. Adored her.' Another brisk shake of the head. 'I don't know how we're going to cope.'

Cynthia waited for him to make clear what he meant.

'She's not going to get over this. She's always been a bit, well, unstable. She . . .' He paused, looking hard into Cynthia's eyes. 'She needs me, Cynthia, for a while at least.'

It was the wrench of his pain she felt, not her own. And it was to his pain that she responded. She clutched his hands. 'Of course she does, Josh, of course she does. I can see that. I understand.' Her own concerns must wait, at least for a little while.

And for the first time he smiled, and reached out to stroke her cheek. 'I was hoping you would. Thank you.'

Had she said more than she meant? Had she hinted at some compliance she didn't feel? She felt something had been concluded without her full consent. 'Er . . . yes. You must take care of her. She deserves it.' Suddenly she was talking nonsense fast, in panic. 'Please give her my sympathy, and look after her. Look after both of yourselves. We've had a great day at the ship. Robert has been an excellent guide. I think he's going to marry Polly. Did you know that? No, of course not. How could you? You've been at sea. There's lots you don't know. You'll be sailing soon, won't you? How quickly the time passes. So . . . take care of yourself. Let me know, won't you, when there's more news? Of Peter, I mean. Be in touch when you can . . .' She was gabbling now and rising from her seat.

'Cynthia, thank you for being so understanding, thank you . . .' She fled the Kardomah café without any more being said.

Josh watched her go, wondering what had happened.

Mrs Murgatroyd convened the meeting. She was seriously concerned. It was certainly important to set aside differences and local enmities for the sake of victory. And it would need all their efforts to restore the country to the way it had been before it was so disrupted. But she saw now that she had been naïve. She had been blind to what others were planning, which might well subvert the things she held precious.

There were public warnings everywhere about spies and loose talk costing lives. At first she had imagined Germans in disguise skulking down alleys and wheedling their way slyly into Churchill's bunker and Derby House. But now she had heard men she trusted talk about people who wanted to change this society from within, who were working to bring about a socialist state, to go the way Russia had gone. Her son-in-law, the editor Jocelyn Frobisher, had hinted, over the Sunday roast, of one person he knew who had created a network of contacts who might or might not be plotting together. And wasn't she, his own mother-in-law, in some way responsible? After all, she was a governor of the very school where this might be happening. The gravy had congealed on the Yorkshire pudding as she defended Ashworth Grammar School. But afterwards she began to think.

Even on a sunny June evening the driveway to her home was shadowy, the bulk of the great laurel bushes casting a sinister green light. Frank Pierce, who had sown her first suspicions, was always flattered by an invitation and snaked his way up the front doorsteps eager to do her bidding. The chairman of the governors, Councillor Desmond, was less delighted. He resented having to dance attendance on this bossy, bulky woman. But his seat on the council would be challenged one day, and Mrs Murgatroyd's influence made her valuable to his campaign. He donned his bowler and took the Hillman Minx out of the garage, using precious petrol for a rare trip to the long avenue of Victorian villas.

'My son-in-law, Mr Frobisher of the *Staveley Gazette*, thinks we should be aware of what is going on among the sixth-formers of Ashworth Grammar School. It seems that under cover of some sort of society, the headmistress is promoting undesirable ideas. Frank, here, experienced a fierce encounter with some of the members. I myself arrived unexpectedly one day to find a sailor – not of the Royal Navy, I should say – enjoying the privacy of the headmistress's study. I had seen him somewhere before in, I seem to recall, most unfavourable circumstances. And now I hear that a member of the Co-operative Movement has been given a free rein to spread socialist ideas among the impressionable girls. I think we should ask ourselves whether Miss Maitland is less patriotic than she should be, not working in the interests of the country as we see them.'

'Er, well, I've always thought Cynthia Maitland was a real live wire.' Councillor Desmond had a soft spot for Miss Maitland. He took out a folded linen handkerchief from his top pocket, shook it open and wiped the sweat from his shining bald head. He knew that Old Murgs, as he referred to her behind her back, was inclined to bouts of self-righteousness. 'I think the parents like her, the staff, too. As for socialist ideas, well, Russia is one of our two great allies. Remember earlier this year, our celebrations for Stalingrad Day? It's natural to discuss such things,' he caught a scowl gathering on the formidable brow, and added hastily, 'within limits, of course.'

'I've been to the school in question. I've suffered at their hands. I found them less than courteous, I can tell you. Downright rude.' Frank Pierce was fluent in exaggeration.

'But I thought we were here to discuss more important matters than courtesy. I thought it was serious.' Councillor Desmond was cross that he'd been dragged from the BBC's *Monday Night at Eight o'Clock* to discuss the manners of schoolgirls. 'Mrs Murgatroyd, you seem to think something more dangerous is going on. Of course we have to be watchful, you're quite right about that. Quite right.' A fulsome smile disarmed Old Murgs. 'But we should be wary of seeing subversion where none exists.'

'Quite, Councillor. Which means we should be watching what Miss Maitland gets up to with particular attention. Keep a close eye on her. I'm glad you agree.' And, feeling she had carried the day, she rewarded them with some of her home-made dandelion wine.

Knowing

Certain things were clear and all of them were terrible. Cynthia left the Kardomah café up the Dock Road scarcely seeing the world around her. She walked slowly, hugging her handbag, her arms round her body for comfort. Going nowhere, glad to be in a city where she wouldn't be recognized. She needed anonymity. She seemed to be facing all sorts of tragedies at once and she needed to be rational and sensible when she felt panic and distress. She kept walking until her shoes began to pinch and rub in the heat, and the sweat made the flimsy floral frock cling to her armpits.

She reached an old bench that had somehow survived the bombing and the collectors of salvage. The green paint on its wooden seat was blistered and peeling. She lowered herself gently as though taking care of herself. Someone had to. In the heat, with the waters of the Mersey dancing blue towards the sea, she was overcome by a delicious lethargy. It was possible to think that someone in her situation – a young girl, perhaps, desperate

272

and alone – might sit here and consider how enticing the deep, forgiving waters of the river looked, and how peaceful it would be to fold into their depths, all cares washed away for good. Cynthia thought of such a person thinking such thoughts, and knew it was not her.

So what was to be done? Slowly she gathered her thoughts, watching, without seeing, the ferries come and go across the river, and the regular traffic of cargo ships putting to sea. She had fallen in love and she was having a baby. When she had realized she was pregnant, she had believed that Josh would somehow deal with it, with their problem. But he was gone now. His concerns were elsewhere and burden enough. She shuddered at the thought of telling her mother and felt cold, despite the afternoon warmth. She dragged a green cardigan out of her bag and buttoned it to the neck. Time to leave the blue moment of calm.

She caught the train back to Manchester and booked herself into the Melville Hotel.

It had been awkward at first. Josh had always signed the hotel register for them both while she stood in the shadows. What name had he used? She knew it wouldn't be his or hers. But the girl behind the desk, biting her nails, recognized Cynthia and hailed her at once by name, 'Ooh, Mrs Jones! It's nice to see you back again.' She had turned to the hotel's board of keys and fetched the one to their regular room. Cynthia was too grateful for the gesture of friendship to wonder what staff gossip had made of their visits. With an unnerving steadiness she climbed the stairs, marvelling to recall the exhilaration of earlier times spent there. She entered the spare bleak room and threw herself on to the bed, kicking off her hot shoes and undoing her clinging dress. The air was dense with dust: the frail curtains let in enough light for her to see the specks dancing in the dim beams. It had been cold when they had been here together. Now she was stifling with summer heat and with worry.

She didn't sleep: she lay naked on her back below a single threadbare sheet, feeling like a body on the slab in a morgue, a life over, waiting for whatever was to happen next. Her hand roved her body, her still-flat stomach.

In the night she got up and peered into the blacked-out night. There was a war going on, a war still to be won. People were fighting and dying. And her own life hung, confused and messy. She went back to the tousled bed, and a troubled half-sleep.

She woke in a sweat, trembling. She had many things to decide.

At seven o'clock she pulled on the dishevelled dress and the painful shoes, waved an almost cheery goodbye to the receptionist and caught the bus back to Staveley. Within two hours she was in her study, in neat navy linen, running the school. She called Grace in and delegated to her the appointments she had in the school diary. She explained she was feeling a little queasy, as indeed she was, a malady that Grace attributed to the excitement of the visit to the ship. Then Cynthia telephoned Councillor Desmond, the chairman of the school governors, and made an appointment to see him the following afternoon.

In the morning Councillor Desmond had folded a crisp linen handkerchief in the top pocket of his smartest suit.

The lively, relatively young headmistress had the safe attraction of a woman in authority, elegant but unapproachable, agreeable but not familiar. It would give him the chance to reassure her that Mrs Murgatroyd's vendetta would get no further.

'I regret that what I have to say will come as a shock to you, Councillor.'

He had scarcely had time to offer her a chair in the small dark room from which he conducted the affairs of his factory, which was currently engaged in making small parts for tanks. Through the walls was heard the steady hum of machinery and the occasional gruff call from man to man. His assistant, Mrs Shorrocks, brought in a cup of bright orange tea already dosed with two spoonfuls of sugar. Scarcity made the gesture a generous one. 'Thank you, that's very kind.'

Cynthia wasted no time in coming to the point. She knew that what came from her mouth would make it an irreversible fact, so if she once got the words out, the rest would follow. 'I have come to tell you that I shall be tendering my resignation from the school to take effect at the end of this term.' There, it was done. Her life's work sealed and set aside. She felt giddy with the impact, and took a welcome gulp of the over-sweet tea.

'Oh, Miss Maitland – Cynthia, if I may?'

She nodded above the rim of the cup.

'I can't believe it, I really can't. You are the pride of the school and its governing body.' At this point a wrinkle of doubt crept in, as the seed Old Murgs had planted sent out a tiny shoot. 'Is there anything else, some other part of the war effort, to which you are committed in any way?'

'I feel I have achieved a good deal at Ashworth Grammar School, and I have learned a great deal there myself. So, it is time for us both if I go elsewhere to continue my work.'

He took out the linen handkerchief and mopped his head, searching for a way to keep her at her post. 'I believe that sometimes professors at top universities take something called a sabbatical, leave of absence for a year, to refresh their ideas. The governors might consider such an arrangement, if you wanted to stay.' Even as he said it, he knew Old Murgs would block the idea, but he felt concern for this enigmatic and beautiful woman. Though perhaps she was a spy, after all. One of ours, of course. Come to think of it, hadn't someone seen her scurrying into a rather scruffy hotel, the Melville, at the back of the railway station in a rather dubious part of Manchester? That might explain it.

Cynthia paused. Was this a compromise, a way out, promising a possible return to the school? But she was in resolute mood. No compromise. Everything about her life was changed utterly and that was how it must be lived. There would be no clinging to vain hopes, lame attempts to salvage whatever might survive. She was a woman alone, a woman who had chosen love and did not regret it. Of that she was proud. She had not made the same mistake twice. The long years of her lonely life without Brian had, she saw now, been haunted by withering self-denial. It had made her a formidable headmistress, capable and respected. She had deflected her generosity of spirit towards her girls, seeing in them the hopes she had denied herself. But now she was more completely her own woman. Loving Josh had taught her that. She would bear their child and bring it up on her own. It would be difficult but she would move away: she knew that that was what happened to luckless girls, saving their parents the shame and humiliation. If this was the price of love, so be it. Perhaps Maud would help her.

'No, thank you so much for the thought, Councillor, but I'm thinking of making a complete break. I would like to start something new. Something I can't yet disclose.'

Ah, yes, he thought. That's it. Secret war work. Several brighter spirits he knew had been 'seconded' to mysterious exploits, no questions asked. Good for them. And good for her. Cynthia was one of the chosen. If the time ever came and if she asked, he would write her a brilliant reference.

The SS *Tremullion* sailed in mid-June on a day of blazing sun, glittering water and bright blue sky. It was the best that a day on board could be. But with him Josh took the cargo of his loss: thoughts of Peter weighed on his heart. So, too, did memories of his second mate, Tim, who would usually be enlivening the bridge and the saloon with his argumentative chatter. His replacement, a taciturn Geordie, was the exact opposite. Now his only friend was Robert, his other surrogate son. Their friendship flowered easily in the hard days. There was time at sea, now U-boat attacks were fewer, to enjoy small delights: a school of playing dolphins, the seamen entertaining them on the harmonica and a squeeze-box, uncomplicated pleasures that brought easy smiles when he was in their company. Back in his cabin, the sorrow returned.

He had taken Jessica to her parents in Surrey. Even as she had struggled to carry on, the yawning purpose-lessness of life without her son had capsized her. She was found crying in corners; she was suddenly and often impatient with her staff; she had thrown things around the flat when Babs had been tactlessly cheerful. Finally she had crawled into her leather chair, curled up in an ungainly ball and stayed there sucking an old linen hankie. The doctor's sedatives were not enough. Derby House had allowed her generous compassionate leave.

At home, she had been reluctant to let go of Josh, hang-ing on to his arm as he passed her into the care of her worried parents. Yes, he would be back. Yes, he prom-ised. No, he wouldn't leave her. The words echoed in his head on the train to Liverpool, and he knew they sealed his future. One day, perhaps, he told himself, he would search out Cynthia again, and be with her somehow. But he made no plans.

Cynthia accompanied her mother to evensong. It wasn't a special Sunday so the congregation smiled with sur-prise to see her there. She must be joining them, planning to come regularly. They welcomed her into the fold.

It was an uneasy tactic. She had decided to appeal to her mother's Christian feelings and seek at least some calm and contemplative moment to break the news. She had no idea how far devout ideas or considerations of the Christian life entered into her mother's thinking. They had never spoken of the sublime. Even at her father's death they had mentioned only how much he would be missed, quickly followed by concerns as to who would now fetch in the coal and wind the clocks.

They returned in the light evening air, admired briefly the growing vegetables that now replaced the garden lawn – they could expect some good-sized onions and a fine crop of runner beans – and went inside to make the nightly Ovaltine. Cynthia stood over the pan as the milk rose to the boil and steeled herself for what was to come.

'Mother, there's something I need to tell you.'

Her mother tipped some of the hot drink into her saucer and blew on it to cool it.

'It's serious, and I want you to consider before you . . . well, before you react.'

'What is it, Cynthia? Are you ill?'

'No, not ill, Mother . . . not actually ill. Though I do sometimes feel a little off-colour. You see . . .' She paused. A moment hence and all would be different. 'I'm expecting a baby.'

The reaction was slow in coming. Her mother set the cup on the now empty saucer and stared at her with cold eyes. 'What did I hear you say?'

'I'm expecting a baby. I'm pregnant.'

'Don't use that word. Don't say such things. Are you mad? Have you lost your senses?'

'No, I haven't. I'm expecting a baby.'

'Don't repeat it. I don't want to hear – I don't want to hear, I say.'

'You need to hear, Mother.' A long and ominous pause. 'I would like your sympathy . . .' The hope died on the instant.

'You? Having a baby? I can't believe my ears.'

'It's true. I'm sorry, but I am.'

'My sympathy? You slut, you! You talk of sympathy! You dare talk of sympathy? Get out of my house! Get out of this house now, I tell you.'

'No, Mother.' Cynthia marvelled at how, in a crisis, people reverted to the stock responses of Victorian melodrama. It was what happened. She and Maud had talked together of what might be said, and Beryl was running true to form. 'No, Mother, this is my home too. I need you to understand and help.'

'You don't belong here, you cheap rubbish, you. This has always been a good home, and now you dirty it with your sinful ways.' And then, her eyes widening in wonder, 'What have I done to deserve this? Tell me! What has brought this shame on us? What did your father and I do wrong?' Her rheumy eyes brimmed and ghastly tears splashed on to the cable stitching of her cardigan. 'Oh, it's not true. It can't be true.'

'I don't suppose you want to hear this but I'm in love with someone who loves me—'

'Quite right I don't want to hear it. I don't want to know, whoever he is.'

They sat in silence among the debris of their lives. 'You can't stay here, Cynthia. That's for certain. How could I ever hold up my head again?'

'I appreciate you feel I will damage your reputation.'

'You certainly will, my girl. You selfish child! Did you ever think what they'd say at the church? And you have standing in the community! What will people think? What will they say?'

'I don't intend to tell them, Mother.' Perhaps if she called her 'Mother' often enough it might remind her to be kind. 'Perhaps you won't want to, either.'

'Don't play games with me, you hussy. Don't tell me what to do, who to speak to. I shall decide that. I shall have to—' Tears became loud sobs. 'I thank God your father isn't alive to know about this. What would he say? He's well out of it. If he'd been alive the shock would have killed him – it would have *killed* him.'

Cynthia bowed her head. This was almost a blow too far. Her memory of her father was dear. She numbered him among the few men she had truly loved. She resented her mother for involving him. 'Well, he *is* dead, isn't he? So that's one thing we don't have to worry about. He's dead, and I'm alive and pregnant. We're in the middle of a war, with people being killed all over the place. This is an episode in our lives that counts for little outside. Yes, I'm sorry it's happening. But we need to talk about what to do. It will not destroy your life. I'm certainly not going to let it destroy mine.'

'Oh, my God, my God! Listen to her!' Her mother had become pathetically dependent once again. Her hand rested dramatically on her heaving breast. 'How can you be so cruel? Look what you're doing.' She gasped for breath. 'Fetch me the *sal-volatile*. It's in the bathroom cupboard.'

Cynthia took her time in walking upstairs to the bathroom. She felt weary that her mother had so deftly turned the attention to herself. Certainly this was a raw world. Coming back downstairs she paused in the hall and dialled a number on the black telephone. 'Maud, I've done it. I've told her.'

'Attagirl. Feel better for it?'

'Not yet. But I will.'

On the morning that she would make the announcement, Cynthia took care with her appearance. She had a secret to conceal, and much as she chose to ignore what was happening to her body, she knew she must dress to cover its changes. She had bought a stout corset, made in a garish pink silk mottled with flowers, stiffened with whalebone from loin to waist, and fastened with small metal hooks. Without too much strain she could keep the appearance of her torso as it had always been. She would have to bear the discomfort. Later in her pregnancy she would, perhaps, as others did, keep out of the public eye or, if she had to go out, conceal the embarrassing bulk under voluminous flowing clothes. But that was later, and she gave no thought to later.

She took the platform for morning assembly with a deliberate sense of occasion. The school moved with assured good spirits towards the climax of the school year. The sixth form had nearly finished their exams. Polly, as head girl, was organizing the tennis tournament between the school's six houses. Brenda Alsop had declared herself official liaison with the staffroom over the end-of-term sports day, and Jen was making plans to spend the summer with a family who had escaped to Britain from France and would help her improve her French.

'This morning I have something important to tell you.

I have decided that I have now fulfilled many of the hopes I had for this school and that it is time for me to leave. I have therefore tendered my resignation to the governing body and will be leaving the Ashworth Grammar School for Girls at the end of this term.'

The news brought a gasp across the hall. Her face gave nothing away. Indeed she felt the tension and excitement of concealment. Was this how spies felt, creating one impression while knowing that something quite other was the truth? Maud had urged her to think like a spy in foreign territory, and she was feeling almost a defiant glee. She wanted to make the days of her leaving as rich, warm and happy as she could. She spoke without solemnity, knowing that it was for her a solemn occasion. It gave edge and immediacy to her words.

'Many things are in flux during a war, and it is a time when other opportunities open up. I hope very much to find one that suits the next stage of my life.'

At this point Brenda Alsop nudged the girl next to her and silently mouthed, 'Spy!'

'In my last weeks here I hope to have the chance to say a personal goodbye to each of you. I love this school and all it stands for. I think together we have made it a strong and true community, where people care for each other and learn how to serve our country. I'm proud of each one of you. I believe you share the principles of honesty and integrity that are so dear to me and all other members of the staff. This terrible war has put a great strain on all our lives. Some of you have lost those you love, others have suffered separation from fathers and brothers, seen sisters take up war work and mothers struggle to keep families cheerful and steady. I, too, have shared some of these experiences and I feel it brings us closer together. These are years I shall never forget.' Cynthia took a little breath, then steadied herself to go on.

'But ahead of us there is the rest of the term to enjoy. Let's make the most of it. We'll have a rousing sports day, an important speech day and go our separate ways, rejoicing.' Her Biblical phrasing caught Cynthia by surprise, but on reflection she felt it expressed the upbeat spirit of her departure. Her private regrets were another matter and not something she wanted to inflict on her girls. Or anyone else, for that matter.

Back in their classrooms there was a buzz of speculation.

'She loves the ship – she's probably going to join the Wrens.'

'I think she's going to do secret war work. She's been seen around the Melville Hotel. It's a dump. Why else would she go there?'

'Yes, but she's been visiting Maud Sheridan, too, and she's a conchie. Perhaps she's going to be an artist.'

'I think she'll be a nun – all that about going her way rejoicing.'

'A nun? Don't be daft. She wants us to win the war. She'll be doing something to help, I'm sure of that.'

'But it'll be secret, you can bet. I agree with . . . She'll probably be on a secret mission. All those people who came to the Tea Club, they were probably her secret contacts.'

'And Mrs Murgatroyd didn't like it, did she? She's probably on the side of Germany. Yes, it's all beginning to make sense.'

With delight in their own mysteries they slowly got back to lessons.

Beryl's conversation with her daughter had been terse and practical since Cynthia had broken the news. She had been reading about such events in romantic novels for years. The words of outrage she had used had come to her from their pages, and confirmed her sense of right-ness. But both had been shocked by their vehemence. And there were consequences to such conversations, and books were no help with those. Beryl wrapped herself in a large crocheted shawl and sat, with a dish of mint impe-rials, to consider what she should do.

Briefly, and only as the sweets were running low, she allowed herself to speculate on who had got her daugh-ter into trouble. There were no men at the school, apart from the caretaker, but there were some important ones among the governors. There were people in the town Cynthia met and talked to, people of standing, heads of libraries and other schools, managers of large shops, even owners of the town's several factories. They all crossed her path and were, no doubt, impressed by her looks and demeanour. There was this business of the school adopting a ship, but it was a merchant ship, and the crew must be pretty rough. Besides, they were at sea most of the time. No, Cynthia had been seduced by some grandee impressed by her style and position. The thought made her feel a little better. She would go and see the vicar.

Mr Potter was used to keeping lady parishioners such as Mrs Maitland at arm's length. He ushered her into the shadowy chill of his study, a room padded with an array of books serious enough, she thought, to minister to her own dilemma. Her eyes lowered, she spoke quietly, just loudly enough for the books to hear. Mr Potter's eyes widened at the unexpected tale. Her voice broke as she talked of her own disappointment and failure, and he reached across the desk to take her hand, and reassure her that her own soul was not touched by her daughter's sins.

Finally he got down to practical matters. 'There are ways that the Church can help, Mrs Maitland. If you put yourselves in our hands we can bring the comfort of Christian charity to bear on such a distressing situation. We have places set up especially to deal with such unhappy events. You'd be surprised how often they crop up. The war is making things worse.'

Beryl balked at her daughter's fall being lumped in with the waywardness of shop girls and factory workers. She bit her lip.

'I can put Cynthia in touch with someone, if you would like that. There's a place in North Wales I can recommend. But there are, of course, conditions. She must acknowledge her error and agree to the solution they offer.'

'Oh, that's the least she can do. We agree to all the conditions. I'm sure she'll feel grateful. Thank you, Reverend, thank you so much.' And Beryl went home feeling the bedrock of the Church, the certainty of its precepts, the breadth of its understanding, all being brought to bear on her personal suffering.

Josh and Robert seized the respite of New York like starving men falling on a heap of food. In late June, the

SS *Tremullion* had delivered a load of coal to Halifax, then come south to pick up foodstuffs, copra, even tanks and cased aircraft. Soon they would be joining a convoy home. Time off in New York was like stepping through a veil of fog into a dream of lights and people. They ambled down the long, bright streets, feeling they deserved some fun. It was great to free-wheel. Was this what the land called Peacetime might be like when they got there?

February's appalling storms had kept the damage to the convoys low, but March had been a ferocious month for attacks and losses. Then, slowly, through April, the pattern of the war had begun to change: the radio officer was getting better information; there were more aircraft; the midway gap was narrowing. Admiral Doenitz was losing the initiative.

Josh and Robert had taken themselves to the Stage Door Canteen, a place teeming with life and laughter. They had tried the British Merchant Navy Officers' Club and found it polite and efficient, but it was not what they needed. Word was that the Stage Door welcomed all services. It was the famous one. They were even making a film about it in another part of the city, with stars and glamour. But after the drab austerity of home all Josh and Robert wanted was a warm welcome, food, drink and company. It was crowded, noisy and dense with smoke. When they emerged in the early hours of a July morning, the city was full of dust and heat, and they were full of bourbon.

'Oh, Robert, this is the life. For a moment or two, at least.'

'Yes, sir, it certainly is. It takes your mind off things.'

'A whole host of things . . . yes.' The phrase hung in the air.

Robert let images of Polly drift across his mind. A future with her was waiting for him, after this lot was over.

Josh had fleeting thoughts of the sobbing Jessica pressing towards him, while the pale beauty of Cynthia floated away. He shook his head, thrusting them both from him. Much of the time he felt closer to his crew, officers and men, than to any woman. They must wait while the war was won. He reached out his arm to Robert, relishing the unsteadiness of the drink, the dipping and swaying of the tall buildings. Robert – like the son he'd lost. He loved Robert. He could tell him things. They tottered happily back to the docks, singing 'An' will ye no' come back again', Josh forgetting at last whatever it was he had to worry about.

'Adoption. That's the condition of the Church's help. I have to have the baby adopted.' Cynthia sat glumly in Maud's only chair. Just beyond her sandalled feet two long windows opened on to an untidy cottage garden, as tousled and colourful as the indoor paintings. A petal or two had drifted on to the bare studio floor and Cynthia kicked at them casually, noticing her ankles had swollen. 'He was very nice about it, the vicar, almost gleeful to have such a full-scale sinner on his hands.'

'Well, where would they be without the likes of us sinners, eh?' Maud gave a deep, throaty laugh that owed a good deal to her heavy smoking.

'Oh, we mustn't joke about it, Maud. My mother's so upset, she's almost ill. She believes she's to blame, that all her church-going and flower-arranging haven't been enough to keep sin from our door. I do believe she wanted me out of the way at once. As it is, I've managed to hold on until now. It's terrible what shame does to you, isn't it? She feels socially crippled by it. She almost dreads going to church now. The vicar comes round to see her instead. At least that stops her crying, and keeps her busy making butterfly buns for his tea.' A quick smile came and went.

Maud handed her a cup of tea, still without milk. She felt for Cynthia's misery, but almost as a formality. After all, Cynthia was part of that official world, a head-mistress, a top person in the town. Had she not, as such, tacitly agreed to abide by its rules? There could be no surprise at her mother's anger when she broke them. What else could you expect? What touched Maud was Cynthia's love affair. There was beauty in that. Maud had even sketched the languorous shape of her friend's body, loosed and free.

'How much do you actually want this baby, Cynthia? Are you really being honest with yourself?'

'I don't know . . . I can't imagine it at all. I know I have to try.'

'And how honest . . .' this was an unfinished earlier conversation '. . . how honest have you been with the father?'

Cynthia stared into the cup, hoping to gather her strength. Instead her shoulders shook, and the grief leaked out.

'He doesn't know . . . I couldn't tell him.' She looked up into Maud's appalled face. 'I met him, meaning to tell, honestly I did, but his son is missing at sea. The Royal Navy. They're distraught, both parents. How could I . . . well, I tried, but I just couldn't.'

'You mean you're five months' pregnant and the father doesn't know?'

'He's at sea again now. There's a war on. What else could I do?' Cynthia was shouting now, angry with Maud, angry with herself, angry with Josh. 'This goddamned awful war. You can't meet, you can't write, you can't talk. We're reduced to automatons – obey or be punished. There's no spontaneity any more. And when there is, look what happens.' The tears came fiercely.

Maud handed her a paint rag.

'I wanted to tell him – I want to tell him now – but sometimes it seems like a dream. It's drifting away from me – I'm having to clutch at a few happy memories, while the world condemns me.'

Maud poured her a small glass of brandy. 'Come on, girl. You're made of sterner stuff than this. Women are the stronger sex, you know. We can see this through.'

'Adoption! My baby – our baby – to be adopted! Must I? Is that what must happen?' An ugly wail filled the room.

Maud waited in silence, then spoke. 'I think you have to accept it. It's the only help you can get.'

Cynthia sipped the brandy. She looked out at the green garden. A long sigh. 'I suppose so.'

Maud waited, then said what Cynthia was thinking: 'I don't think you could cope if you went ahead and kept it.

Just be practical for a moment. Think of the problems. Finding somewhere to live – an unmarried woman with a bastard child, not easy. Then working and caring for a child at the same time. No woman can do that without neighbours and a mother to help out. I don't see that happening, do you?' Silence again. The garden, the petals, the friendship.

'The churches arrange these things. They have places to go . . . You'll be taken care of.'

Then Cynthia spoke, in a quiet, thoughtful voice. 'I suppose you're right. I accept that.'

Maud saw her out, pausing at the studio door to make Cynthia the gift of a small bright watercolour, one of her best, one she was proud of.

'I hope you'll write. Please write to me, Maud.'

The girls took their leave of the school. Sad goodbyes, promises to stay in touch, sudden affection for previously neglected teachers, excitement and confusion about the future. Satchels filled with fountain pens, blotters, the library book not returned, an old pair of plimsolls, a clutch of addresses written on scraps of paper. Then out through the gates, shouting farewells into the hopeful summer air, they went into their future. Melanie Grout, who had read 'Cargoes' to the captain, Enid Carter who had fallen from the horse in the gym, Madge Prendergast, Muriel Grainger, Elsie Dawson, who loved Beethoven and Goethe, Brenda Alsop, who hated so hard, Jen Wainwright, who had lost her love and Polly, who had found hers. Off they trooped and the teachers turned with faint sadness to prepare for next term's intake. It seemed an eternal cycle, year round, of young lives coming and going.

Cynthia left too. Grace, shocked by her departure, helped pack away the books from the shelves in the oak-lined study: the lacquer tray that held the three fountain pens, the cigarette box, the paperweight. Cynthia folded them away with the Indian rug and the run of bright silk cushions from the small sofa where the Tea Club's guests had been alternately nervous and forthright. Finally she retrieved from the drawer the old sepia photograph in its silver frame. It had no meaning in her life now, but she could hardly leave it behind. Grace phoned Reg, who ran a taxi out of Staveley station, and Cynthia drove away from her past without looking back. She held in her lap a small silver dish – a present from the sixth-formers.

Within weeks two things would happen of which she was unaware. Josh, back in Liverpool, would ring her home and, getting no reply, come to the house: Robert had procured the address from Polly. He would pause at the door, scuffing his shoes fretfully, running his hand through his wiry grey hair, then ring the brass bell, notic-ing its tarnish and the disarray of the front garden. Slowly he would hear the slap-slap of slippers slithering towards the door, see it open a crack to reveal a long, sad face under a nest of white hair. Pale, watery eyes weighed him up. 'Excuse me. Is this the home of Cynthia Maitland?'

A voice, more forceful than the frailty of its owner sug-gested, coughed out a reply: 'I don't know who you are. Nor do I want to know. But it is certainly not her home.' And the door slammed.

Later that month there would be another ring of the same bell, newly polished. This time it was expected, and Beryl had on her silk afternoon dress and a white pinafore: she would be serving tea. At the door, George Potter, eager and officious, was about to complete his intervention in the lives of this fallen household. With him he had a young woman, neat and nervous. Someone from church, devout and disciplined.

Discovering

2003

'The cards are to you – they were sent to you!'

'How can you know that? There's no name.'

'Yes there is – on the baptism card. You must have missed it.'

'Really?'

'So that means all the cards are to you. How weird is that?'

'Not all that weird. Mothers do keep mementoes of children. I had one for you once, a pink book full of bows and rabbits.'

'Ugh! Ma, that's not you at all!'

'I think it must have been my hormones going crazy and affecting my judgement.'

'Where is it now . . . this pink job?'

'Pa threw it out . . . said bad taste would have no place in your life. He never liked it when you got that tattoo.'

'He never said.'

'He was like that.' They exchange smiles for the much-loved dead. 'So who sent these cards? And why was I baptized in Llangollen? And all those so-called god-parents, who are they? I've never heard of any of them.'

'Gran must have known, mustn't she, to have kept them all these years?'

Millie decides to find out. She takes the train to Chester and hires a car. She drives slowly, winding her way out of the tight little city and steering by the distant Welsh hills. But the motorway is like any other. She's enclosed within the car and within her own thoughts. She wants to shake them loose, think new things. She opens the windows to let the brisk mountain air refresh her, but the speed of the car defeats her.

She parks briefly at a small service station and considers taking a walk, finding some random path and heading off across a field for an hour or so. But what path, what field? And what would she, a stray motorist on a strange quest, make of what she found there?

She is heading for Llangollen. The old black-and-white map with the two red marks lies on the passenger seat beside her and a moleskin notebook is in her bag. She is idling along the way, avoiding getting there too soon. She is curious, eager to unravel her mother's conundrum, but not just yet.

She drives into Llangollen around midday and turns left across the old bridge into the bustling little street at the heart of the town. A recent shower has left the roads shining and driven people into the scattering of cafés. A small museum huddles in a side-street. A former church, now an information centre, displays local artists' work. Millie decides to walk, taking her time. She is beginning to feel good about being here. She has a connection with the town and will seek it out.

The postcard shops are full of the Ladies of Llangollen: two friends who lived together long ago in a house they beautified with strange wooden carvings. They were either eccentric or forced to be so by nosy townsfolk. Millie feels a sense of fellowship with them, living on their own terms, by their own rules. She admires that. She admires their low-built home, too, overrun with fantastical carvings.

It is somewhere along this road that the cross appears on her map. She asks the woman taking the tickets at Plas Newydd the whereabouts of St Martin's Church, and is directed further up the road to where it runs into the lush countryside.

'Very quiet it is, these days. Not so busy as it was.' The church is there, closed and bleak, and beside it a small modern bungalow with 'Vicarage' in black wrought iron on a white picket gate. But the second cross on the map indicates the building next to it. Two Victorian villas have been clumsily knocked together with plasterboard, badly matching red brick and a PVC window or two. A damaged door is held on by a single rusty hinge over pale blue paint.

There is no one around. The whole thing is boarded up with planks nailed across windows, and a rotting rope, intended to keep people out, lies in the mud of the neglected garden. There are the remnants of an old noticeboard, warped and curled, traces of old paint and lettering beyond reading, but making an attractive pattern on the surface. She takes out her digital camera and snaps, then goes back to record the doors and windows, though she's not sure why.

The Reverend Silas Jenkins is not at home, but his wife – she introduces herself as such – says he won't be long, and would Millie like to come in. She crosses the front step of the vicarage into a cloud of household smells – the density almost makes her gag: washing being boiled, onions being cooked, the singeing smell of a hot iron, the tang of furniture polish. The smells bustle for her attention as the round, smiling woman escorts her to the front room, set aside, it is obvious, for parishioners and their problems. Here, household smells are dissipated by a large bowl of pot-pourri, giving off its own chemical fumes. Millie coughs and takes out a handkerchief.

'Would you be liking a cup of coffee while you await him? I hope he won't be long as his dinner's on.'

The coffee has almost no taste, so overwhelming is the assault from the air. There is a digestive biscuit, half soggy from the spill in the saucer. It is comforting, and the welcome is genuine. Millie feels safe. She sips the pale, tepid liquid, grateful that some things haven't changed.

What Mr Jenkins tells her will make her glad that many things have.

He comes bumbling in, carrying a tattered briefcase, rimless spectacles on the tip of his nose, and bright red cheeks, indicating either haste or good humour, possibly both. He dumps his wobbly bulk in the opposite arm-chair and asks what he can do for Millie.

She takes a deep breath and explains about the map, the cross, her walk along the road, her scramble round the derelict building. 'I hope your wife will excuse my mud on the carpet.' She has picked up the habit of conciliation. Finally she tells him of her mother's legacy of papers and mystery and, lulled by his kindness, discloses more of her family background.

'Mother was a keen churchgoer, you see, but rather strict with me. Too strict, in fact. When I was at university, well, I . . . er . . .'

'You lost your faith. Of course you did! Everyone does. I did so myself. It's quite common. The thing is, has it come back? Mine did, even stronger than before. But don't worry. The Church doesn't go in for blame, these days. Thank God. Quite literally, thank God,' and he shot a glance towards the ceiling and made a little pyramid of prayer with his hands.

Soon Millie's old half-inch-to-the-mile map is spread, for want of any table space, across the floor. She is aware of a vague stickiness on the carpet, either from its synthetic texture or an archipelago of ancient spills. On all fours the two scramble around tracing where, Millie believes, the two crosses mark the church and the derelict building she has just visited. 'What did that place use to be?'

'Oh, it's been empty some twenty years now, but for many years before then it was used as a hostel of some sort. The property belongs to the Church.'

'But back in the nineteen forties, what was it then?'

'As I said, it belonged to the Church. Not to this particular church, but to the diocese, answering, of course, to the authorities of the Church of Wales. It was a place called the Cradle of Hope. They don't have such places nowadays. No call for them.'

'And what was the call for them then? Do you know?'

'Oh, yes, of course. I know all right.' He is petulant at her suggestion of ignorance and bits of him wobble in protest. 'Of course I know. I may not have been here at the time, my dear lady, but everyone round here knows.'

He fumbles with his tattered briefcase, plucking from it papers he doesn't read, rearranging them, then putting them back. He is not looking at Millie.

'The Cradle of Hope was what it suggests – a place where children were born and cared for, and found good Christian parents to adopt them. The Church was active in that field, you know, very active.'

'And their mothers? You don't mention their mothers.'

'Well, they were glad of somewhere to come, usually through a family connection. They knew their babies would be given to good homes. Lucky for them, with the alternatives . . .'

'What alternatives did they have?'

'Well, I don't know exactly. But having an . . . er, illegitimate child was reprehensible in those days. People wanted it hushed up.'

There is silence in the room. Millie can hear kitchen sounds in the distance and the heavy chime of a large grandfather clock in the hallway.

'But what did the mothers want? That's what matters to me.' Millie's voice was measured and temperate, with a deliberate and false emphasis.

'Oh, Mrs . . . I'm sorry, I've forgotten your name. Please, I don't quite know . . .'

'I have reason to believe . . .' She wants almost to laugh at the absurdity of coming all this way in search of her mother's secret, tracing her ancestors and uncovering this. She would have been happy to join the notorious Ladies of Llangollen. Instead the box, the map, brings her a truth she has never imagined. '. . . I have reason to believe I was born here.'

Mr Jenkins transforms his bumbling self into a figure of love and wisdom. He takes the baptism card Millie pulls from her large leather bag in his chubby hands and nods benignly. 'Yes, it's from this church. And now you know why it's set out like this. Your mother's name is not here in order to save embarrassment.'

Millie is breathing fast, anger surfacing from deep within, deep in her past. 'No, not *her* embarrassment. The embarrassment of others who sent her here, who wanted her out of the way. And I was brought up believing a lie. My so-called mother wasn't my mother at all. She came here and took her pick.'

Mr Jenkins waits patiently for her rage to subside. 'It was another time, wasn't it? Please consider that the mother who adopted you must have wanted you very much. Adoption isn't easy, but the Church found good homes.' He is speaking from the heart, the simple truth of what he knows. But to Millie he is speaking in code.

Facing her steady gaze he persists with his inadequate comfort. 'We can't know what happened and I'm not sure any good would come of finding out. I'd like to think your own life has been a happy and satisfying one. And your own family?'

'I have a daughter, yes, Kate. But my husband died two years ago. He never knew.'

'Please, remember, you are as precious in the sight of

God as you ever were before you learned your story. It makes no difference in His sight. The Church is always wrong to condemn without love. I am sure it found you a good Christian home.'

'Oh, yes, it did.' How can she explain to this mild, gentle man her mother's exacting faith? She rises to go. 'I'm truly grateful for your kindness. You can imagine the surprise. You have both been very kind.' Suddenly she feels love for Mr and Mrs Jenkins, a rush of warmth for their homeliness and simple lives. She recognizes in them genuine goodness and bafflement at the world around them, but they offer gentle comfort where they see it is needed.

Mrs Jenkins emerges from the kitchen in a soiled apron and stands on the step beside her roly-poly husband to wave goodbye.

Millie drives into the hills, beautiful against a lowering sky. At the summit of the Horseshoe Pass, she parks and gets out. She feels the wind lift her hair, and looks out across the broad horizon of landscape and sky. In its immensity she tries to let the pain slip away. In the vastness of the countryside certain things resolve themselves in her mind.

Remembering

1975

And back they came. Melanie, who had once read 'Cargoes', Enid, who had fallen from the horse in the gym, Elsie, who had loved Beethoven and Goethe, Mona, who had admired Aneurin Bevan, red-haired Mandy – grey now – who once had a swing to her hips, Brenda, who had hated so hard, Jen who had lost her love, and Polly, who had found hers. Back they came, with numerous others, all middle-aged and excited, surprised and disbelieving. They had imagined that Ashworth Grammar School for Girls would last for ever. Now it was being closed.

The reunion had been Enid Carter's idea. Her invitation began, 'Dear schoolmates . . .' Its tone was robust, even boisterous, and went straight into several wastepaper baskets. Others sent refusals:

Dear Mopsy (isn't that what we called you?),
    I think you must have gone to a different school. I really hated my days at Ashworth Grammar, with all

302

those rules and regulations, and those stuffy old spinster teachers. I was always in trouble and in detention. Thank goodness things have changed so much since then. I'm a teacher myself now, and work in a noisy, friendly and happy school, nothing like the Dickensian regime we suffered. I'm not at all sorry to hear it's closing.

Yours, Pippa

PS Perhaps I'm being harsh. We did have some good times, especially during the war. And Miss Maitland was OK. But how long ago that seems now. The world's a different place.

Most surprising of all, a neat letter from Cynthia Maitland explained with what pleasure she would see her old school again: 'So much has happened'.

Jen found her invitation wedged among her post in the mailbox on the back of her neat olive front door in a shabby part of Islington. She read it last among the flyers for the King's Head Theatre and serious legal magazines urging her to take out subscriptions. Since Oxford, she had forged ahead as a lawyer, her high heels clicking sharply on the expanses of the Royal Courts of Justice. Her speciality was employment law and she was eager to see the new Equal Opportunity Act on to the statute book. She had been consulted about relevant clauses by Barbara Castle's civil servants and attended its celebrations at London's Banqueting House. She was well pleased when, earlier that year, the Tories had elected a woman as their leader. She had never married. She had loved Tim when she was a schoolgirl, but she had made no effort to find another love. She had sex whenever she wanted it, with fellow students, pop musicians, the occasional professor, but she wanted none of them at the centre of her life. The centre was her work.

She was sorry her old school was to close. She regretted the cull of grammar schools before the tide of comprehensives. But in her day it had been a strict and uncompromising place. She remembered, with a sort of squiffy fondness, the ageing spinsters who had been her teachers. She owed them not for the things they had taught, which she had discovered at Oxford had been routine grammar-school fare, but for the ambition and self-reliance that had shaped her life. She owed a good deal to the elegant headmistress who had encouraged them to debate, and even disagree, organizing those awkward get-togethers in her study, which had caused such a fuss. How completely innocent they had all been. Miss Maitland, that was her name. She had left suddenly in Jen's final year. Talk was that she'd gone to do a secret job for the government to help win the war. The gossips had called it spying. Almost all war work had involved secrecy so the idea wasn't far-fetched. She'd liked Miss Maitland: she'd had the air of a delicate animal, whiskers tense and sensitive, ever poised to escape the burdensome conventions of the day. Well, those conventions had gone for ever. She wondered if Miss Maitland was still alive. She decided to go.

Polly accepted her invitation immediately. The date went at once into her sturdy diary, among details of family visits – brother Gerald had survived the war and become a teacher – and of farm activities – a visit from the local vet, recruitment of casual labour for the hay-making. Her willowy young self had broadened into a wide-hipped, heavy-breasted farmer's wife with a bevy of children and a kitchen whose warmth and chaos were similar to what she had enjoyed as a child. Hans had become farm manager as soon as he was old enough. His English still had the stilted perfection of the studious foreigner, and his impeccable manners still startled new-comers, but once they realized he had stayed on after the war they were sympathetic to the German who preferred England.

The farm thrived. Robert had left the Merchant Navy in the 1950s, taking it over as his father's rheumatism laid him low. But the old farmer was still watchful of the Friesian herd, which had long reclaimed the land that had gone under the wartime plough. The place was a country idyll; the old manor house – half-timbered with its historic priest's hole – featured occasionally in local articles about Cheshire's heritage. They took that with a pinch of salt. Tourism in their part of England? Not likely. Not with everyone now flocking to Ibiza and Benidorm.

Robert was still in touch with Josh. The Old Man had stayed at sea until the late 1950s and went on loving it, feeling more alive the moment he passed the harbour bar, his face set towards the waves and the wind. Then, as he neared sixty, he had been elected a Younger Brother of Trinity House, delighted to discovered that the culture of the sea that lived in his bones was cherished on land.

Robert had still been his first mate when Jessica was killed in a car crash, driving too fast and over the alcohol limit after one of her weekends away with Babs. Josh had been ravaged by her loss: he had given his life to her against his heart's inclination, and felt the pain of her departure all the more. But as he aged he was a busy and able spirit. He joined the Honourable Company of Master Mariners, followed their affairs and publications with close scrutiny, and occasionally made forays to their lectures and lunches on the HQS *Wellington* moored on the Thames. He sent out a swathe of their Christmas cards – always some stalwart vessel breasting the waves – to a wide range of friends, including one over which he paused a little longer when he wrote the message.

The grown-up schoolgirls, now about to enter into their fifties, arrived in pastel shades and sensible shoes. Many peered through glasses, not sure that they recognized the faces, smiling and nodding for fear of offending a former close friend. They convened in the tiled vestibule and the headmistress's room, whose golden oak had darkened with the passing of years; it looked dirty somehow to those who remembered its earlier glow. Had time or too much Mansion polish brought it down? The invitation had indicated that there would be a reunion lunch, then an address by Jennifer Wainwright QC. Everyone reckoned that if it proved insupportably dull they would steal away. At least they had come.

Polly and Jen were talking together when Cynthia walked into her old room. At first they didn't notice her. She stood alone, surveying the scene, taking pleasure in what was familiar. Being alone was comfortable. It felt good to stand where she had once held sway, and muse on the wayward path, so unanticipated, so painful, that her life had taken.

In the event it was Polly who strode across to greet her, she it was who had forwarded the invitation. In her mind was the memory of that encounter in Liverpool's Kardomah café, Robert hinting that something might be going on. In their wilder moments they'd imagined a full-scale love affair, though surely the headmistress and the captain were too old and conventional for such things. They had left it at that.

'Miss Maitland, it's good to see you. So many people here will be delighted you've come. You remember Jennifer Wainwright, don't you? She's a barrister now. Perhaps you know that.' One or two others noticed and moved across to join the group.

'My dear Polly, I'm delighted. I was hoping to find some of my girls here,' she smiled inclusively at the gathering numbers, 'and, Jen, what a successful career you're having. I've read about you in the annual school magazines. But they don't say much, do they? I allow myself to be enormously proud of you.'

Cynthia still had an air of understated elegance. She was now in her seventies but had neither the stoop nor the density of an old woman. If anything she was thinner, with a network of wrinkles mapping her cheeks. Her clothes had shifted in style to the relaxed comfort of dark trousers and discreet silver jewellery, reflecting the easy composure of the retired. The unspoken question was what had she made of her life. That would have to wait.

Meanwhile Enid, Melanie and Elsie told of satisfactory, if unremarkable, lives. Cynthia had a smile for each.

Only one person noticed Grace Boyd arrive and stride briskly into the gathering, asking immediately about the seating arrangements for lunch. She had grown bossy with age. Few remembered who she was and her terse enquiries received curt replies. One or two bothered to ask when she had been there. 'Never as a pupil, only as secretary to Miss Maitland during the war.'

'Ah, yes, the ship adoption. Do you remember it?' Conversations sprang up recalling Captain Percival, the Admiral, and his tall blond first mate.

'Ssh,' someone said. 'Didn't he marry Polly, and isn't that her over there?'

Across the room, Cynthia had seen Grace. She had been expecting her. She had wondered whether or not the encounter should be avoided, but had come to the conclusion she had reached every year since the adoption of her daughter and the sending of the annual unsigned birthday card. She reasoned that she had a place, however shadowy, in her daughter's life. She had long ago come to a calm accommodation with her loss, though the prospect of the turmoil erupting again made her uneasy. Nonetheless, the school and her days as headmistress were the most vivid she had known. She would accept the invitation and whatever happened.

In the event Grace Boyd came across to her, drawn by her original devotion, then her revulsion and now their shared secret. She, too, had been apprehensive of what might happen. Well, she had nothing to be ashamed of. Her actions had saved a sorry situation. She and

308

Roderick had helped avoid what would have been a terrible scandal. When she first learned the whispered news from Mr Potter, she had sobbed into her pillow at the shame and horror. Miss Maitland, whom she had served with such impeccable care, turned out to have been living a life of depravity – depravity that had had scandalous consequences. When she had calmed her nerves, and conveyed to Roderick what was going on, they had prayed together. Only then had they realized, at Mr Potter's prompting, that it offered them a God-given opportunity. Their hearts sang at the prospect of their own child.

Grace was proud of the home they had given Millicent. They brought her up in a godly household, instilling Christian values, even as young people rebelled and took up hideous music, screaming at popular musicians, wearing denim jeans and marching against the Bomb. The vicar who succeeded Mr Potter had taken them with him into a more exacting sect of their faith. She had no regrets even though Millie – as she preferred to be called – had grown into an ungrateful teenager, finally delivering a blasphemous tirade against her parents before slamming out of the house to live in some unspeakable squat. She was back, of course, when Roderick fell ill, making hospital appointments, driving Grace to sad appointments with specialists, as should be expected of a daughter. And now she was making something of her life. She was in her early thirties and already a university lecturer. Given the chance, Grace would boast of it to those around her. Except, perhaps, to Miss Maitland.

Cynthia saw her coming and eased herself away from the surrounding circle.

'Grace Boyd. I had imagined you might be here.' Her gloved hand was taken and given a firm and formal shake, but Grace's gaze was clouded.

'I feel as much a part of the school as anyone, you know. I gave it some of my best years.'

'Of course you did. I have reason to know that, and . . . to be grateful to you.' Cynthia was leaving things vague. Better to be as generous as the tension of the moment would allow. 'We had such a busy time, during the war, didn't we?' Others standing by nodded at this. Reminiscences about wartime were cropping up all over the room.

'We did, indeed.' Grace managed a weak smile – Miss Maitland was coming wilfully close to events best not mentioned. She jerked her head, as if to ward off an uneasy conscience, and launched, with a false laugh, into her own reminiscence. 'I remember having to organize the Tea Club. It was an awful lot of extra work. And, as I recall, caused a good deal of fuss.' The implied censure went unnoticed.

'Oh, it did. I was so proud of it. It helped all my girls grow up, don't you think? To know about the wider world. It helped make a difference to the way they thought. To me, too, I suppose.' How shameless a statement was that? Grace thought. She wondered at Miss Maitland's cool audacity in showing herself at the very place she had disgraced. Grace held her faith more strongly every day. It sat at the very heart of her, reinforcing a tight and exacting conscience. She saw with alarm that the world around her had grown casual and easy of behaviour. Ten years earlier she had signed the Clean Up TV petition started by a Mrs Whitehouse. She was pleased when Brenda Alsop spoke up to disparage Cynthia's claim.

'But it really wasn't a wider world, after all, was it? Local bigwigs showing off their petty views to gaping schoolgirls,' she declared, with a high, bold laugh, her powerful scent and flamboyant dress setting her apart. She had arrived in a pale blue Jaguar, parked under the overhanging beech trees along the road. She'd come because there might be a newspaper feature in it – 'What became of girlish hopes?' 'Not a lot' was her foregone conclusion. Her arrival confirmed as much. Here she was, a dazzling Fleet Street peacock among a flock of hens, so much wiser to the real world of money and influence and success. 'You must know it was just a swap shop for obvious ideas. I had to learn that pretty damned quick.'

'And so you did.' Cynthia wouldn't take offence. She was both appalled and amused that one of her *protégées* should have become the high priestess of reactionary polemics, dubbed 'the Diva of the Dailies'. 'We've all marvelled at your success, Brenda. Perhaps you owe some of it to your schooldays. You certainly held strong opinions even then. And here you are, still hammering away at anything you disagree with.'

'And the world listens! D'you know we have a readership of three point four million?'

'And to think it all began with the Tea Club! I'm so pleased for you.'

Cynthia turned to Jen. 'I dare say you've been a target, haven't you, Jen? After all, you always were.'

'More an adversary, I'd say. I don't agree with Brenda any more than I ever did. But I enjoy her engagement with battles she can't win.' It was spiky now and the laughter tensed. Someone reminded them it was time for lunch.

As they moved away Cynthia stayed at Grace's elbow, contrived yet unobtrusive. Gently she took her arm, letting the others move ahead. Her voice was soft and sure, but a nerve twitched in her cheek. 'I would be pleased to know how your . . .' she forced the word out, clear and unhesitant '. . . your daughter is.'

Grace looked at her blankly. 'I'm surprised you ask, Miss Maitland. I'd hoped you might let the past stay private. But I'm happy to tell you,' she indicated neither warmth nor disapproval, just neutrality, 'our daughter, Millicent, is a university lecturer in the history of art.' Cynthia made to respond but Grace went on, 'We learned last week that she and her husband have had a baby daughter, seven pounds at birth. Mother and child are doing well. They are going to call her Kate.' With a bleak smile, Grace followed the others towards the dining hall.

Cynthia swallowed hard. She had learned what she had come for. Here was a new and momentous development. She had become a grandmother. Things that had gone wrong in her life could now, in the fullness of time, be put right. She had never set out to keep a diary, a deliberate attempt to set the record straight. She wasn't sure what 'setting the record straight' meant. Life was too confusing for that.

Her memories of her humiliation remained vivid. She had been back to Llangollen to retrace her steps, marking on a black-and-white map exactly where the Cradle of Hope had been. Only she knew her story, and only she ever would. How the strict regime had kept six pregnant women virtually under lock and key. The others had been girls in their teens. Without any sense of irony, they had called her 'Ma' and had laughed and cried together over having made an unforgivable mess of their lives. Occasionally the matron allowed her to go for a walk and she would follow the road along the river until she came to the spot where she could watch it roaring and churning under the bridge, gushing yellow-white foam across huge slabs of rock. Day after day she had gazed down at it, thinking of being at sea in the wild Atlantic. The war scarcely reached this far; the way of life was simple, with oil-lamps, lumpy meals and churchgoing disapproval. She always left the river reluctantly, knowing that nature was strong, certain and didn't condemn her.

No, there would be no diary. There was no plan, no evidence, no proof. But she had kept a few things with her: random items from days at school, gifts from the ship, occasional photographs, the record of her humiliation, the baptism card, and a few remaining papers; they all had a future. They would leave a light trace through the years that only she knew and understood. She had once dreamed they might pass to her daughter. But now someone new might one day find out her story without judging or feeling wronged. Cynthia would do nothing as damaging or direct as to intervene. She would leave her memorabilia to chance and, yes – she paused as the idea came to her – to her family. She would check with Enid that Grace hadn't changed her address.

Jen had been asked to make a speech. Brenda Alsop glowered from the front row as Jen delivered just enough reminiscence for comfort before some seriously challenging stuff about the role of women. She was witty and forthright. She cited Dorothy Parker one minute, Betty Friedan the next. Her quotation from Germaine Greer won a ripple of recognition, if not always sympathy. She ended on a tide of warmth that embraced them all. Eager to be identified with Jen's success, Brenda set aside old rancour and led the applause. Here they were, the girls of Ashworth Grammar School, grown middle-aged and grey, with memories that were happy if never quite accurate. A number had made a place in the world, but most had done what the school implicitly expected: they had made homes for families and stayed in them. Jen's smile – meeting their applause – reached out towards Cynthia Maitland, who raised her clapping hands to her star pupil.

Polly gave Jen a lift to the station.

'We were all so innocent then, weren't we? Much more innocent than girls of sixteen are nowadays.' Polly was thinking of her own daughter, Joanna, travelling with friends to India, her son Joel doing VSO work in

Bangladesh. 'With the war on we couldn't even cross the Channel.'

Jen smiled in agreement. Memories insisted on spilling out. 'I remember going to France as a student in 1948 and being amazed by the street cafés, everyone smoking Gitanes, drinking wine at every meal ... a totally different world.'

'And you know the story, don't you? About Miss Maitland and the captain?'

'No. Should I? He was very kind, wasn't he? Sensitive face.'

'Oh, more than that. According to Robert, they were passionately in love.'

'Cynthia Maitland and Captain Percival? You're kidding. I never noticed anything.'

'You were in love with Tim.'

'Yes.' They both paused.

'Well, they had a kind of *Brief Encounter*, a full-blown affair. That was why she left the school.'

Jen gazed, open-mouthed, as Polly turned the car into the station approach. 'But how did they ... And we never ... What happened?'

'Don't know – nothing much. Apparently he tried to trace her after she vanished. You remember that.' She applied the brake and turned to Jen.

'Yes, it was odd. We thought that at the time, didn't we?' They fell silent, each searching for scraps of memory, any indication.

'Robert stays in touch with him. Josh, he's called. He tried to find her for years after the war. Especially after the Admiral was killed in a car crash.'

'Oh, I didn't know. What happened?'

'It seems she became a bit of a soak – that's the rumour. She shouldn't have been driving.'

'No, I mean the captain's search for Miss Maitland.'

'I don't know. Men don't talk much, don't go into detail.'

'And we were with her just a moment ago.'

'She's a mystery, isn't she? Keeping it to herself.'

'And we didn't know, did we? Not a hint.'

'Well . . . not exactly. No, I suppose we didn't.' Polly didn't mention the Kardomah. 'You know, sometimes things happened that you knew nothing about – but then it's as though you've known all along.'

'Did we have an inkling, d'you think?'

'Who knows? Who knows any more what any of us thought?'

Deciding

The call comes as she is bathing Freya. A Madonna track is blaring through the flat, the woman's zest making Kate smile. What energy, what power. Kate is tired: today's dialysis and the journey to the hospital were dispiriting. She pats Freya and, keeping an eye on her, leaving the door open, moves to the bedroom and slumps on the bed. She picks up the phone.

'Er, yes . . . hello. It's Kate.' She waves to Freya.

'Kate, it's Ma. I'm just back from Llangollen and, well, I've had something of a shock and I must tell you.' Millie's voice is odd, her usual calm edged with fretfulness.

'What is it? Are you ill?' Panic gathers. 'Has there been an accident?'

'No, no, I'm fine. I'm OK. It's something . . . you remember when you found that baptism card in Gran's basket? The card with my name on it? Well . . .'

Kate takes the phone into the bathroom and sprays Freya with foam from a coloured can. The little girl's

317

whoops of pleasure reach Millie. Madonna is still throbbing in the background.

'Look, I can't talk over the phone. I need to see you. Can I come round?'

'Ma, are you OK . . . come round. Yes, of course, come round.'

Kate's flat is brisk and bright: she had shared it with Laszlo for a couple of years and her father had given her the cash to buy him out when he'd left. Now there are traces of another man. A leather jacket hangs on the coloured IKEA pegs in the hall, and through the bedroom door Millie sees jeans and a bulky sweater tossed on an unmade bed. Not conclusive, she thinks. She tiptoes in to kiss the sleeping Freya, hair wet from the bath straggling over her pillow.

'So, tell me. Let's start with the baptism card.' Kate is folded on a shapeless canvas chair that shifts and moves as she does. Her mother sits forward, in a red bucket chair focused, intense.

There's only one way to say it. 'Kate, I've discovered something terrible. I'm adopted. Gran adopted me. Gran wasn't my real mother.'

Kate laughs at the absurdity of it, then screws up her face, trying to decipher the degree of her mother's distress. 'Adopted? What are you saying? How on earth do you know?'

'It started in Llangollen – well, of course it started earlier, with the baptism card, but going to Llangollen did it. I found the place where I was born.'

'Well, how damned silly is that! Why the hell didn't she ever tell you?'

'I don't know. People didn't tell their children anything in those days.' Millie shakes her head.

'Is that what all the stuff in the box is about? A paper chase for her descendants, telling but not telling?'

'Oh, I don't think she was thinking of me . . . I think she couldn't bring herself to destroy the truth. Maybe she felt guilty and unconsciously took the trouble to leave a trace . . . all those bits and pieces.'

'Why would she feel guilty?'

'Well, she could never come out with it . . . or Daddy either.' Millie is clutching her knees, leaning towards Kate, a sad parent appealing to her child. 'I never felt I belonged. I thought their piety shut me out but . . .'

'You need a stiff drink.' Kate goes to the kitchen and returns with tumblers of gin, tonic and a lemon. 'So you're saying your mother – your real mother – was some sad young girl thrown out to cope on her own? Is that it?'

'Apparently it happened a lot then. I was born in Llangollen.' Millie sits back in the awkward bucket chair. 'I found the place: it's derelict now, all boarded up and overgrown. So I asked around. Back in the 1940s it was called Cradle of Hope, a home for unmarried mothers. It's where the baptism card comes from.'

'Cradle of Hope – bloody hell!'

They manage a smile, but Millie is thoughtful, smoothing the grey cashmere of her dress. She is glad of Kate's reaction, so forthright and loving. A complicit silence as the story sinks in and tenderness swims between them. Millie is looking at Kate with new eyes: her own flesh and blood, how much that matters. Separate but of the

319

same stem, the fruit of her love for Dominic. Her eyes consume her daughter, the thin body, the coloured boots and dangling beads, the careful choice of clothes to conceal her damaged body.

Millie suddenly realizes that she has made her decision. It was easy after all.

They sit together, mother and daughter, worn down by the story and the gin.

'I wonder about that young woman . . . my mother.' The word is hard to say. 'What was so terrible that she couldn't care for me, couldn't love me enough like – like I love you.' Millie's composure breaks and a sort of low growl rumbles to the surface, the groan of a wounded animal. She holds on, breathing deeply to control the tears.

'Well, this is all very extraordinary, I know. But how much does it actually matter?' Kate lives in the day, the present, for the moment. Illness makes her do that. 'I mean it is shocking all right, but it doesn't affect who you are, and you are still my wonderful talented gorgeous ma. Nothing can change that.' Kate gives a frantic grin. She rocks in the canvas armchair, wanting, on impulse, to enfold her mother in her arms. Instead she lurches forward, plumps herself on the floor at her mother's feet, and puts her chin in the soft folds of her lap. 'Oh, Ma, you're who you are, clever, strong, elegant – wife of Dominic, mother of Kate, granny of Freya. What more can you want?'

Millie reaches for a tissue and blows her nose.

'I know. I know. But, well . . . thank you.'

'So there it is, out in the open. No more secrets.'

'Oh, but there are. Who were they? I want to know who they were, my parents. Mummy was so strict and severe. Was she making up to God for the sins of that wretched slip of a girl?' She takes a good blow into the tissue. 'I want to find out.'

It is Kate who cracks it.

Friends Reunited comes up with Ashworth Grammar School, and sets out the names of subscribers year by year. Back in 1943, the date of Millie's birth, there's a list of only four: one is Enid Carter. Meanwhile Baz has been checking DNA sampling on the web. Would anything from the hamper retain the DNA of whoever had handled it? The telegram, perhaps. It would be good if something had cut the skin and caused a trace of blood to catch a fibre, a shred of paper. Not likely – and anyway how would you know? Nothing in the hamper holds guilty stains. But so what? The DNA of a total stranger is your own: where does that get you? Nowhere.

After a week Enid Carter replies:

Thrilled to hear that you have a connection with the school. Sorry not to have replied earlier. I'm living in New Zealand. We farm sheep here. Have done for years. And, just fancy, I knew the person you mention: Grace Bunting married a Roderick Boyd – your mother's maiden name. But she wasn't one of the pupils. In fact, I think we mostly ignored her. She was a mousy little thing, devoted to the head, ran around her like a pet dog. Came as a bit of a shock when the head left. She was her secretary, you see, very proud of her title: secretary to the headmistress, Miss Maitland. Miss Maitland left in 1943, to go to another job. Mrs Boyd left around the same time to have a baby. I remember we gave one a silver dish as a leaving present, and the other a set of baby clothes. Things were scarce in those days. Please let me know if I can help further.

Yes, she certainly can. Kate hangs on to this precious link. Soon she has more news for her mother: 'I'm going to meet someone called Mrs Warburton – Polly Warburton. She's a farmer's wife in Cheshire and says she can tell me all about the school, Miss Maitland and Grace Boyd. Sounds intriguing, eh? D'you want to come?'

'No, I – I'll stay here. There's so much to think about. This discovery is shaking everything up – shaking me up. You'll be all right, going to meet her?'

'No problem.'

Millie surveys her study. It's late at night and Stravinsky's *Pulcinella* is playing. Lamps sit on low tables casting a glow across the room. The weather is unseasonably hot and the sash windows thrown wide to the late-night air. A car purrs home and the small noises of neighbours attend the turning of keys and slamming of doors. She feels calm, rested.

This is proving hard to deal with. She is trying to be fair, but she doesn't want to be fair. They must have been desolate, her so-called parents, not to have their own child. And taking her into their lives must have made them happy. But she is angry not to have shared what they knew. She wants to blame them. She looks at the comfortable room full of her life, the life of a professional woman in her late fifties: educated, rational and thoughtful, capable of judgements, secure in her values, sure of her place in the world, proud of the books she has written. Why should all this be clouded by the matter of who had fathered and who had borne her?

A chasm may have opened up into the past in the last few days, but set against that there is her life today, the warmth and comfort of the family she takes for granted. Kate, her flesh-and-blood daughter, is even now dredging the past to bring her reassurance. Yet she herself is demonstrating a desperate falling away. A sense of shame and regret sneaks up on her. She walks round the familiar room, touching familiar objects: a Japanese fan, a small Indian box and the framed picture she has taken from her mother's hamper – it turns out to be by the Royal Academician Maud Sheridan. Here is the home she has created. Her identity isn't in doubt, it's all around her. Her genetic identity might be other than she'd thought but her sense of self transcends it.

Kate lies in bed looking at her arm on the bright blue duvet. It is scarred from elbow to wrist: a raw, meaty scar, tinged with blue and mottled at the edges. It seems unlike any other part of her: her freckled neck and shoulders have a milky paleness, her body is neat and white. But she loves this arm, this stalwart arm of hers. It is keeping her alive. It is where the exchange of blood happens when the dialysis machine is hooked into her. The exact place where the artery links directly to the vein gives out a buzz. It is mechanical, like a toy bee trapped under her skin, buzzing, keeping her going.

Baz is still asleep beside her. All is quiet. Freya is with friends. It is early morning and the summer sunlight is filtering through the flimsy curtains. This is the day things begin to get better. Tonight she will check into the hospital. She has slept fitfully, excited by the prospect. Her arm, will it return to normal once she has the new kidney? The other, which was used first to accommodate the tube, is better, but the bruises have left traces. For a long time she felt defiant about their appearance, wearing trim little camisole tops with shoelace straps and shift dresses that left her arms bare. But strangers sometimes gave her odd looks, and once in a club a tipsy girl had asked whether her fella beat her up. After that she covered herself. Helpfully, fashion moved on to skimpy little cardigans.

Baz stirs and reaches round her waist. She smiles and waits for him to wake. She thinks about her mother and wonders how she's feeling. She wants to ring her but it's far too early. It's an amazing thing they're to go through together. How like her mother not to say anything, going to all those meetings with the consultant, then deciding to go ahead. It seems so practical and efficient. She's like that, of course.

'Are you sure you want to do this?'

'I am, Kate. Quite sure. Now let's have no agonizing about it. Please.'

'I am ... well ...'

'I know ... but the time to be grateful is when it's over and done with. We're not there yet. Till then it's work in progress.' She had grinned with the sense of purpose she brought to her lectures, to family plans, to writing her books.

Suddenly awake, Baz takes her arm, and brings it to him. Tenderly he strokes the skin, soft and taut, over the blotched stain. Slowly he kisses the spot where the buzzing happens.

'Pervert! You just like its funny feel!' Kate laughs.

He seizes her. 'I like the funny feel of you.'

Millie wakes with a sense of joy. How odd. She'd expected to feel afraid. And, in a sense, she does. Yes, she can feel the fear lurking, slithering at the back of her mind. But it's an old fear now. Something has disarmed it. She makes herself a cup of rooibosch tea and flavours a bowl of fat-free yoghurt with honey, then adds some grains. Her nerves are steady at the prospect of the day. This is now what she wants to do above all else. She is shocked she could have hesitated. She packs a small photograph of Dominic in her hospital bag, with a postcard of the Ladies of Llangollen.

Later in the day Kate and Baz take the tube from the Angel: Millie calls a minicab. High summer isn't far away and the leaves are bright green on the London streets. They meet in the hospital's broad and busy entrance, passing a couple of furtive smokers standing well clear of the building. There is a magazine shop, a

325

flower shop and much coming and going: wheelchairs and family groups, professionals in different-coloured coats moving purposefully, arriving patients and visitors, lost but determined.

Kate is familiar with exactly where to go: third floor, along the glowing blue linoleum, following directions she knows well. Millie pauses at paintings on the walls, surprised they are by well-known artists, donated in the hope that art will soothe nerves and fears. Nobody is paying them much attention.

Kate and Millie check in at the nurses' station, where several young women attend to laptops. They wait to be shown to beds in separate wards. Each has her own consultant, one of the renal specialists in the department. Mother and daughter make different journeys towards the same end.

Millie lies back on her pillows. She has brought with her a book by Mark Haddon. She has heard it is good, but she doesn't feel the urge to open it. Why enter another's world when your own is so full of change and surprise? She looks at the other three beds. One woman is watching television with earphones clamped to her head. Another is fast asleep. The third is sitting up writing letters and listening to an iPod. So, no contact there.

She sighs. It's such a family event that it seems strange Dominic isn't part of it. She thinks of Kate's birth and how he hovered round the bed. It was relatively daring, in those days, for fathers to be in attendance. 'I'll stay away from the sticky end,' he said, as if delicacy mattered at such a moment. But the instant Kate was out and lying, blotchy and wet, across her body, his eyes had filled with tears – as they would have now.

Baz is allowed to see Kate into her bed. He leans across and looks into her bold blue eyes. Her face is slightly puffy. She is tired, very tired. Her body is exhausted by all the dialysis, her ankles swollen. Over the weeks he has loved her, he has grown to know the rhythms of the illness, how she feels queasy and tired after each afternoon session, how she insists she's well enough to preside at the funerals, usually in the mornings, then goes home, tiring fast, to rest and eat a depressing diet. She takes real comfort from helping the bereaved. At first it had struck him as odd that she had chosen such work, but he has grown to understand that she sees the world as a place where people must help each other. It's a sort of happiness in itself. And now Millie, the formidable scholar and powerful mother, is doing the same. They are all three on a high of expectation. Let's hope it goes well. He kisses her softly, tiptoes from the ward and makes his way home.

In adjacent theatres, their bodies lie under wraps, except for the crucial area. They do not know with what deftness their surgeons move, how the kidney taken from Millie's side is placed tidily in a dish and conveyed within minutes to where Kate's body is waiting to receive it.

Three hours later Kate wakes woozily from the anaesthetic. The nurse says her mother is already alert and fine.

'Mother and daughter are doing well.' When were they last so close?

Next day, Millie is well enough to sit in the chair beside her bed. In the other ward, Kate opens a get-well card from Polly Warburton.

Meeting

2003

Josh has woken to the crashing of waves against the sea wall, the spray reaching the house windows. He loves the sound. Later he will wrap up warm, then stand at the door and let it touch him, wetting his face, tasting of the world's seas and his life's story. But it takes him a long time to get up and dress these days. His back is stiff, his joints gnarled. He reaches slowly to put on thick sea socks and boots. He drags a familiar checked shirt across the grizzled grey hair of his chest, tucking it clumsily into corduroy trousers. Living on his own for so many years has made him frugal, rationing his movements, limiting the range of his activities. He doesn't wash very often either.

He walks along the harbour each morning, pauses for a pint at the Ship Inn on the quay, watches a few boats coming and going, holiday trade mostly, but an occasional local fisherman serving the little restaurant on the bay. The villagers treat him as their own eccentric, keeping an eye on his comings and goings, and pointing him out to their B-and-B customers – 'He's well on in his nineties, you know, been at sea all his life. A bit forgetful, these days, but somewhere inside he's as bright as a button.'

He looks back on that life often. There is plenty of time. He has long mastered the petty domestic arrangements that keep the little clapboard cottage trim. His own needs are few. When he could still take out the little dinghy and cast a few lines he'd bring back, if he was lucky, a few fat mackerel for his tea. For more than ten years he's not been able to do that, though. Walking is the only physical activity left. He enjoys feeling the stretch of his limbs, which creak as he climbs out of the armchair but ease into a slow stride as he makes his way into the blow and bluster of the weather. He enjoys weather, too. It has governed so much of his life. As you get old you can still enjoy it. He listens to weather forecasts, imagining the onset of storms and swelling seas; he sleeps without curtains, savouring rain or sleet, the dawning sunlight, fog shrouding the shore. He can't be out there much any more but he comes as close as memory will allow.

Old age is like that. The parameters draw in, and the mind focuses on nearness. In the years after he'd left the shipping line and had settled on the coast, he took up painting. He'd sit in the front window upstairs with a newspaper spread on the table, tubes of paint and jars of brushes. He had plunged right in, painting what he saw, ships coming and going, the deep red sails of coastal barges, the noisy colours of spinnakers, children on the beach running and shouting, the little houses across the bay, painted different colours by new arrivals with money and fancy ideas. They look like so many sugared almonds. Places are so much more colourful than they were when we were younger – or does memory paint the past in black-and-white? And is it photographs that keep it sepia for ever? Josh's paintings are vigorous and full of colour.

The meals-on-wheels lady had been the first to notice them. Then some official called to ask if they could have a couple to put in the local artists' annual exhibition where they'd sold for twenty pounds each. But he was sad to see them go, and didn't offer any more for future shows. Instead they stack up round the place: he swaps them about sometimes for variety, but it's getting difficult to lift them. Perhaps he'll take one along to this event he's been invited to in London. Robert and his wife have organized it. It's all a big fuss. Something about long-lost relations wanting to meet him. But he's pleased it's happening. He's proud to be in his hundredth year and grateful there's someone left to notice. He chooses a picture of a seagull on the sea wall, with a boat on the water in the background. Robert will like that. It's good to give people things.

Robert meets him at Paddington station. He's been in touch with these people but Josh has chosen where to meet them: the HQS *Wellington*, home of the Honourable Company of Master Mariners to which he belongs. If he is to meet strangers, as Robert says, he prefers to be in familiar surroundings. It's where he still keeps in touch with one or two who've known the same life as him.

Robert Warburton gave up the sea for farming long ago, but by the time he left they were good friends. Sometimes they speak of young Tim, who went down with the *Treverran* all those years ago. He stays in touch with Charlie Rawlings, too, the apprentice he'd taken to Ashworth Grammar School and embarrassed among all those gawky schoolgirls. Charlie's a member of the Worshipful Company. It will be good to see him again. Were the war years good or bad? Terrible in many ways, but vivid in the memory. His senses had been alert, reactions sharp, passions heightened.

He remembers with fondness the love he had known with Cynthia, how it had lit up his life and how its glow lingers. The war had been cruel to them, and left its regrets. After Jessica's death, in the reckless car crash on a weekend away with Babs, he had tracked Cynthia down. He visits the memory often. He wants to keep it alive. He had sought Polly and Robert's help in finding her. She was living with Maud.

The cottage the two women shared was down a curving lane not far from the private school where they had taught, a small art college for girls, founded by husband-and-wife philanthropists in the 1930s. Maud had already been a visiting lecturer and when a vacancy arose for a history teacher she had recommended her friend. Cynthia had wanted nothing more than to live quietly away from the world she had known. The chance to teach again renewed her spirits: she began to smile, make plans, be glad. She shut the past out of her daily thoughts. There was a life to be lived and she got on with it.

The garden gate creaked as he had swung it open. A

332

woman's head popped up at the window but she didn't recognize him. Then Cynthia opened the door and stood quite still. 'Josh.'

'Hello, Cynthia.' She was clearly stunned. 'Well, are you going to invite me in?'

'Well, yes, I suppose I am.'

She wasn't sure she welcomed this reminder of the past. So many events jostled together and she knew she had kept from Josh something he had a right to know. It hadn't been deliberate. But it had happened. There was so much to explain, but she found she couldn't do it. She fetched tea, she showed him the garden, all the time wondering whether to open old wounds. She fussed over the cushions, the flowers, the cups and saucers, wondering whether now was the right moment . . . or this . . . or this. But it never was.

He remembers still the sweet chime of a clock striking four. It had cut across his speaking to her, his asking her to come to him, to come and live with him. The chime finished before he did. And he waited for her reply.

'No, Josh. Life is so different now.' She had laid a solicitous hand on his arm and given him a dry, passionless kiss on the cheek. And she had said nothing more, told him nothing. But her eyes glowed.

He remembers the chime. It sounds in his dreams. Later, when a large grandfather clock fills the small space of his seaside home, its sonorous sounds mark the hour, and he sometimes thinks of that light sweet chime that had sealed his fate. It was the last time he had seen

Cynthia. After that she grew in his imagination: the love of his life, the woman of his dreams. Safe from reality, he lived a life of high romance, talking to her in his empty home, saying goodnight to her before he fell asleep. He lived more closely to her then than he ever had in fact.

He hung on to the contact, writing, exchanging Christmas cards. Until one day a letter had arrived from Polly. She had heard from Maud that Cynthia had died in the local cottage hospital. She had suffered kidney failure.

And now here he is on the station platform, clutching the painting, Robert grinning from ear to ear, taking his elbow, steering him towards the car. But Robert wants to talk in private. They go to a small coffee-house on the Embankment. Josh manoeuvres his stiff limbs into the spindle-legged chair and waits. This is a nuisance. Why doesn't Robert simply take him to the event? It's his event, after all. But he says there's something he needs to explain and fetches cups of tea.

What Robert has to say is confusing for Josh to take in. His conversation seems to meander, recalling the grammar school where he had met his wife, Polly, and the Ship Adoption Scheme they had joined. Then Robert takes a deep breath and plunges on with what he warns will be a great surprise. Does Josh remember the headmistress, Cynthia Maitland? he wonders. Well, there's no surprise about that: she's often in Josh's mind, though it isn't always clear what is a genuine memory or what is an imagined one. And he doesn't care. It doesn't much matter any more.

334

Robert tells him Cynthia had a child.

Perhaps Robert's confused. Josh was the one who had a child – Peter – lost with his ship. He winces at the thought, recalling Jessica's hysterics and the deep pain of what followed. But Robert persists, and slowly Josh begins to understand. Cynthia had a child, a child who was Josh's daughter. That was why she had given up being headmistress. Josh stares at him. The old face stays still, its parchment skin sucked in round the cheekbones and the withered mouth. He reaches for a handkerchief and wipes saliva from the corners of his mouth.

'Why didn't she tell me?' The voice is slow, the brow more furrowed. Then, with what passion he can muster, 'Why didn't she tell me? She sent me away. In the end it came to nothing.'

But it seems it didn't, after all. There is more. Josh's daughter is called Millie, and she has a daughter of her own, Kate. And there is a granddaughter too.

Seeing his blank stare, Robert wonders whether it's too late, whether Josh is too old.

Josh can hear what he says well enough, but his mind can't. Instead it hears the chiming of a clock from long ago, and the soft touch of Cynthia's dry lips on his cheek.

'They're your family, Josh. Millie and Kate. They're waiting to meet you.'

There is briefly panic in Josh's eyes. Then a single tear trickles over the broken veins. Slowly he makes sense of all he's being told, and isn't surprised. Events to him are remote, long ago, over and done with. But here are some new ones and that pleases an old man. Struggling to his

335

feet, he senses urgency as though the world waits upon him to put it right. 'We'd better go, then. My daughter, you say? My own daughter?'

They wait at the top of the curving banister that leads from the deck into the *Wellington*'s saloon. Millie smiles nervously at everyone who arrives, whether she knows them or not. Kate is preoccupied with a restless Freya, in a crisp blue dress. Most of those arriving are strangers, old men of the sea, some younger ones. And then, Josh: tall, very thin and stooped, gaunt with a sinewy strength despite his age. His hair is spare and grizzled; his long nose gives his face strength; his pale eyes, behind the clouds of age, are still keen and pene-trating. He bears himself as a handsome man commanding respect. He looks from Millie to Kate. Then to Polly.

'Polly. Robert's been telling me such things . . . sur-prising things . . .'

'Yes, Josh. I want you to meet . . .'

Suddenly his mind leaps and spins. He reaches out to steady himself. He is poised between here and there. So many places. A vortex of memories. So long ago. Did they really happen? But the images whirl closer. The golden oak-lined study, blonde hair beneath a pert little hat, thin curtains in the summer breeze, the creaking gate, the silver chimes. He looks from Millie to Kate, then back again. Taking his time, then, 'Yes, that's right . . .' He remembers so much – blue eyes, pale hair. He steps towards them and takes Kate's hand. 'Yes, of course . . .

'Do you remember that woman . . . I don't recall her name . . . who was so rude in the Midland Hotel? During the war, it was . . . She had no right. But you rescued me. You were lovely then, really lovely, still are lovely. I'm glad . . .'

Acknowledgements

Throughout my researches into the battle of the Atlantic I have had the unstinting help of Richard Woodman, author of many books about naval history, most recently *Neptune's Trident*, a history of the British Merchant Navy (The History Press). He has given generously of technical advice and professional comments. I am equally grateful for the professional advice of Robert Elias, a specialist registrar in renal medicine at South Thames, who took the time to explain polycystic kidney disease and how patients and donors deal with donor transplants. He also arranged for me to visit the renal unit of St George's Hospital (Tooting). The fictionalizing of all such matters is entirely my own responsibility.

School contemporaries have been helpful with shared memories and I draw on surviving copies of the *Stockport High School Magazine*. I also quote from *Seafarers, Ships and Cargoes*, edited by Leonard Brooks and R. H. Duce. Urban Strawberry Lunch provided extensive oral histories of Liverpool.

I have enjoyed continuing support from Geoffrey Cannon, Laurence Marks and Olga Edridge, and help with a translation from Harry Guest. Above all I owe a huge debt to the team at Virago: my editors Lennie Goodings and Vivien Redman, to Rosalie Macfarlane Hazel Orme, and, as always, to my agent Ed Victor.

Bibliography

Beardmore, George, *Civilians at War: Journals, 1938–1946* (London: J. Murray, 1984)

Blakemore, Ken, *Sunnyside Down: Growing Up in 50s Britain* (Stroud: History Press, 2005)

Broad, Richard and Suzie Fleming (eds), *Nella Last's War: The Second World War Diaries of 'Housewife, 49'* (London: Profile, 2006)

Brooks, Leonard and R. H. Duce (eds), *Seafarers, Ships and Cargoes: First-Hand Accounts of Voyages by Ships of the Mercantile Marine* (London: University of London Press, 1951)

Calder, Angus, *The Myth of the Blitz* (London: Jonathan Cape, 1991)

—————, *The People's War: Britain 1939–1945* (London: Cape, 1969)

Gershon, Karen (ed.), *We Came as Children: A Collective Autobiography* (London: Victor Gollancz, 1966)

Hartley, Jenny (ed.), *Hearts Undefeated: Women's Writing of the Second World War* (London: Virago, 1994)

—————, *Millions Like Us: British Women's Fiction of the Second World War* (London: Virago, 1997)

Hennessy, Peter, *Having It So Good: Britain in the Fifties* (London: Allen Lane, 2006)

Hillary, Richard, *The Last Enemy* (London: Macmillan, 1942)

Homes, A. M., *The Mistress's Daughter* (London: Granta, 2007)

Howard, Elizabeth Jane, *Slipstream: A Memoir* (Basingstoke: Macmillan, 2002)

Howe, David, Phillida Sawbridge and Diana Hinings, *Half a Million Women: Mothers who Lose their Children by Adoption* (London: Penguin, 1992)

Howe, Leslie, *The Merchant Service To-day* (London: Oxford University Press, 1941)

Johnson, Audrey, *Do March in Step Girls: A Wren's Story* (Sandford: Audrey Morley, 1997)

Kershaw, Ian, *Fateful Choices: Ten Decisions that Changed the World, 1940–1941* (London: Allen Lane, 2007)

Knyaston, David, *Austerity Britain, 1945–1951* (London: Bloomsbury, 2007)

Monsarrat, Nicholas, *The Cruel Sea* (London: Weidenfeld & Nicolson, 1951)

Nicolson, Harold (ed. Nigel Nicolson), *Diaries and Letters 1907–1964* (London: Weidenfeld & Nicolson, 2007)

Partridge, Frances, *A Pacifist's War* (London: Hogarth Press, 1978)

Pym, Barbara (ed. Hazel Holland and Hilary Pym), *A Very Private Eye: The Diaries, Letters and Notebooks of Barbara Pym* (London: Macmillan, 1984)

Rowe, Jane, *Yours By Choice: A Guide for Adoptive Parents* (London: Mills, 1959)

Waters, Sarah, *The Night Watch* (London: Virago, 2006)

Wing, Sandra Koa (ed.), *Our Longest Days: A People's History of the Second World War* (London: Profile, 2006)

Woodman, Richard, *The Arctic Convoys 1941–1945* (London: John Murray, 1994)

——————, *The Real Cruel Sea: The Merchant Navy in the Battle of the Atlantic, 1939–1943* (London: John Murray, 2004)

Wyndham, Joan, *Love is Blue: A Wartime Diary* (London: Heinemann, 1986)

——————, *Love Lessons: A Wartime Diary* (London: Heinemann, 1985)

THE LITTLE STRANGER

Sarah Waters

Shortlisted for the Man Booker Prize 2009

In a dusty post-war summer in rural Warwickshire, a
doctor is called to a patient at lonely Hundreds Hall.
Home to the Ayres family for over two centuries, the
Georgian house, once grand and handsome, is now in
decline, its masonry crumbling, its gardens choked with
weeds, the clock in its stable yard permanently fixed at
twenty to nine. Its owners – mother, son and daughter –
are struggling to keep pace with a changing society,
as well as with conflicts of their own.

But are the Ayreses haunted by something more sinister
than a dying way of life? Little does Dr Faraday know
how closely, and how terrifyingly, their story is
about to become entwined with his.

'Sarah Waters' masterly novel is … gripping,
confident, unnerving and supremely entertaining'
Hilary Mantel, *Guardian*

**You can order other Virago titles through our website: *www.virago.co.uk*
or by using the order form below**

☐ The Little Stranger   Sarah Waters   £7.99

*The price shown above is correct at time of going to press. However, the publishers
reserve the right to increase price on the cover from the one previously advertised,
without further notice.*

Please allow for postage and packing: **Free UK delivery.**
Europe: add 25% of retail price; Rest of World: 45% of retail price.

To order the above or any other Virago titles, please call our credit card
orderline or fill in this coupon and send/fax it to:

Virago, PO Box 121, Kettering, Northants NN14 4ZQ
Fax: 01832 733076   Tel: 01832 737526
Email: aspenhouse@FSBDial.co.uk

☐ I enclose a UK bank cheque made payable to Virago for £ . . . .
☐ Please charge £ . . . . . . to my Visa/Delta/Maestro

Expiry Date ☐☐☐☐   Maestro Issue No. ☐☐

NAME (BLOCK LETTERS please) . . . .

ADDRESS . . . .

. . . .

. . . .

Postcode . . . . Telephone . . . .

Signature . . . .

Please allow 28 days for delivery within the UK. Offer subject to price and availability.